ESCAPADE

DIANA PALMER

ESCAPADE

ISBN-13: 978-1-335-00805-3

Escapade

www.HQNBooks.com

Printed in U.S.A.

To my sister, Dannis Spaeth Cole

Dear Reader,

I wrote *Escapade* in 1992. It seems like forever ago. Back then, I still had many of my contacts in the newspaper business, and access to many sources who were willing to help out an old reporter who needed detailed information for a fictional novel. Ah, glory days.

The plot revolves around a young woman, Amanda Todd, whose parents left her half interest in a small newspaper. It's run by a former reporter who thinks the job press is useless and wants to get rid of it. She, on the other hand, thinks the job press has great potential and she goes to work, behind his back, to make it pay. Seething about controlling interest of her inheritance being left in the hands of Joshua Lawson, a millionaire playboy, she also has to convince him that she knows how to manage a business. It doesn't help that she's in love with him, and he works hard at keeping her at arm's length because of a tragic secret that he can't share with her.

The newspaper boss becomes involved with a married employee, a circumstance that will put the heroine in great danger of losing her life and finally convince the hero that, in the end, love is far more important than business.

It's like going back in time for me. The visiting journalists who come to see the newspaper are the family of my Georgia boss, the incredible Amilee Graves. There was a photo of her on the wall, having breakfast with JFK in Washington, DC. She was one of the first female newspaper publishers, one of the first female mayors. She was elected mayor one time by acclamation when she wasn't even running for office! She and my best friend, Ann, who worked there with me, were my inspiration. Ann still is. Best traveling companion on earth. Our husbands wouldn't travel, so we did. So many adventures. They would truly fill a book! Thanks, Ann, for being my friend for so many years. Fedora hat, whip, bad attitude—that's us. Female Indiana Joneses, lol.

As always, I am your biggest fan.

Diana Palmer

CHAPTER ONE

The colorful, noisy crowd on the docks at Prince George Wharf was a breath of fresh air to Amanda Todd after the sad, somber atmosphere of her home in San Antonio, Texas. She was enchanted with the way the musical accents of British speech mingled with native patois in the European-class boutiques. Usually she would have had time to shop and enough money to indulge her whims. Since her father's funeral three days ago, however, her finances had become an unholy tangle. She worked at her family's weekly newspaper and job press but her father's will had stipulated that she wouldn't inherit the company until she reached the age of twenty-five, in two years, unless she married first. Harrison Todd hadn't held modern views concerning women in business. In fact, he'd screamed bloody murder when Amanda had pursued her dream of a degree in accounting at college, but Josh had prepared her for that.

It was Joshua Cabe Lawson, her late father's business partner, who had always supported her while her father was alive, and even now he was watching over her. He had arranged for

her to fly to Nassau's Opal Cay in the Bahamas on one of the
Lawson Company's Learjets. So she could spend one week on
his island recharging her emotional batteries.

Drained and worn out, Amanda hadn't argued with him.
Besides, Josh was executor of Harrison Todd's will, which
meant Amanda's financial future was temporarily in his hands.
She was certain that would lead to a lot of arguments, for Josh
was no less strong-willed than she. In spite of the fact that
Josh had always championed her cause, they had lately become sporting adversaries.

The Lawson Company of San Antonio, Texas, was a computer conglomerate that produced both mainframe and personal computers. Its international success meant that Josh, as
its president, traveled often. His brother, Brad, was vice president of marketing, and had the charm and charisma his older
brother sometimes lacked.

Brad and Amanda had known each other since childhood.
Although they'd gone to separate grammar schools, they had
attended the same private high school in San Antonio while
Josh had been dispatched to an exclusive military academy,
learning the stiff-backed discipline that had enabled him to
take charge of his father's company at the age of twenty-four.
Josh had increased the company's profits fifteen percent the
first year he had control. The board of directors, dubious in
the early days of his tenure, had become allies, though they
still weren't sure what to make of Brad. Amanda had always
felt like a sister to Brad, a sentiment that had deepened when
old man Lawson had died ten years ago. She was glad he'd
come to pick her up when she arrived on Opal Cay. Josh was,
of course, tending to business.

"Josh never slows down, does he?" Amanda asked the tall,
handsome man as they strolled along the dock in Nassau. "It
isn't as if he's going to starve."

Brad chuckled. He lifted his sharp-featured countenance to

the warm sea air and closed his eyes. "That's a fact. Making money is all Josh lives for. At least since Terri cut out on him."

Amanda didn't like her most vivid memory of Terri. She wasn't a bad sort, but Amanda wanted someone special for Josh—and although she wasn't sure why, she knew that someone wasn't Terri.

She turned toward the bay, where several lumbering white cruise ships were setting in port. She'd been on a cruise ship only once. She'd been seasick the entire trip. These days she flew when she had to travel.

Amanda paused by a straw stall, smiling at the shy girl who was watching it for her grandmother. "How much?" she asked, pointing toward a particularly lovely hemp hat with purple flowers woven around its wide brim.

"Four dollars," the girl replied.

Amanda pulled a five-dollar bill out of the pocket of her white Bermuda shorts and handed it over. "No, no, keep that," she added when the girl handed her a colorful Bahamian dollar in change.

"Thank you, ma'am," the Bahamian girl replied, laughing.

"You spoil these vendors rotten," Brad muttered. "You've got a closetful of hats already, and you won't bargain."

"I know how long it takes to make one of those hats, or a purse. The tourists are only concerned with saving money. They don't realize how much it costs to live here, or how hard these vendors work to make a living. I do."

"I suppose you think a million dollars is too much to pay for a beachfront cottage?"

"Rich absentee owners have certainly priced the Bahamian people out of their own land," she said noncommittally.

Brad stopped and studied Amanda through his sunglasses. Tall and slender, with black hair down to her waist and pale green eyes, she wasn't exactly a beauty, but she dressed to emphasize her best features. And she had a warm heart and a loving nature. If her father hadn't been such a strict parent, Amanda would probably have been long married at twenty-three, with a houseful of children.

"We were all sorry to hear about your father," Brad said solemnly. "Rough, your being an only child."

She shrugged. "He was hardly ever at home, until he got so sick. Even then he preferred the company of his nurse to me. I only saw him when we argued over my choice of possible futures."

"So I recall," Brad said, chuckling. "Harrison wanted to ship you off on a cruise with a new business contact, and you went to college to study accounting."

Amanda felt cold all over. "It was the first fight I ever won, and I've still got the scars. But I knew if I didn't stand up to him then, I never would. It seems that I was the number one contender for Dell Bartlett's fifth wife. I shiver at the very thought."

"So do I, and I'm not even a woman!" Brad muttered.

She laughed. It changed her face back to the impish, radiant one Brad remembered when she was in her teens. Amanda and her father had never been very close, even after her mother died, leaving Harrison quite a nice inheritance from her family. Yet despite her tyrannical father, Amanda had retained some small part of her mischievous nature over the years. But she'd missed out on a lot of fun. Harrison Todd had guarded his daughter as if she were the crown jewels.

"You look wicked when you laugh, Amanda," Brad commented dryly. "Remember that vicious Siamese cat you used to have?"

"Oh, how could I forget?" She giggled. "He knocked Josh into a prickly pear cactus!"

"And you spent half an hour with a flashlight and tweezers pulling the spines out of him." He smiled at her. "He hated being touched. Nobody got near him in those days. That military training made him so aloof. But he let you close enough to undo the damage, and he made you his pet. Now he thinks he owns you."

"Not me, buster," she said, grinning. "I had enough coddling while my father was alive. Besides, Josh is my friend, just as you are. That's all."

Amanda hailed a carriage driver whose horse wore a colorful straw hat. "Take us around Bay Street?" she asked, waving a ten-dollar bill.

"You bet!" the driver said, giving her a blinding white grin. "Climb aboard!"

She and Brad slid into the cart and held on as the driver urged the horse into motion. They rode past breathtaking eighteenth-century architecture mingled with high-rise banks and hotels.

"How's the job?"

"Murder!" she exclaimed. "The *Todd Gazette* was part of my mother's estate, you know, but Dad put it up as collateral on a loan to buy stock, and he defaulted. He had terrible business sense. Josh says he has an insurance policy that will pay it off, but until I'm twenty-five or married, I have no say in its operation." She grimaced, thinking about how poorly the operation was presently being managed. She had wanted to tell Josh, but he had been so busy that she couldn't even get him on the telephone. Aside from needing the rest, she hadn't argued about this trip since it might afford her the opportunity to make Josh see that she stood to lose her inheritance if he didn't give her some control over the paper.

"Your father should have listened to Josh on those stock options," Brad pointed out. "Josh warned him not to invest in the airline in the first place."

"I know. Even though Dad respected Josh's business sense, he wouldn't listen that time." She glanced toward a white jasmine hedge with pure delight, reveling in the smell of it.

"There wasn't really much left to lose. Josh salvaged the good investments, but Dad owed every penny he had. He lived to the very limit of his credit."

"And now you resent being left in the lurch."

"Of course I do," she replied. "But brooding won't solve anything. I have a very nice little cottage all my own in San Antonio and job security. At least," she added with a rueful smile, "until the *Gazette* folds. It isn't doing very well these days."

Brad took that in without comment.

"What I couldn't do with that job press it's attached to, given the chance," she murmured almost to herself. "It's got such potential."

"Josh thinks it's redundant," Brad remarked. "He favors shutting it down and retaining the newspaper."

"But he's wrong!" she said fervently. "Brad, it's only being mismanaged! It's—"

He held up a well-manicured hand. "Stop! We're here to enjoy the scenery and drink in atmosphere." He closed his eyes and sniffed. "Just smell that sea air! It's invigorating, isn't it? No amount of money can buy back clean air and viable land."

"I can't argue with that," Amanda agreed.

"This is the life," Brad murmured lazily. "Sand, sun, and a congenial companion. To hell with business."

"Don't let your brother hear you, or you're going to be out of a job."

"Josh and I are the only two Lawsons left. He couldn't fire me if he wanted to. I'm a marketing genius."

"And so modest!" she commented playfully. "I'm only a working girl, not a self-serving layabout like you!"

He tried to swipe at her hat, and she ducked, laughing. She gave in gracefully after that, letting herself relax and take in the lazy, lovely atmosphere of Nassau.

Ted Balmain met the launch at the marina late in the afternoon. If Josh Lawson had a factotum, Ted was it. Indispensable as valet, bodyguard, and general organizer, the tall, swarthy Texan officially was overseer for Opal Cay, one of seven hundred islands in the Bahamian chain.

"Ted, someday you're going to be delegated to death," Brad remarked as he helped Amanda into a seat.

"That's what I keep telling Josh," Ted agreed pleasantly. He cast off the line from the pier and cranked the engine. "Hang on. I feel reckless."

"I'll throw up," Amanda threatened.

Ted gave her a teasing glance. "No stomach," he told Brad. "She's always going to be a landlubber at heart."

"That's why we went into Nassau. You can forget you're on an island when you're browsing down the streets."

"It was wonderful," she agreed. "Thanks, Brad."

"My pleasure, squirt. Don't I always look out for you?"

Her eyes smiled up at him. "Yes. As usual."

"Josh is back," Ted remarked as he pulled out of the bay.

Amanda's heart beat faster. Josh was so vital, so alive, that his very presence started her blood churning. He could put her in a vicious temper with a few terse words and then make her laugh two minutes later.

Josh was a big brother to both Brad and her. But to everyone else he was "Mr. Lawson," the man who entertained CEOs and diplomats on his yacht, in his San Antonio manor, and on Opal Cay. He had the ear of money moguls on Wall Street, and he was a millionaire many times over because he took risks that sensible men avoided. Sometimes he pushed the boundaries of ethical conduct, but Amanda was the only one who wasn't shy about voicing her disapproval. While Harrison Todd had certainly sheltered his daughter from much, he had encouraged her to stand up for her beliefs. Her father had been happiest when she had fought him tooth and nail, and

now Josh reaped the benefit of her in-house combat training. So to speak.

"What kind of mood is he in?" Brad asked for both of them.

"He brought a houseful of people with him."

Brad let out a long sigh. "Protection," he told Amanda
with a grin.

"Good thought," she agreed. "I'm glad he realizes how
dangerous I am…"

"I wasn't talking about you!" Brad grinned, because he
knew that Josh never ran from a fight with anyone.

"I hope the two of you haven't done anything to set him
off," Ted commented. "He got off the plane breathing fire.
That Arab he's trying to sell his new computers to is giving
him a hard time. I wouldn't mention anything upsetting to
him, if I were you."

Amanda thought about the job press.

Brad considered his latest gambling debts.

She glanced at Brad and frowned at his guilty expression.
"Brad…you haven't been to that casino again?" Amanda asked
slowly.

Brad wouldn't meet her eyes. "No," he said quickly.

She didn't believe him. Brad didn't lie well, and he loved
to gamble. She'd seen him when he had the fever, so intent
on the game that he'd bet anything. Josh had been trying for
months to get him into therapy. But Brad refused to admit
he had a problem, despite the fact that he lost thousands on
the spin of a wheel or the turn of a card.

Amanda stared toward the cay, where Josh's gray Lincoln
was parked at the two-story garage along with at least three
other luxury cars. Two launches were moored at the long pier
that led up to the white stone house. Dozens of blooming
shrubs surrounded the mansion, everything from bougainvillea to hibiscus and jasmine. Opal Cay had satellite cable, an
international network of telephone and fax lines, a computer

system with its own power supply, and a larder that was always full. Even Amanda, who was born to wealth, couldn't remember seeing anything comparable to Josh's island estate.

"Isn't it beautiful?" she asked lazily.

"Isn't it expensive?" Brad teased.

She glanced at him over her shoulder, pushing her wind-blown hair out of the way as she smiled. "Cynic."

He shrugged. "Maybe I am. Josh is rubbing off on me." He moved toward the bow of the launch. "Ease her up to the pier, Ted, and I'll tie her up."

Amanda felt self-conscious in her white Bermuda shorts and simple gray tank top and sandals. Brad was at least wearing white slacks and a designer shirt, but neither of them was properly dressed to mingle with the crowd Josh was entertaining today. She caught sight of Josh's blond head towering over dignified men in suits and women in designer dresses, and she beat a hasty retreat upstairs to change. Anyone who was privileged to get an invitation to the cay was automatically included in parties and even social business meetings.

"Did you see the Arab's wives?" Brad whispered as they darted up the staircase.

"How many has he got?" she queried.

"Two. Don't put on anything too sexy," he cautioned with a grin. "You might be targeted for number three."

"He'd fall short of the mark," she replied mischievously. "I've got it in mind to become a corporate giant, not a used wife."

Brad burst out laughing, but Amanda was already behind her closed door.

CHAPTER TWO

The din of voices and the kaleidoscope of mingled colognes and perfumes gave Amanda a roaring headache. She'd come back downstairs long before Brad, who returned with a worried look and went straight to the bar.

Amanda, clad in a silver sheath with diamanté straps and matching shoes, put on her best party smile for the curious elite of Josh's business group. Most of these people were executives of his company and bankers. But two of the men were Arab entrepreneurs whom Josh was hoping might introduce his newest business computer into Saudi Arabia for him. Even Brad's personable coaxing hadn't budged the men, so Josh had invited them along with the bankers and two of his executives back to Opal Cay for a buffet dinner. It provided him with a more congenial setting in which to wheel and deal. But this time his hospitality didn't seem to be working, because the Arab's black eyes were as cold as anything Amanda had ever seen.

Josh had nodded to her when she came downstairs, but his attention had been on his victims. She felt a little slighted, and that only aggravated her headache. Because she had always looked up to Josh, he could hurt her as no one else ever had. Over the years she'd managed to keep him from knowing it, however.

She watched his guests as they inspected the house with covetous eyes. The enormous white stone mansion in its grove of acacia and silk cotton and sea grape trees was a showplace, tangible evidence of Josh's business acumen. The Lawson Company had branches in every major city in the United States and was moving slowly into Europe and the Middle East. This year Josh was adding a software division line to the Lawson offerings. His was a profitable public company, listed on the New York Stock Exchange, and although he was answerable to stockholders and a stiff-necked board of directors, he ran the whole organization himself, with key executives from every branch answerable only to him.

He ran his business with the same arrogant bearing and cool efficiency of a military commander. His employees stood in awe of him, as did Amanda. Some of the time.

In the beginning of Josh's partnership with Amanda's father, it was Harrison who had the business acumen and the contacts. But for the past few years Joshua had been in almost complete control. That had angered Harrison, who hated the thought of being outdone by a younger man. As a result, he'd tried to break away from the Lawson Company.

The attempt had been disastrous, culminating in Amanda inheriting a minority forty-nine percent of the newspaper that had been in her mother's family for a hundred years. Before Amanda's birth, and her own death in childbirth, Amanda's mother had given Harrison Todd control of her part of the baby's inheritance until the unborn child was twenty-five, but now Joshua had it. Amanda knew she was going to have to fight to convince him to let her inherit a controlling interest.

She also knew Josh didn't usually fight fair, but that he

would with her, because of their friendship. There had been no hope of her gaining control while her father was alive. But Josh would see things differently now. The *Gazette* was the only bright spot in her life. She would no longer have her family home because her father had mortgaged it, and the insurance that had saved the newspaper wasn't going to save the house. Amanda had moved into a small cottage on the property that was free and clear.

Surely Josh would not let her lose control of the newspaper by a tiny percentage after all she'd been through. She desperately needed to retain that precious family heirloom.

She pushed back her long black hair and let it fall against her bare shoulders. Despite the fact that she was still a virgin at twenty-three, she sometimes felt a sensuality as overwhelming as night itself. She felt it most often when Josh was nearby.

Cradling her fluted crystal glass in her slender hands, she walked out into the hall. Secreted in a small alcove, all alone beside a potted palm, she watched Josh hold court in the grand living room.

The sound of footsteps close by broke her trance.

"Mr. Lawson wanted me to ask if you needed anything," Ted Balmain asked with a smile.

"No, thanks," she said, grinning up at him. "I have advanced training in this. I spent a lot of time sitting in the hall outside the principal's office in high school."

"Not you!" he chided.

"I never stopped talking. Or so they said." She peered around him. Brad was trying to charm a young Arab woman. "Ted, do you know what some societies in the Middle East do to you for seducing innocent women?"

Ted cleared his throat. "Well, uh…"

"I think they cut off body parts," she continued. "You might get Brad to one side and jog his memory."

"I'll do my best, but women love him," he murmured.

She laughed. "Well, he's handsome and kind and rich. Why wouldn't they?"

He didn't remind her that Brad had gone through two nasty paternity suits over the years. "I'll educate him," he promised. "Hopefully this party won't go on too much longer. We've had this Middle East computer deal in the works for weeks, and today they wanted to discuss closing it. But, unfortunately for us, not in Nassau. They had a yen to see the house. Josh didn't really have much choice, but it must be difficult for you to mingle with all these people right now."

"Well, I suspected the house would be full. Isn't it usually like this?" she asked gently. "Josh is always surrounded by business people."

"In his income bracket, who isn't?" Ted asked with a chuckle. "Staying rich is demanding. And I don't need to tell you how many people depend on the company's solvency."

"No," she agreed. "I'm only a guest myself, remember. I don't expect preferential treatment."

"All the same, your father just died."

"Ted, I lost my father a long time before he died," she said wistfully. "I'm not sure I ever had him in the first place. But I do know that if it hadn't been for Josh, my life would have been unbearable. When Dad got hard-nosed about things I wanted to do, Josh was my only ally."

"He thinks highly of you," Ted had to admit. He glanced over his shoulder. "They're not going to be here much longer," he promised. "Then we might have a whole day of peace and quiet. Well, you will," he amended with a grimace. "Josh has a meeting in Nassau tomorrow and in Jamaica the day after."

"He needs to delegate more," she mused.

"He can't afford to," he said. "Not on his level. His father did, but he was something of a playboy. In the process, he almost lost the business."

"Balmain!" an impatient voice roared down the hall. It was deep and commanding, rough with authority and just a hint of a Texas drawl.

"Be right there, Josh!" he called back, flushing a little. Obviously he'd strayed too far.

"You'd better go," Amanda murmured. "Thanks anyway, but I'm fine. I thought I might walk down on the beach for a few minutes. I need a little peace and quiet, even if that does sound ungrateful." She leaned forward and glanced toward the elegantly dressed and jeweled women present. "Some of these women smell as if their husbands make a living from selling perfume! I've got the most dreadful headache."

Ted laughed politely, but he hesitated. "Josh won't like you going alone."

She stood up, tall and elegant. "Oh, I know that," she said with a gamine grin. "But I'm going anyway. See you."

She walked toward the front door, her mind blocking out the sounds, the noise, the smells. Ted grimaced, because he would probably catch hell for this. He turned and, stomach tied in knots, went back to join his boss.

"What kept you?" the elegant blond man asked curtly. His dark eyes were intimidating in a darkly tanned face as sculptured and aesthetically pleasing as a Greek statue.

"Amanda wanted to talk," Ted said reluctantly. "She's lonely, I think."

Joshua Cabe Lawson glanced around him impatiently at the Middle Eastern businessmen and their expensively dressed wives, chattering and laughing and drinking his best imported champagne. He wanted to be rid of the lot of them, so that he could comfort Amanda. He knew it was difficult for her just now. That's why he'd insisted she come down here. He hoped a rest would help her get over the shock of her father's death as well as the reality of her financial situation. But it wasn't working out as he'd planned. He was smothered by business demands that had all seemed to come due at this inconvenient time. And these talks were the one thing he couldn't postpone.

"I'm almost finished here," he told Ted Balmain. "Tell her I'll be along in ten minutes."

"She, uh, said she wanted to walk on the beach. She has a headache."

"I'm sure the noise bothers her." He glared at his guests. He lit a cigar and puffed on it irritably, his blond hair catching the light of the chandelier overhead and burning like gold. He was tall—very tall, with a broad, muscular body that was as powerful looking as if he spent hours a day in a gym.

His thick, dark blond eyebrows collided as he considered that he hadn't spent five minutes with his houseguest since she'd arrived. Not that she complained. She never did. She was spirited, but she was the least demanding woman he'd ever known. All the same, he felt vaguely guilty.

"Start hiding liquor bottles," he told Ted. "And jerk Brad away from that terminal fascination in the corner and tell him I want to talk to him. Now."

Ted whispered something to Brad, who quickly excused himself to join his brother.

The difference between the two brothers was striking: one blond and tan and handsome, the other a little shorter with brown hair. But both had dark eyes, and their builds were equally strong.

Brad held up his hand and grinned before Josh could speak. "I know I'm risking assorted body parts, but isn't she a little dish? She speaks French and likes to go riding on her father's Arabians, and she thinks that men are perfection itself!" He wiggled his eyebrows.

Josh was amused, but only briefly. "She's engaged to one of the Rothschilds, and her father has an army."

Brad shrugged. "Easy come, easy go. What do you want?"

"Wrap this up," he said, jerking his head toward the balding sheik he'd been talking to all day. "Tell him the last price I quoted him is rock bottom. He can take it or go home and dust his camels. I haven't got the time to bargain any further."

"Are you sure you want to do that?" Brad asked. "This is an important market."

"I know it. So does he. But I'm not going to sacrifice my profits. There are other marketing avenues open to us. Remind him."

Brad chuckled. He loved watching his older brother in action. "I'll make your wishes known. Anything else?"

"Yes. Get Morrison on the phone. Tell him I'll want him to fax me those last cost estimates for Anders's new operation in Montego Bay by midnight. I don't care if he's not through," he interrupted when Brad started to speak. "I want what he's got by midnight."

"You got it," the younger man said with a sigh, his mind drifting away to a disturbing phone call he'd made before coming downstairs. His worries were playing on his mind, but he couldn't afford to let his brother find out what they were. At least not yet. He forced his attention back to Josh.

The older man misread his expression. He narrowed his dark eyes and smiled sardonically. "You think I'm a tyrant, don't you, Brad? But business is best left to pirates, and we've got two in our ancestry. Cut and thrust is the only way."

"As long as you're sure the other guy isn't wearing plate armor," Brad reminded him.

"Point taken. I'll be on the beach with Amanda. How is she?"

"Putting up a good front, as usual," Brad said. "She's hurting. Harrison wasn't much of a businessman and less of a father. Still, blood is blood."

"Maybe she's mourning what Harrison never could give her—a father's love."

"When I have kids," Brad said firmly, "they may not get much else, but they'll get that."

Josh turned away abruptly. "I'll be on the beach." He nodded politely to the balding Arab and left.

Moonlight sparkled on the softly moving water near the white sand. Amanda was standing in the surf, her shoes in one hand, her hair blowing in the breeze. There was the scent of blooming royal poincianas and hibiscus and jasmine in the night air.

Because of the noise of the surf, she didn't hear him approach until he was right beside her. She looked up, her green eyes faintly covetous on his tall, powerful body in the elegant dark evening clothes. The white of his shirt made his tan seem even darker. She'd known this man forever. All the long years of her cloistered childhood she'd admired him. Through his public and private affairs, through the anguish of her home life, it was dreams of Josh that had kept her sane. He didn't know. That was her secret.

"Sorry I ran away," she said, feeling the need to apologize in case she'd seemed rude. He'd been kind to her, and she felt ungrateful. "I've got a rotten headache."

"Don't apologize," he replied. "I hate the damned noise myself, but it was unavoidable. They'll all be gone soon, one way or the other." He looked down at her. "Why did Ted take so long to ask if you needed anything? Is he the reason you came out here?"

She stared at him blankly. "I beg your pardon?"

"Did he do something to make you uncomfortable?" he asked impatiently. "He's too outspoken sometimes."

She laughed in spite of herself. "As if he ever would. Don't you know how you intimidate your employees?"

He cocked an eyebrow and smiled. "I don't intimidate you."

"Ha, ha," she said. "Then why am I here?"

He shrugged. "You needed a rest. Mirri couldn't get you out of town, so she called me." His eyes narrowed. "She's a good friend. I can't figure out her wild taste in clothes, but I like her."

She smiled. "So do I." She stretched lazily, feeling as safe with Josh as she always had. "I love it here."

She looked at ease, and that relaxed him. Turning back to the sea, he stuck one long-fingered hand into his slacks pocket and lifted the cigar he'd just lit to his mouth. "I bought Opal Cay for this view," he remarked. "Prettiest damn stretch of beach and horizon in this part of the islands."

She had to agree. In the distance, the dark outline of trees on the next island was plainly visible, along with the colorful neon lights of the casino that had been built there. It was one of Josh's holdings, and he liked looking at it at night. The brilliant lights shone in the thick darkness that clung to the horizon, yet the complex was barely visible in daylight.

"I like trees and sunsets," she remarked.

"I like the look of money being made," he mused, watching her.

"That's rotten, Josh!"

"I love to watch you rise to the bait." His dark eyes admired the low cut of her sleek silver dress with its thin straps. "You shouldn't dress like that around this sophisticated crowd," he cautioned. "No wonder Ted took his time getting back."

"It's very modest, compared with what that redhead had on," she accused, though it pleased her to know he noticed. She wanted to impress him, and she wanted him to see her not as a child, but as a woman.

"That redhead is a stripper."

"Why did you invite her?"

He shrugged. "One of the sheiks took a liking to her, as they say back home. I didn't imagine it would hurt the deal to let him bring her along."

"That's disgusting," she said shortly.

His face went bland and vaguely wicked. "No, it isn't. It's business." He lifted an eyebrow. "Don't worry, they won't be staying the night," he said knowingly, and smiled.

She flushed, glad he couldn't see the color in her face. "Why do you always put me in the room next to the main guest room? The last couple you entertained kept me awake all night. She was a redhead, too. And she screamed," she muttered.

"And that brings back a memory, doesn't it?"

She hadn't expected him to bring it up. In eight years they'd never talked about it. She shifted her stance, trying not to let him see her face.

"Aren't you going to answer?" he chided.

"There's nothing to say. What I saw happened a long time ago."

He put his smoldering cigar in his mouth and forced the broad tip back into bright orange life. "It isn't a memory I like," he said gruffly. "It shamed me to know you'd seen me with Terri on the beach. I was aroused enough to be careless."

"I didn't even realize you were out there with her," she replied tersely. She tried to blot out the memory of Josh's aroused, nude body poised over Terri's writhing form, but it was impossible.

She looked away, shivering with reaction. How that memory had haunted her, the sight of his big hand on Terri's hips as he'd jerked her up to him in a sharp rhythm. When she'd cried out and convulsed, Amanda had been horrified. Then Josh had found his own satisfaction and the sight had burned into her brain like acid. She'd run away, so fast, trying to escape the erotic images.

She closed her mind to the rest of it. Turning, she walked along the beach. Her body felt oddly on fire.

"I know it was traumatic for you," he said quietly, falling

easily into step beside her. "Maybe I should have brought this all up at the time, but you were pretty naive at fifteen."

She wrapped her arms across her chest, trying to forget the memory of his face as he'd suddenly given in to his own pleasure. In all her life she'd never seen anything like it.

"There's no need to explain it all, Josh," she whispered in anguish, turning her head away. "I understand now what was happening."

He took a sharp breath and jammed one hand into his pocket. "All right," he said angrily. "We'll skirt around it some more, just as we have for the past eight years. I just wanted to clear the air. You brought up the noisy, amorous guests next door to you, so, it seemed like the right time. But I guess you've had enough to deal with lately without my bringing up embarrassing memories."

She stopped walking and turned to him, her face shadowed as she looked up. "Dad protected me so," she began slowly. "I'd...never even seen a naked man."

"Your father sheltered you too damned much," he said.

She lifted her hair away from her hot face without looking at him. Her body felt funny. Hot. Clammy. Throbbing with some sensation she couldn't understand.

Josh paused in front of her and reached out and touched her shoulder. His fingers fell lightly on her heated flesh. She caught her breath. His touch was the most erotic she'd ever felt, and she couldn't hide her reaction.

His dark eyes slid down to her thin gown, to the small, hard peaks that betrayed what she was feeling. That, and her ragged breathing and the set of her exquisite body, told him things he didn't really want to know just yet.

"You're vulnerable," he said curtly. "The night, the strain of the past week, the excitement tonight...maybe even the memory we share, it's all knocked the pins out from under you."

"Yes," she said, her eyes wide as they searched his in the flood of light that came from the house.

His fingers trailed along the throbbing pulse in her throat, and further, to the faint outline of her collarbone. Her breath caught, but she didn't protest or push at his hand.

His lips parted as he watched her face. Somewhere in the back of his mind he knew this was dangerous. She was unguarded, and he was aroused. It had been a long time since he'd been with a woman. Just after Terri had left, there had been a Latin heiress with whom he'd conducted a very lukewarm, long-distance affair. And yet the tiny sound that suddenly escaped Amanda's throat aroused him more than Louisa Valdez's naked body in a bed ever had.

Amanda shivered. In one moment she'd recognized the years of frustrated longing she'd felt for him, and suddenly she needed him more than ever.

He couldn't quite believe the look of desire he saw on her face. It unsettled him. The cigar dangled in his free hand, and he fought the sudden shift in his perception of her.

She still hadn't moved, but his mind had. His fingers lifted as if her soft skin were white fire. He didn't dare touch her again. He didn't move. His face poised above hers as if it had been carved from stone.

"Joshua?" Was that husky whisper her voice?

His gaze fell to the taut thrust of her breasts against her bodice, down to her smooth hips and her long, elegant legs, to her pretty bare feet. Her silver shoes lay scattered on the white sand, the foaming surf just touching them. He had to remember why he couldn't get involved with a woman, especially not with Amanda.

With a soft curse, he moved away from her all at once. "Here," he said gruffly, "you've left your shoes in the surf. They'll be soaked."

His words brought Amanda back to reality.

"They're old," she said. "I touched them up with some of Harriet's silver hairspray."

He looked for his cigar and found it lying in the water. He sighed and shoved his hands in his pockets. He smoked too much, anyway. "Harriet's hairspray?!" he replied suddenly.

She laughed. He sometimes seemed to be listening when really he was miles away. "That will teach you to pay attention when I talk to you," she said, and in seconds he was smiling and everything was back to normal.

Afterward Amanda could hardly remember when or how they'd gone inside. But once she was upstairs, she almost collapsed with burning heat on her bed. Her head was really splitting now, and she was feeling particularly vulnerable.

She wanted Josh. She could no longer deny the sensations she felt. But she'd make sure that she stayed in control from now on. Having only just escaped her father's domination, she was in no hurry to rush back into emotional slavery.

At least Josh wasn't going to take advantage of her weakness. He'd rejected her, but not unkindly. She'd heard some of the rumors about his lovers. A lot about Terri, the woman she'd seen him with on the beach so long ago. She knew he didn't want to get married, but that he was an honorable man. He knew Amanda too well to lure her into his bed for a few minutes of pleasure. Maybe that was a good thing, but all the same her body throbbed until dawn. The worst thing was that she hadn't even had the presence of mind to mention the job press at the newspaper office to him.

Josh gave up on the idea of sleeping when his company finally departed. He'd won his deal with the oil sheik, and he should have felt satisfied. But he didn't.

He felt as restless as ever. Imbued with an ongoing urgency about life, he often wore out employees who simply couldn't meet the demands he placed on them. Like many overachievers, he was impatient with people who lived at a normal pace.

"Go to bed, for God's sake," Josh said to Ted. "You're asleep on your feet."

Ted chuckled as he rose from his comfortable chair. "I don't mind keeping you company," he said. "But a few hours of sleep sounds great. You seem to live on catnaps."

Josh shrugged. "In the early days it was the only way I could manage to save the company. Now, it's a habit." He frowned. That wasn't quite true. What he'd felt with Amanda bothered him. He lit a cigar impatiently.

"That will kill you," Ted remarked at the door.

"Life kills people, too," came the sardonic reply. "Dina's enrolled me in a stop smoking seminar," he added. "I'll kick the habit. But not tonight."

Ted shrugged. "Suit yourself. See you in the morning."

The door closed, and he was alone with his thoughts, his memories.

He was going to miss Harrison Todd. Amanda's father had not been a perfect human being, but Joshua had learned a lot from him in the early days. Knowing he wouldn't have Harrison around had been a blow. Brad was a good salesman, but Harrison had years of experience neither Lawson brother had had a chance to accumulate.

Business, he mused. Even when he was alone, it dominated his mind. Better that than Amanda's soft, pretty body, he reminded himself. His young life had been a kaleidoscope of affairs not unlike his parents' adulterous adventures. He could remember his father flirting openly with other women, and it wasn't a rare occurrence. His mother had been a little more discreet, but there were always men half her age traveling with her, helping her spend her money.

Sent off to school at the age of six, Josh had never known a family environment or honest love. Amanda's tender concern for him over the cactus so many years earlier had surprised him. He wasn't accustomed to people caring about him more than his money.

Amanda stayed near him at the worst times of his life. When he'd broken his leg on a skiing trip, it had been Amanda who'd come to see him in the hospital with potted plants and sympathy. She'd fussed over him when he was sick, teased him when he was well, become an integral part of his life. But in all that time he'd never touched her. Not even under the mistletoe at Christmas.

Everything had changed a few hours earlier on the beach. Now he didn't recall her nurturing ways. He wanted her, but he didn't know how to reconcile that with his affection for her, with their friendship.

With other women, relationships were simple. His lovers were experienced, sophisticated women who could settle for sex without emotional involvement. He knew that wouldn't be possible with Amanda. He equated Amanda and sex with marriage and children and forever after. Since marriage had become an impossibility for him, he had to reconcile himself to keeping his hands off Amanda. Tonight had been a moment out of time. She'd sensed his rejection at once and with grace and dignity. He had to make sure that he didn't put her in that position twice, because he didn't like seeing Amanda humbled. It didn't suit her spirited nature at all. He'd spent years prodding her temper, helping her stand up to her father. Now he had to keep her on the right track.

He flung open a file folder and buried his thoughts in business.

CHAPTER THREE

The ocean off Opal Cay was every shade of mingled green and blue in the color spectrum. Like the rest of the Bahama Islands chain, the water was crystalline, unpolluted. Virginal.

Amanda smiled at the unspoiled beauty and hoped that this exquisite sugar-white beach would never go the way of so many other beautiful coves that now boasted casino and hotel complexes.

She pushed her hands deeper into the pockets of her short white robe. She'd just been swimming, and her slender body was still wet, like her long black hair. She lifted it to the ever-present breeze, feeling the hot, wet wind pull at it, drying it. Under the robe was a yellow bikini with red stripes, the first unconventional statement she'd made since her father's death.

She knew she should have felt something. Sadness. Grief. Loss. Emptiness. There was only relief. What a eulogy for Harrison Sanford Todd.

"I must be heartless," she said aloud.

"Why?" came a deep, cynically amused reply from over her shoulder.

She turned, her pale green eyes wide. They softened helplessly at the masculine perfection of the man who approached
her. She pushed back her long, windblown hair to keep it out
of her mouth in the crisp breeze. "I thought you were going
to Nassau."

"Not until eleven-thirty. It's barely seven. Why are you
out so early?"

"I dreamed about Dad," she said. It wasn't the whole truth,
but it was close enough. She rammed her hands deep into her
pockets. "I wish I could miss him."

"He wasn't exactly a family man, Amanda. Don't waste
time on unnecessary guilt. He gave what he could, and so did
you. Let that be enough," Josh said in his soft, deep Texas accent. His dark eyes flashed like the reflection of the ocean in
sunlight as he looked down at her from his imposing height.
"Didn't I mention the undertow and the danger of swimming alone?"

"You probably did," she agreed with a grin. "And I probably didn't listen. But I only went out a little way. I'm not
terribly adventurous. Yet," she added.

He smiled. "You'll get around to it. It's a big world."

"And full of sharks," she mused.

His eyes narrowed as he glanced seaward. A smoking cigar
dangled from one lean, darkly tanned hand, its only adorn-
ment a thin gold watch buried in the thick hair of his strong
wrist. He was wearing white slacks with a sedate gray T-
shirt, tediously conventional. It was like flying a false flag,
because there was nothing, absolutely nothing, conventional
about Joshua Cabe Lawson, as his business adversaries had
learned to their cost.

He towered over her, despite the fact that she was tall and
slender. His blond good looks and superb physical presence
drew women like a magnet. His scandalous reputation had
dimmed only briefly during the time he was seeing Terri. Al-

though Josh had genuinely loved the woman, she'd left him because he didn't want to get married. He was incapable of commitment except when it came to business matters. Then he was as dedicated as any workaholic.

Amanda, fresh out of college and brimming with ideas, had some small understanding of the aphrodisiac that a career could provide. She wanted desperately to have a chance to make the *Todd Gazette*'s small job press grow to its full potential. The present manager, Ward Johnson, had been in his job so long that he just slogged along from day to day in the same old rut, never bothering to change anything at all. His first love was the weekly newspaper. The job press was only a worrying sideline to him, and like Josh, he wanted to close it down or sell off the equipment. Amanda didn't. She knew it could pay for itself. If only it were run right!

Amanda loved working at the paper. Although she didn't have a journalism degree, she did have one in business, and she had some innovative ideas about how to upgrade the antiquated equipment, reorganize the print shop, and structure the job descriptions of the staff who overlapped both businesses. But repressed from childhood by her overbearing, domineering father, she hadn't yet learned how to be aggressive without being offensive, and when she made gentle suggestions, no one would listen to her. Least of all the man at her side.

She looked up at him and wondered idly why he never made her feel smothered even when he did exercise his protective instincts. For a year after she'd come home from a finishing school in Switzerland, he'd hounded her until she'd entered a local San Antonio college, late, at the age of nineteen.

Joshua had steered her toward college when her father hadn't even noticed her lack of occupation. Women needed to train in a profession, Josh had insisted, and not be dependent on anyone else for a living—even a husband, if she ever married. She'd taken that one piece of advice and gone on to major in business and minor in marketing. She'd graduated summa cum laude while Josh watched her accept her diploma. Her father had been closing a deal in London.

Josh had gone into business with her father eight years before, and despite the fact that he seemed to hate almost everyone he associated with, he'd been kind to Amanda since the first time he'd seen her.

She remembered that meeting with amused delight. Tough Joshua Lawson had fallen into a prickly pear cactus because of her cat, Butch—a fourteen-pound monster of a cat with the disposition of a rattler. Amanda had been horrified that her pet was going to be strangled, but her compassion for Joshua had been even stronger than her fear for Butch. She'd rushed to get a pair of tweezers, and it had taken her twenty long minutes to pull out every cactus hair. She'd done it painstakingly, while a surprised and then amused Joshua sat docilely and allowed a personal invasion that he would have tolerated from no one else. Amanda hadn't known that until years later, when he'd confessed it with rueful amusement.

"What are you smiling about?" he murmured.

"The prickly pear cactus," she said immediately.

He chuckled. "Yes. The prickly pear. What ever became of that blue-eyed cat?"

"He died, remember? While he was staying with Mirri last year," she replied, a little sad.

"Tiger Lily," he muttered.

His reference to Mirri made her smile. "Her temper is no worse than yours," she pointed out. "And she's the best friend I've got."

"She's a lot like you," he said disgustedly. "Incredibly repressed and hopelessly locked into a self-destructive pattern of solitary living."

"Well, thank you for that professional analysis," she said

sarcastically. "And you aren't supposed to notice that Mirri's repressed," she reminded him gently. "She certainly doesn't give that impression to strangers."

"I know," he replied. "She puts on a good act when she's dressing like a third-rate prostitute, piling on makeup, flirting outrageously, and publicly announcing that she wants to have some man's children." He chuckled. "And how they run! But one day she's going to find someone who'll mistake that image for the real woman. And I'll feel sorry for her when she does."

"I hope it never happens," Amanda remarked.

"So do I. Her scars are deep enough. Like yours." His eyes narrowed on her face. "Someone should have taken a horse-whip to Harrison years ago. I considered it a time or two, on your behalf. What he did to you was criminal. I could never make him see it."

She was surprised and touched that he'd cared enough to try. "He could be cruel," she agreed. "But he wasn't all bad. He did find good people to take care of me, and I always had everything I wanted."

"Everything except love," he agreed. He touched her chin, and his fingers felt hard and cool against her face as he lifted it. "Some lucky man is going to enjoy you one day, Amanda, with all that love and need welled up in you, just waiting to pour out."

She smiled at him, ignoring the sweet explosions that were going off all over her body. "Just as long as he can cook and use a vacuum cleaner," she teased.

He laughed, not offended at all. His eyes went back to the horizon. "At least you won't be hiding out anymore."

"No, I won't," she replied, realizing this was the perfect opportunity to assert herself further. "Joshua, what about the job press? Are you really going to side with Ward Johnson and close it down?"

"Here it comes," he grumbled, glaring at her. "Can't we get away from that damned job press? What do you know about running a job press, anyway?"

It was impossible to wring a decision out of him. She'd long since learned that he was a past master of the Socratic method—answering questions with questions.

"I know more about it than Ward Johnson seems to. He's running the operation into the ground. Josh, I'd like to take over management of the newspaper and job press in San Antonio," she blurted out.

"We had this conversation before Harrison died. The answer is still the same. No," he said.

"You might hear me out before you make any snap decisions. I've thought about it a lot. I have a degree in business administration. I know how to manage a business."

"You have the education, yes." He turned to her, his face hard and unyielding. "You don't have the experience, the ruthlessness, to handle people."

Management doesn't always require ruthlessness. "I've been working at the paper for two months. I've managed everything recently, and I've noticed a lot of flaws..."

"You've been substituting for Ward Johnson when he was out of the office," he returned. "That's a far cry from managing on a day-to-day basis. And what do you want me to do with Ward, fire him after fifteen years of loyal service just so you can play Madam Executive?"

She flushed with temper, her green eyes darkening, her face flushing. "You're forgetting that I own forty-nine percent of the paper," she said through clenched teeth. "And that it's been in my mother's family for almost a hundred years!"

"You'll get control of that forty-nine percent only when you comply with the terms of the will," he said with a cold smile.

"I'll contest it!" she raged.

"Your father's mind was as sound as mine. You haven't got a legal leg to stand on."

She felt as if her face had gone purple. Rage sparkled in her pale green eyes, making them as glassy as ice.

"Until you reach twenty-five, or marry," he reminded her bluntly, "I suggest you follow Ward Johnson's lead. Then we'll talk."

"Ward Johnson can go to hell," she said icily. "And you can keep him company, Joshua!"

His wide, masculine mouth curled up at the corners in amusement. "When you were about seventeen, you had all the spunk of a two-hour-old bunny rabbit," he remarked. "That was when I started to needle you. Remember?"

"Made me furious," she corrected, almost choking on the flash of temper. She took deep breaths to regain control. "Made me mad enough to throw things."

He nodded. "It was what you needed. Harrison had made a puppet out of you," he added, his face hard. "A damned little doll whose strings he pulled. I taught you to fight for your survival."

Slowly the rage left her. Yes. He had done that for her. And once she'd started to challenge her father, her life had changed. She, who had never raised a hand in class in school, who had never spoken back to an adversary, was suddenly able to stand up to anyone.

"It seems I learned well," she said after a minute. She glanced up at him with a rueful smile. "But it's uncomfortable to fight, just the same."

"Or lose. But both experiences teach valuable lessons," he returned. His eyes were almost transparent for a few seconds. He could have told her that he knew as much as she did about being overwhelmed and dominated. His childhood had been no joy ride. But that was something he never discussed. Not even with Brad.

He stepped away, taking a long draw from the cigar. "Disgusting habit," he muttered. He pulled a tiny tape recorder from his pocket and depressed the record button. "Dina, remind me about that no smoking seminar at the Sheraton next week. I've got a board meeting that morning, so I'll forget otherwise."

Amanda smiled secretly, amused at his gesture. Dina had been his secretary since his father's untimely death from a heart attack ten years ago. She knew where all the bodies were buried, and she was efficient in a frightening way. Amanda had once wondered, quite seriously, if Dina was psychic, because she seemed able to anticipate every move Josh made. Even now she probably had an alarm programmed into her computer to remind him of that seminar he'd just remembered.

"Why are you grinning like the Cheshire cat?" he asked curtly. "Another dangling thought?"

The smile vanished. Her hands clenched in her pockets as she prepared for yet another fruitless argument. "About the job press..."

"No," he repeated with cold emphasis.

She threw up her hands. "I could get more out of a stone wall!"

"There's one." He indicated the sea wall that protected the front of the house. "Try it."

Her shoulders sagged. She was too worn out to fight any more today. "Will you at least look at some figures on the press before you kill it?" she asked quietly, determined to set at least that much accomplished.

"All right. But that's all I'm promising." That deep south Texas drawl of his was deceptive. It didn't denote an easygoing disposition. Quite the opposite, in fact. "And I'm not kicking out Ward Johnson."

"I wouldn't really want you to go that far," she confessed. "He has problems at home."

"And you collect broken things and broken people," he said perceptively. "Like the stray cat that was badly bitten by a neighborhood dog and had to be taken in," he recited. "And the pigeon with a broken wing. Then there was, of all things, a garter snake that the gardener cut with a weed eater!"

"It was only a little snake," she defended herself.

"The bleeding heart of the world," he scoffed. "You care too much about the wrong things."

"Somebody has to."

"I suppose. But don't look at me. I've got a business to run." He turned his wrist abruptly and glanced at his watch. "I have to get ready to go into Nassau."

"You wouldn't like to take a day off?" she asked. He looked surprised. "A day off," she began, a grin lighting up her face. "It's when you don't work for an entire day. You go snorkeling or sunbathe or sight-seeing…"

"A hell of a waste of time!"

"You're going to wear yourself out from the inside," she pointed out. "First your brain, then your stomach, then your heart. In no time you'll be a walking bone-and-skin frame with nothing inside."

"You don't say?" He took a handful of her long black hair in one hand and tugged on it as he had done when she was a kid. Only now her head eased back gently, and his eyes dropped to her soft pink mouth and lingered there before he spoke. "You're sassy," he said.

"I learned by watching you," she said. Her voice sounded husky. She couldn't breathe properly when he was this close, and she was afraid that it might show. "Joshua, you're hurting my hair," she whispered unsteadily.

His grip lessened, but only slightly. He actually leaned toward her, so that his coffee-and-smoke-scented breath cooled her parted lips. "Be careful that I don't decide to take you over," he said deeply. "You'd make one hell of an acquisition."

"Don't be silly. I wouldn't match the decor in your office at all," she said with forced lightness. Her body was already burning. "You like dark Mediterranean, and I'm French provincial. Besides, you're too busy."

"Is that what you really think? That I only have a cash register for a brain and a slide rule for a heart? You, of all people on earth, should know better," he added, his voice as sensuous as velvet against bare skin. "I taught you to fight, but I guess you'll have to learn just about everything else on your own. I'm too jaded to make a proper tutor." He let her hair fall back to her shoulders and turned away from her.

She studied his long back with pure pleasure. "I have to get my education somewhere, Josh," she murmured, striking just the right note of amused honesty to raise one of his eyebrows. "If you won't sacrifice yourself for me, I guess I'll have to advertise for someone who will."

"No, you won't. You don't know how to play that kind of game. When you give yourself, it will be for keeps."

She looked up at him openly, appreciating the hard lines of his face, the faint weariness there. "You're tired. Why don't you send Brad to Nassau and get some rest?"

Her concern almost pushed him over the edge. He didn't want it; he didn't need it! His hand clenched at his side. He took a draw from the cigar and sent up a cloud of smoke.

"Because Brad wouldn't get any farther than the casino across the bridge on Paradise Island, and you know it," he said flatly. "I'm going to keep him away from temptation, at least until we close this Saudi Arabian contract."

Amanda had her own suspicions about how well Brad was avoiding temptation, but she couldn't sell him out to his brother. Josh made no allowances for weakness.

"You're hard to argue with," she commented.

"Then stop doing it. I don't have time, anyway." He checked his watch again. "I'll try to be back in time for dinner."

"I haven't seen you for thirty minutes at a stretch since I've been here. And I really do have to think about getting back to San Antonio."

"It's only a week since the funeral," he said. "Stay a while longer. Why not fly over to Jamaica with me tomorrow? I'll make sure I have time for you."

"Don't strain yourself," she said, annoyed at his patronizing one.

"Don't worry. I won't," he said with a pleasant smile.

She threw up her hands. "Every time I'm around you, I feel as if I've been dragged backward through a hedge."

His face seemed faintly troubled. He touched her hair again, but this time he drew his hand away at once. He searched her eyes intently and held them until her heart ran away.

"I'm not a child, Josh," she said huskily.

"You aren't superficial, either," he replied. "You're as deep as the ocean, as enigmatic as a budding rose in a briar patch. I admire your values as much as I admire your spirit. I could never soil that."

"You pirate," she accused softly. "You're as old-fashioned as I am."

He nodded slowly. "Don't tell anyone," he said with a half smile, and started walking again. "I'd hate to ruin my image."

CHAPTER FOUR

Brad didn't go to Nassau. Josh went himself. But that evening at dinner, Josh did ask his brother to travel to Montego Bay.

"All right," Brad said pleasantly. "I'll go to Jamaica for you. But I do need to be back in San Antonio by the end of the week. I've got a prospective client to court, an aerospace executive."

Amanda caught the flicker in Brad's eyes that Josh missed. Perhaps she simply knew him better, but his reason for going home to Texas didn't sound completely honest.

"Suit yourself, as long as you hold up your end," Josh replied. "I have to admit that you've made some startling gains in new territory this year."

Brad fingered his wineglass and didn't look up. "Enough for a raise?"

"You still owe me six months' salary," Josh reminded him. "And you're paying off a hell of a loan."

Brad's dark eyes flashed in anger at his brother. "Go ahead. Rub it in. So I lost. But sometimes I win. When I do, I win big!"

"Nobody wins at a gambling house," Josh said coldly. "It's a narcotic. You're addicted, but you won't admit it."

Brad tossed down his napkin and got to his feet. "I'll take the Learjet to Mo' Bay in the morning. When I've finished there, I'm going home." He dared his brother to argue.

Josh didn't. He simply stared at the younger man, ending that argument. Brad glanced at Amanda with a strained smile and left the room.

"You ride him hard," she told Josh.

"Try the quenelles," he said, ignoring her comment. "They're delicious."

"He's your brother."

"That's why I want him to wake up, before he squanders his inheritance and ruins his life."

"You can't drag him into some clinic, Josh," she persisted. "He's not a chair that you can send off to be reupholstered."

He cocked an eyebrow. "You don't want to start this tonight," he said firmly, a faint threat in his voice.

She wasn't going to change his mind. As usual, it was already solidifying as quickly as concrete. She lifted her fork to her mouth. He was right: the quenelles were delicious.

While a taciturn, uncommunicative Brad flew to Jamaica, Josh took Amanda out in the launch to another island, an uninhabited one near Opal Cay.

"You yourself said that I needed some time off," he reminded her when she seemed surprised at his choice of location. "Harriet packed us a delicious picnic lunch and a bottle of wine."

She smiled. The prospect of an entire day with Josh was devastating to her senses. Heaven.

Josh dropped the anchor and they disembarked. It was autumn back in San Antonio, but here it was eternal summer. The beach was as white as refined sugar. The sea was every shade of aqua and blue in existence. There wasn't a cloud in the sky. It was, Amanda thought as she waded ashore, a perfect day for a picnic.

She glanced at Josh, trying not to be obvious as she noticed his long, muscular legs in white Bermuda shorts. He was wearing a blue knit shirt with them, one that showed off the breadth of his chest and shoulders. He wore deck shoes and deftly unloaded their things in a few, easy strides. Amanda enjoyed watching him. She loved his hands. They were large and powerful, his fingers ending in broad, flat nails that were immaculately clean.

She'd tied her long hair back in a ponytail for comfort, but she felt smaller and younger than ever as she walked along in his shadow to the shelter of palm trees and sea grape trees along the beach.

"Was this an impulse?" she asked.

He spread the white linen cloth on the ground and put the big wicker hamper on it, leaving Amanda to get out the plates and silverware while he removed the covered containers of food.

"Yes. I do get them every once in a while," he said. He glared teasingly at her over a tub of chilled tuna salad. "If you make one false move, so help me, I'll bury you up to your pretty neck in the sand and leave you here."

She laughed, because he looked so menacing. "Would you, really?"

"Probably not."

Her eyes met his. "I was only teasing, you know," she said gently. "I don't think of you as a…well, I really am old-fashioned about some things."

"I know." He took a plate and handed her an open container with a service spoon. "Here. Eat something. You've been living on your nerves for too long already."

"It still hurts, a little," she confessed, looking up. "Dad didn't care very much for me, but he was all I had."

"That isn't true. You still have Brad and Mirri and me."

"Yes. Yes, I do." She took the container and filled her plate.

Josh hadn't brought swimming trunks, but that was just as well, because Amanda was more than content to lie in the sun. She was determined to get an even tan before she went home.

Josh had stripped off his shirt and was lying on the beach bare-chested. She stared at him covertly, enjoying the power and masculine beauty of his body. He was very tan and muscular without being misshapen, as some overenthusiastic bodybuilders seemed to Amanda. He was long and lean, but not thin. His chest had a wedge of dark blond hair that ran in a wide band down to the waistband of his shorts. And probably beyond.

"Are you tanned all over like that?" she asked without thinking.

He didn't open his eyes. He smiled, and one big hand went to the fastening of his shorts. "Want to see?"

She laughed. The sound was silvery and sweet in the quiet of the island, unbroken except for the bubbling of the surf and the sound of sea gulls sweeping down onto the beach. "No. Thank you," she added politely.

He yawned. "Brad and I don't bother with bathing suits when we've got the island to ourselves." He glanced at her. "I don't doubt that you've got white stripes all over, though."

Without looking at him she said, "With my luck, one of my neighbors would be hiding in the bushes with a videocamera, and I'd be on the six o'clock news for indecent exposure."

"There are spoilsports everywhere," he murmured. "I'm tired." He sounded faintly surprised.

"You never sleep," she said. "I'm amazed that you haven't collapsed."

"I'm indestructible."

"Nobody is. When was the last time you had a physical?"

"I've got one scheduled in two weeks," he said. "My board of directors insists on it once a year."

He didn't add that this year he'd gotten the courage to request an additional, private test. He wished now that he'd left it alone. Part of him didn't want confirmation of something that he'd suspected for several years; another part wanted to be sure.

"Good for them," Amanda said. "None of us want you to drop dead, you know."

"Are you sure about that? I'm the only thing standing between you and the *Gazette*."

"You and my father's will," she emphasized. She sat up, looking down at him with soft green eyes. "And I wouldn't want anything to happen to you. Not ever. Not for money or any other reason."

His eyes were very dark. They narrowed and ran slowly down to the V neck of her sleeveless T-shirt and back up again to her oval face with its exquisite expression. He found that looking at her gave him pleasure. It also kindled a curiosity that he was tired of fighting.

Something inside him caught fire, burned. She was untouched, and he wanted her. Needed her. Was desperate for her. He could stand only so much, and the temptation she'd unwittingly offered him had made him restless and unable to sleep, even to work these last few days. He let out a slow breath and gave in to it. Just once, he told himself. No heavy stuff, and just…this once.

He sat up, very slowly. His hand went to her mouth. He drew the tip of his forefinger softly over the curve of her lower lip, smearing lipstick and nerves as he held her eyes. His gaze fell to her soft mouth, and he bent his head. "This is not the best idea I've ever had. But kiss me anyway, Amanda," he breathed as he leaned forward and his hard mouth fit itself slowly over hers.

Amanda's whole body clenched with tense pleasure. It was the first time—the very first time, despite her dreams of years past. The sweet shock of his mouth on her soft lips made her whimper and curl into him like ivy. She reached up, straining to get her arms around his neck. The kiss she'd wanted so badly was hers now, and she was drowning in it, being seared by it. Her body felt as if it were on fire. It throbbed and ached in the oddest places, and she felt her long, elegant legs trembling as he drew her across his body and began to deepen the kiss.

The only men she'd ever kissed had been, for the most part, students at college. One or two of them had been experienced, but the majority had been like her—shy and introverted and not very experienced. She couldn't ever remember being tempted to go to bed with any of them.

But with Josh she felt differently. Perhaps their long friendship made him more acceptable to her, or perhaps it was the barely tamed sensuality of his mouth that devastated her senses. Whatever the explanation, she collapsed like an alcoholic drowning in liquor the minute he touched her.

He seemed to know it, because he tempered his ardor to match her lack of experience. She stiffened when he gathered her hips against the aroused thrust of his own. He loosened his hold, concentrating instead on teasing her mouth with his tongue, nipping it gently with his teeth. She relaxed, and when she did, his hands slid back to her hips and tugged coaxingly until her belly was completely against his.

Memories of his hands on another woman's hips, pulling her to him as he loomed over her in the moonlit darkness filtered through Amanda's mind.

She gasped under his mouth, and he lifted his head with obvious reluctance.

"Does it disturb you that I'm aroused?" he asked huskily.

"Yes," she confessed with embarrassment, hiding her face in his chest.

He took deep breaths. His heartbeat was shaking his powerful body, but he didn't try to force her to accept anything she didn't want.

He lifted her chin and searched her eyes slowly, seeing the desire and fear mingling there. That, and the adoration that she was too inexperienced to hide. She was deeply infatuated with him. He'd known it for years, but until now he'd managed not to do anything about it.

He drew in a long, ragged breath and moved away from her. "No," he said quietly. "I can't handle this, Amanda."

She licked her lips and tasted him on them. He looked as unsettled as she felt, but he was fighting the feeling. And winning. He got to his feet and lit a cigar as he walked down to the surf.

By the time he came back, Amanda had everything in the hamper. She tried to act as if nothing had happened.

He reached down to pick up his shirt, knowing Amanda watched his nude torso.

Still aroused, he turned away, dragging the shirt over his head. This wouldn't do. It really wouldn't. Her mouth was the closest he'd ever been to heaven, but he wouldn't start something he couldn't finish.

"We'd better go," he said quietly. "Brad should be back soon. I want to know how he made out."

"I'm ready when you are," she said pleasantly.

He took the hamper, and she walked silently beside him back to the launch.

On the way back, their uncomfortable silence was broken by a sudden gale. It wasn't at all frightening to her. Nothing was, with Josh at the controls. She'd seen him in all sorts of dangerous situations over the years. Once, a sudden squall had come up when they were in the twin-engine plane he'd owned before the Learjet. His cool nerve and unruffled competence had stayed with her as he'd turned what could have been a tragic accident into an adventure.

"What are you thinking about?" he asked on the way across to New Providence, his voice sounding odd in the purr of the engines.

"About how well you handle danger," she replied honestly. "You're very cool under fire."

"I had extensive training, having to face my board of directors with expansion proposals," he said dryly. "It takes nerve to make money."

"Don't I know it." She grimaced. "I don't know if I'll have anything to inherit when I'm twenty-five. It looks as if Ward Johnson is going to lose it all," she said irritably. "His mind isn't really on the job lately."

"Give it up," he advised. "You ought to know by now that I don't budge when I think I'm right." His fingers danced over the controls as Opal Cay came into view on the horizon. "Hold tight."

He pushed the throttle forward, and his dark eyes danced as he fought the squall and the whitecaps on the way in to the small marina.

When they were on the pier, he smiled with wicked amusement at the look on her face. "I thought you trusted me at the controls."

"I do. But I really don't like getting into anything that's over my head."

"Don't you?" In his dark eyes there was a soft, sensual threat that made her pulse leap. But he didn't follow up on it. He took her arm and the hamper and walked briskly toward the house.

Dinner that night was delicious, but Amanda had no real appetite. The lethal combination of Josh's sexy company and the certainty that she had to go back to Texas soon took the edge off the pleasure of the evening.

"Do you want something else?" he asked with concern.

"It's not the food. It's wonderful," she said. She put down her fork. "I really have to go back."

"Why?" he asked irritably. "Are you afraid the business will fail in a week if you aren't there to save it?"

"Don't be sarcastic," she said. "And that just might be the case, even if you won't believe me."

"Don't try to live your life in a flaming rush, Amanda," he cautioned. "You've got all the time in the world."

"Have I?" She looked down at his hand on the white linen cloth, with its dark tan and scattering of blond-tipped brown hair. "The most exciting thing I've ever done was to go to a professional wrestling match where the audience became the feature attraction."

He chuckled. "I remember. I had to rescue you. As I recall," he added with malicious glee, "you started it."

She shifted restlessly. "Well, they called my favorite wrestler a bum and started cheering for that madman who was stomping his face."

"And you rushed to his rescue."

"Somebody had to!"

He burst out laughing, his dark eyes soft with indulgent humor. "You're delightful, did you know? You don't primp for hours, you don't demand diamonds and furs, you don't even insist on going the party rounds every night. You're unique as a companion."

"Unique as yours, I suppose," she said without looking at him. "Or don't you usually take your dinner companions to bed?"

"If I didn't respect you so much, I'd take you there in a minute," he replied easily. He finished his cocktail. "But we share too much history. I have nothing to offer you," he said solemnly. "Nothing at all."

The finality with which he made the statement chilled her. The bleak look in his eyes puzzled her, because coexisting with it was a frank, blistering hot hunger.

"You want me," he said suddenly. "But you still aren't quite sure how you want me, are you, Amanda? You're looking for fairy-tale situations, roses and perfume, happily ever after."

"No," she began, unsure of where this conversation was going.

"A relationship isn't all candlelight and soft music, honey," he said quietly. "It's raw and sensual, and people get hurt. A man changes when he's been with a woman he desires."

"Yes. He doesn't want her anymore," she said knowledgeably.

"Not always," he said sharply. "Sometimes he wants her all the time, to the exclusion of business, honor, morality, anything! That happened to me with Terri. I got careless because I needed her so badly. That's why you saw us that night on the beach. I thought of nothing but her body, was so enthralled by it that I couldn't go even one night without having it. She was just as hungry for me. That kind of attraction can blind you, even when love isn't involved."

"Oh."

"That kind of desperation leaves you out of control," he persisted. "It can convince you to make love in a parked car in the middle of rush hour traffic. That's why I don't have love affairs anymore. I have casual encounters that end almost as soon as they begin." He dropped his eyes to her hands, which were locked together on the table. "I hate addiction. I smoke cigars instead of cigarettes because they're easier to give up. I drink brandy, not whiskey, because I can take it or leave it. I never have more than one drink at a party, because I don't want the risk of losing control."

Amanda had known these things, but she also knew he *was* addicted to smoking, whether or not he admitted it to himself. It cut her heart to know that he wanted no deep relationship again. Because she did.

He got to his feet. "I have to meet someone at the airport in Nassau. Ted's going to take me over in the launch."

"All right."

He paused, staring down at her. "You and I have been friends for a long time. I don't want to lose that because we touched each other and flames kindled, or because you want something in business that I don't want to give you."

"You'll always be my friend, Josh," she said, smiling tightly. "I hope I'll always be yours."

He moved closer to her chair and, leaning a hand on the table, bent so that his face was much too near. His breath brushed her lips when he spoke.

"I owe you more than a broken heart."

She reached up and touched his face. It tautened, and his eyes kindled.

"Do you want me?" she asked in a husky whisper.

"I'm bleeding to death for you," he replied, his voice rough with passion. "And do you know what I'm going to do about it?"

Her lips parted on a rush of breath. "No. What?"

"Absolutely nothing." He moved away from her, and the tension in his body was visible. "It's the only noble thing I've ever done in my life. How's that for a joke?"

He laughed bitterly. A minute later he was gone.

CHAPTER FIVE

Brad closed the deal in Montego Bay, but he took his time getting back to Opal Cay. He had real problems. He had to find a way to cover his bets before he lost something more precious than money. He needed cash, fast. His only hope was to persuade Josh to pull his irons out of the fire one more time. But that wasn't really likely. Josh didn't understand weaknesses, because he didn't have any. He wasn't vulnerable. Calculated business decisions were his life. He was one of the world's strongest people, who never leaned or needed to lean on others. How could he possibly understand a passion for gambling? Not, Brad reflected, that he couldn't quit whenever he wanted to. It's just that until now, he hadn't wanted to. Next time, for sure.

He felt something cold suddenly splash against his suit sleeve.

"OhmigodI'msorry!" tumbled out of the waitress's pretty mouth. She was wearing a spandex skirt that barely covered the top of her thighs, with a clinging white body shirt open over the taut swell of brown breasts. She was blonde, blue-eyed, and incredibly sexy. So sexy that he didn't notice the brown stain on his spotless gray suit sleeve or feel the wetness.

"Hello," he murmured sensually.

"Hello!" she replied, grinning. Her hair was full of colorful, lacy bows. "I'm Barbara, your waitress."

"Brad Lawson," he replied, letting his eyes run down her. The five-star restaurant wasn't crowded this evening. Except for himself and about five couples, it was practically empty. There was this walking dessert here, of course.

Her eyes grew big. "Really?" she asked. "Are you Joshua Lawson's brother?"

Big brother was known everywhere. He wondered if Josh had sampled this delight and decided that he probably hadn't. Josh's taste ran to brunettes. In that way, if no other, he was predictable.

"That's who I am," he agreed.

"Your brother had lunch here once," she said, explaining how she knew him. "I was crying because my mother had gone to the hospital with a heart attack. Mr. Lawson squared it with my boss so that I could have time off to sit with her. He's very nice."

He smiled, relaxing. "Yes, he is. So am I, of course. I'm intelligent, handsome, rich, and incredibly modest."

She laughed. "Are you?"

He put his hand over his heart, momentarily taken out of his woes. "Modest to a fault. Bring me a vat of fried oysters and I'll make all your dreams come true."

She blushed, but she giggled, too. "Could you?"

"Can sharks swim? Away with you! Get those oysters. Hurry, we don't have a second to lose!"

She laughed. "All right. Would you like something to drink?"

"A glass of champagne. Champagne and oysters are the secret of Casanova's success, I'm sure of it."

"Well," she murmured with subtle coquetry, "we'll see, won't we?"

His body tautened at the look in her eyes. He smiled slowly. He wouldn't make it back to the cay tonight. He hoped Josh wouldn't scream too loudly.

Amanda went up to her room early, bored with her own company. She heard Josh go out, but she was fast asleep when he came home. And Brad still hadn't shown up by morning.

It was going on nine in the morning when Amanda phoned Mirri in San Antonio, before she went down to breakfast. She hadn't spoken to her best friend since the funeral, and she was feeling fragile. Josh was driving her mad.

"Are you okay?" Mirri asked her immediately.

"I suppose, except for having to fight Josh at every turn," she replied.

"Really?!" Mirri enthused. "How exciting!"

She was glad Mirri couldn't see her telltale blush. "For a foothold at the newspaper, you idiot," Amanda murmured with forced humor. She lay back on the green-and-white-patterned bedspread with a sigh, her long black hair radiating out from her face in soft waves. "I mean, it's not going to be an easy road to upper-level management. My credentials don't impress him."

"All that brainwork wasted." The other woman sighed. "Well, if at first you don't succeed..."

"I didn't really expect him to turn the whole enterprise over to me. He said that I don't have the experience, and he's right. But I can get it," she added stubbornly. "I was at least hoping for partial control."

"Don't step on any toes," she cautioned. "The reigning editor has chopped off more educated and talented employees than you know. He's underhanded and unscrupulous when it comes to keeping his cozy nest. The only reason he keeps

Joshua in the dark is because your new partner hardly ever has time to get a look in."

"You've been working for the FBI too long," Amanda pointed out. "You're beginning to sound like an agent."

"Don't I wish." Again she sighed. "I'm just a paralegal with big dreams and bad eyes. Do you know what Nelson Stuart told me? He actually said my red hair was too blatant for a government agent!"

"I didn't think you were speaking to Mr. Stuart."

"He's the senior agent," she muttered. "I have to speak to him. I thought I might try law school. He had something to say about that idea, too."

"Well?"

"He said you needed a brain for that."

"Maybe they'll transfer him to someplace cold."

"I volunteered him for Yuma, Arizona. I thought he'd feel more at home someplace hot."

Amanda laughed. She'd seen the steely Mr. Stuart once. He was as dark as Joshua was fair, lean and cold-eyed and very much the lawman. He and the vivacious Mirri had been enemies from her first day at the San Antonio FBI office. The situation hadn't improved much in two years. Mirri threatened to quit more often these days, of course. Mr. Stuart had asked that she be transferred. Neither one of them had had much luck. Or perhaps it was more a case of not wanting to have much luck. They were a very volatile couple, and Amanda often thought that it was as much due to a flaming attraction as it was to the hostility they camouflaged it with.

"When are you coming back?" Mirri asked. "You don't have anybody to talk to over there, and I know Joshua can be hard on your nerves. Not that I don't think a lot of him for taking such good care of you."

"That's for old times' sake, I think," Amanda said quietly. "I owe him a lot. He deserves so much more than a life of mergers and takeovers. It's a pity that he never married and had children."

"Joshua Lawson?!" Mirri exclaimed. "Married? Ha! That'll be the day." There was a pause. "On second thought, there was that South American heiress he was squiring around in New York last month. I forget her name, but they made the color insert in one of the grocery store tabloids. Josh is very handsome, isn't he?"

Amanda didn't want to think about Josh's women. She knew he had them, all too well, but it was much more comfortable to keep her head in the sand and not confront the reasons it bothered her.

"I suppose," she replied noncommittally. "Listen, I'll be home at the end of the week," she continued, changing the subject. "We can go shopping. Now that I work every day, I find I don't have enough clothes to cover the whole week. When I was in school I could wear jeans and T-shirts."

"Okay. I'll go shopping with you, *if* Josh lets you come home so quickly. He may think you need more of a break, and I'd have to agree," she added solemnly. "Taking care of your dad and working every day took its toll on you."

"I figure that if you agree to take a job, it's your responsibility," she reminded her friend. "I like working. Dad had private nurses, thanks to Josh. He never paid much attention to me, even when he was so sick."

"He never paid much attention to you, period," Mirri said coldly. "Just like my father. If I'd had somebody to take care of me when I was in my teens, maybe I wouldn't be the emotional wreck I am now. He turned me loose. He never cared that I went out at night alone, and I was too stupid to know the danger." She paused, her voice thin with memories as they came back to haunt her. "Sweet Jesus," she whispered reverently, gripping the telephone cord, "what I'd have been spared if my mother hadn't died. My life changed when your father sent you to my grammar school instead of a private school."

"We had each other, Mirri," Amanda said with a smile. "Even after I had to transfer to that private high school. Even when your worst nightmare came true."

"If it hadn't been for you, I'd have killed myself that night," Mirri said soberly. She was silent for a minute, remembering the details of that horrible night. Too often they played through her mind. But Amanda was the only one she dared tell. "You took me home with you because Dad was out of town. I cried all night long after we got back from the hospital, and you sat up with me."

"You should have accepted the counseling they offered," Amanda ventured.

"Talk about…that…to a bunch of strangers?" Mirri asked, incredulous. "It's bad enough to have Nelson Stuart looking at me as if he thinks I stepped out of a brothel. He thinks I'm one bad lady."

"You might tell him that vivacious persona is a mask."

"Are you nuts?!" Mirri burst out. "Anyway, Mr. Stuart's opinion of me and fifty cents might buy me a cup of coffee."

"You're hopeless."

"And getting worse. Look, I've got to run. You take care of yourself."

"You, too. See you soon."

As Mirri hung up, she became aware of dark eyes staring at her, glaring at her. She was wearing a colorful skirt with a red peasant blouse—wild colors that suited her and disguised the shamed severity of her soul. Her long red hair fell in natural waves to her shoulders, and her blue eyes were big and thick-lashed in a face dominated by pale skin and freckles.

"Using the company phone on company time, Miss Walsh?" he asked without smiling.

"It's my coffee break, and I got called. I didn't call anyone."

She propped her chin on her hands, supported by her elbows on the desk, and gave him a big-eyed stare. "May I ask you something, Mr. Stuart?"

One dark eye narrowed. "What?"

"Is that your real face, or one you glue on every morning?"

The glare got worse.

"It's just that you never smile, sir," she said with an irrepressible grin. "I only wondered if your face would crack if you tried."

"Proper use of the telephone goes with your responsibilities," he told her stiffly. "No personal calls on company time, whether or not you initiate them."

"I still have—" she checked her watch "—two more minutes on my coffee break. And if you aren't certain that I didn't initiate the call, you can always check," she offered. "After all, you whiz-bang FBI guys can get access to telephone company records, right?"

He continued as if she hadn't spoken. "In addition, I would appreciate it if you could dress in an appropriate manner around this predominantly masculine office."

She looked at herself, from her huge dangly gold circle earrings to her jangly gold bracelets. "You mean, you'd like me to go *naked*?! Mr. Stuart!"

She raised her voice just as two of the younger agents came in the door and quickly averted their faces. They disappeared into another office with muffled hysteria while Mr. Stuart's bruised dignity healed itself.

"On the contrary, Miss Walsh," he said through his teeth, "having you naked in the office would be much less of a distraction than having you dress like a kaleidoscope!"

He turned and walked into his office, closing the door with a subdued thump.

Mirri watched the door for a minute. Then she licked the

point of her index finger and, with a grin, made a mark in the air.

"One for my side," she murmured dryly.

Joshua was preoccupied as he made his way out of the Lincoln he'd just driven around to the village on the other side of the island. He maintained a small cottage industry there so that the local people could better their standard of living.

The islanders on Opal Cay, like many of the Bahamian people, were skilled craftspersons. They wove palm fronds into intricately designed baskets and purses and hats and wall hangings. On New Providence, where Nassau was located, a huge warehouse had long since been converted at St. George Wharf into individual stalls where crafts could be sold by Bahamian merchants to tourists on incoming ocean liners that docked at the bay. But this was a notoriously low-paying procedure, especially as tourists felt obliged to bargain the friendly merchants down so low that they were making the equivalent of one US dollar for a purse or hat that had taken all day to make.

This sort of thing had irritated Josh, who knew full well that people who could afford the trip to the Bahamas could afford to pay five dollars for a handmade straw hat or purse. So he'd worked out a deal with a friend in Kansas who ran an import shop. Crafts made by his employees were marketed in a place far from the ocean, where such exotic goods were rare indeed and brought a fair price.

Joshua furnished the raw materials from which the crafts were made by people on Opal Cay and arranged for their transport and sale. The islanders paid no rent. After all, he reasoned when some of them protested, wasn't it their land to begin with? A piece of paper was no claim on land that generations had loved and nurtured. There was a resident nurse and a small clinic where a French physician called twice a week. Joshua made available modern amenities like electricity and running water, but only for those who wanted them. He forced change and acculturation on no one. Studying the Native American experience had convinced him that trying to absorb a culture and change it completely was nothing more than slow genocide. What he was doing on Opal Cay was meant only to give the people the means to do as they pleased with their own culture. They had requested that he appoint a manager for their profits, which he had. With investments and securities, they were amassing a sizable nest egg. If something ever happened to him, or his empire, they would not be at the mercy of some newcomer who might buy the island and value profit over native population.

He felt at an ebb. The death of Amanda's father had put more strain on him, and he was feeling the burden of endless rounds of talks and bargaining that he now had to shoulder alone. Brad was essentially a contact man, a public relations whiz who could charm just about anyone. But, if pushed hard enough, his brother would give in to deal-breaking points. Josh would crack wide open before he yielded an inch.

He paused in the study long enough to pour himself a small brandy. He'd planned to go into Nassau again to talk to the minister of education about upgrading the computers in the school system, but the gentleman was out of town, and he couldn't get an appointment until next week.

He really was tired. Brad hadn't come back from Montego Bay or telephoned, and he knew that meant one of two things: his baby brother had stumbled onto either a willing girl or a high-stakes poker game. He didn't honestly know which would be worse. Brad was careful, but it was a dangerous world for a womanizer. His own reputation was more myth than fact, to keep women at bay. But Brad's reputation was earned.

While he was glaring into his brandy snifter, Amanda came

into the room, in jeans and a white tank top with her long black hair in a braid down her back.

She stopped at the door. "I didn't hear you drive up."

He studied her figure, liking its slender, elegant lines. "Imagine keeping a Lincoln just to drive around a tiny island. Extravagant, isn't it, but visitors are impressed by it."

"No doubt." He liked the way she looked, young and fresh and unpretentious. His heart ached at the sight of her.

Almost involuntarily, he moved forward and touched his brandy snifter gently to her full lower lip, which was devoid of lipstick. "Taste."

"I don't like brandy," she began.

"It's an acquired taste. Acquire it."

He smiled slowly, and she couldn't resist him. She tasted it and made a face as it stung her tongue.

"You're the one indulging in it. Why force me?" she asked, watching him reach out to place the snifter on the bar.

"Because."

She smiled back at him, delighted at his playfulness, then stunned when he casually draped his arm around her. Amanda's heart ran wild at the closeness, at the feel of all that warm strength and power so near. He looked tall and intimidating at this range. Far too handsome for comfort with the overhead light making metallic patterns in his blond hair, with his dark eyes narrow and sensuous looking into hers.

Her breath caught as his fingers stroked down the side of her neck. His voice was deep and soft in the stillness. His eyes searched hers. She could feel his breath on her parted lips. "Being near you makes me hungry."

Amanda quivered and drew in her breath at the suggestion of such intimacy.

He cocked an eyebrow at the betraying gasp and let his gaze fall deliberately to her mouth. He dragged his thumb over it. She wanted him. He wanted her. He kept fighting the temptation to give in to it, but it got worse by the day.

He moved away from her abruptly and picked up his drink.

"I must be more exhausted than I realized," he said dryly as he bent his head to light a cigar. "Where do you fancy eating tonight?" he asked.

Amanda was still trembling inside, but if he could shake off that kind of sensual temptation, so could she.

"I still like seafood."

He turned, with frank admiration in his eyes. He didn't like most women, but Amanda was unique: an independent woman with a mind of her own who could still be very, very feminine when she wanted to. "So do I. Go change and we'll go."

"Okay," she added, and hesitated. She looked worried.

He sighed. "You can trust me. I don't have plans to seduce you on the table."

She sighed. "Pity," she murmured, tongue-in-cheek.

She could learn to play his game if she had to, she thought to herself.

He cocked an eyebrow. "I told you. I'm not that kind of man. I want some assurances, or I'm not leaving the island with you."

She laughed delightedly. She could manage her turbulent emotions with humor. Right now it was the only safety valve she had. "Oh, all right, then," she laughed. His gaze slid over her without expression, although there was an unfamiliar glitter in it. "Whenever you're ready," he said quietly.

He made it sound like a statement of intent. "When I'm ready?"

"Are you going to dress?" he asked with polite interest. He flicked his wrist and checked the time. "Because I've got a long-distance call coming in three hours that I have to be back here for."

"Oh. Sorry. I'll hurry."

He was, she thought as she rushed upstairs to dress, the most exasperating man she'd ever met. He wasn't like Josh lately. He was intense and watchful. He'd wanted to kiss her, but he seemed always to catch himself in time. She wanted to push him off balance and see what happened. Something was bothering him, something deeply personal. She wished she could ask what it was.

Back in Montego Bay, a frustrated Brad had spent a fruitless evening and morning trying to seduce one saucy little blonde waitress. He hadn't had any success, and his own woes were playing on his mind.

The call he'd just received was from Las Vegas, from a flunky who worked for the casino owner to whom he owed a fortune. Perhaps, he thought, if he could speak to the owner himself, he could buy enough time to tell Josh how much trouble he was in. He hadn't managed that much nerve just yet.

He picked up the phone in the suite he'd rented and dialed a stateside number, waiting impatiently for it to ring.

"Desert Paradise Casino," came the reply eventually, in a soft, seductive voice.

"Let me speak to Marc Donner," he said shortly.

"One moment. I'll see if Mr. Donner is in. May I tell him who's calling, please?"

"Tell him it's Brad Lawson."

There was a very long pause before the telephone was answered.

"Donner." The voice was deep, unaccented, and without compromise. It reminded Brad vaguely of his older brother.

"I'm working on the money I owe you," he told the man. "I'm staying on Opal Cay. One way or the other, I'll have it in a few weeks, a month at the outside."

"Do you think your brother will give it to you?" came the amused reply. "Josh Lawson isn't known for a life of frivolity."

"No, but he's known for other reasons," Brad said defensively.

"Sure. His money and his cutthroat approach to business. But he won't save you if you try to duck out of paying me," the silky voice purred. "And just between us, I don't think he'll try. He doesn't like gamblers. Even ones he's related to."

"Blood is thicker than water."

"Strange that you should mention blood," Donner said carelessly. "Don't let me down, Lawson. Don't even think about it."

"I told you. I'm working on it." The man chilled Brad's blood. Donner had been connected with a couple of murders though he'd never gone to court for any of them. Brad was worried, but he had nobody to blame except himself. He didn't really expect Josh to bail him out of this one. No, he'd have to get himself out of this mess. "I'll get back to you next week."

"You'd better. I know where to find you."

"Don't I know it." He sighed and put down the receiver.

He needed to get his hands on a substantial amount of cash at once. He'd tried his luck at the tables, but that hadn't worked. He knew Donner was too intelligent to leave him bleeding in a ditch even if he did look more like a wrestler than a casino owner. He would probably show up at a board meeting, cause a scene, and blow the whistle on him. Josh would then have no choice but to pay the debt and kick Brad out. Brad winced at the thought of it. He had to find a way out—any way out.

CHAPTER SIX

Amanda was sleeping late. Josh had taken her to dinner the night before, but it had been a quiet, uncomfortable outing. Despite his attempt at humor, he was having trouble coping with their new relationship. He couldn't seduce her, but it was impossible to think of her as Harrison Todd's little girl anymore. He seemed to have spent the entire time working to keep his hands off her while he endured the gnawing ache in his loins. By the time they got back home, his nerves, and apparently hers, were shot. They parted company at once.

She'd mentioned going home Friday, which was tomorrow. He hadn't argued. He'd wanted to, but she was right. It was a hopeless situation, and every day they spent together made matters worse. He didn't want to hurt her. For her sake, it was better that she left before he lost his precarious control.

He sat down in his study and reached for the telephone. It might be a good idea, he thought, to find out how things were going with the newspaper back in San Antonio. If, as Amanda had said, Ward Johnson was paying less attention to management than he should, it didn't bode well for the paper's financial future—or that job press she was so worried about saving. He could at least insure that Amanda had a reasonably secure future.

Ward Johnson was making up the front page when he was called to the telephone. Down the long wooden makeup board from him, Dora Jackson was making up a grocery ad while one of the part-time people wrote cutlines for the photographs and headlines for stories as they were pasted up with hot wax on the ruled sheets.

Putting down his scissors Ward walked to the extension phone behind him. As he spoke, he couldn't help staring at Dora. It was inconvenient having a woman who looked as good as she did in the office with him. Once they had been high school sweethearts. Now they were both married and trying to keep up happy facades. It had been impulsive and crazy of him to hire her when she'd come looking for something to keep her busy.

"Johnson," he spoke into the receiver.

"Lawson," came the terse reply. "I want an update on the paper's finances."

It took Ward a long moment to realize that his caller was Joshua Lawson. He hesitated. "Mr. Lawson," he stammered, caught off guard. "The finances…oh, you mean the quarterly report."

"That's right. I need you to fax it to me today."

"I'll get right on it."

"Include an update on the job press, could you?"

"Well, I told you about that," Ward reminded him. "It's a waste of capital. The newspaper will carry us along."

"I've heard rumors that the Morrison group is in the planning stages of producing a throwaway to go in competition with the *Gazette*." That was something Josh hadn't mentioned to Amanda. She'd had enough stress for the past two weeks.

The publication he was talking about was a free newspaper that contained mostly advertising with only a modicum of news. It was a handout, and no weekly newspaper with a subscription list could compete with one. It would rob them of advertisers in no time at all. There was a pause. "Do you know how to cope with competition from a shopper?" he added dryly.

Ward cursed under his breath. "I know all right. If you haven't got an efficient operation, you might as well close the place down. You can't compete with a shopper. It attracts advertisers like glue, and you don't even have to charge for it."

"That being the case, our revenues will have to be pretty good to stand the competition."

"I'll get the figures for you. How's Amanda?"

"Healing. She'll be back to work on Monday."

"Nice girl. Hard worker. A little too involved sometimes. She's full of ideas that won't really work."

"Really?"

Ward smiled to himself. So much for taking the wind out of Miss Todd's sails. He'd felt threatened for the first time in years when she'd walked in the door. He knew that her family had owned the paper and that she stood to inherit a half interest or so at some point. But he'd been running the operation for fifteen years, answering only to Harrison Todd. For the past few years no one had interfered with his methods. Then Amanda had come to work for him. He wasn't amenable to having a girl fresh out of college trying to give him orders. It was just as well that Joshua Lawson knew that, right off the bat. After all, Lawson owned the majority of the paper's stock.

"She's a good accountant," Ward added to soften his criticism. It wouldn't do to sound as if he were threatened, even if he was. "Nice head for figures."

"So I've been told. Are your advertising rates up?"

"No need to raise them," Ward argued. "We're undercutting the dailies. We get enough without driving away old customers."

Josh was too cagey to question that without seeing the figures. He had his finger in too many pies to keep a close check on any of his side interests. For Amanda's sake, he was going to have to get a closer look at the *Gazette*.

"What's the problem about the job press?"

"There are three other print shops with more people and more modern equipment than we have. We've lost a lot of customers to the quick-print place that just opened in San Antonio. It does photocopies."

"I thought Harrison bought you a high-quality copier?"

"The girl who knew how to operate it quit. The new girl just sets type. She doesn't know much about printing, and Tim, who runs the presses, doesn't have time to run out and make copies when he's got negatives and plates to make."

Josh wanted to argue with that. Just as well he'd asked for those figures. He'd keep his counsel until then.

"All right. Get me those figures."

"Late this afternoon, for sure. I'll have to wait until after we put the paper to bed."

"That's fine."

The line went dead.

Josh wondered how much of what Johnson had said was true. Amanda was an eager beaver, but she was sharp, too. There were plenty of holes in Johnson's management theory. It was possible that Amanda was right about the job press. But the competition could be killing their business. It had happened to other print shops. Now that he had access to the entire operation—something he hadn't had while Harrison was still alive—he could keep Johnson on his toes and hopefully keep Amanda's inheritance solvent. He had a feeling the figures weren't going to be particularly pleasing.

Back in San Antonio, Ward Johnson was certain of it. He

ran a hand through his sandy hair and stared with unhappy resignation at the figures as he produced them from the computer. He knew how to run the machine, although Amanda was a whiz at it. But he hadn't bothered to analyze its performance. He just plugged along from day to day, secure in the knowledge that old advertisers would stay with him and a few new ones would come along. The paper was paying for itself. Barely. He'd had so much turmoil in his private life that he hadn't wanted complications or problems on the job. He hadn't wanted to rock the boat and upset people by offering a new price list.

But after he'd studied the spreadsheet, he wished he'd listened when Amanda had first mentioned that things were getting out of hand in the revenue column. Prices had gone up everywhere else, she'd said, and needed to go up here. Ward had laughed at her and said that people would go elsewhere if he raised his prices now, for newspaper ads or job work in the print shop.

But, looking at the figures, he realized that she was right. He was operating in the red because he'd been too involved with his own problems at home to go over the books regularly. Prices would have to be raised, for a certainty. That meant he'd have to put in some late hours working on them.

In addition he had to send this proof of ineptitude to Joshua Lawson. He grimaced. No. He didn't dare. He was thirty-four years old. He wasn't in his dotage, but it would be difficult to get another job at his age, even if he wasn't proven incompetent. Gladys would love it if they fired him. She'd laugh. His wife always laughed at his failures. She enjoyed them. She always had, even before she'd climbed too deep into her bottle of gin to get out again. He didn't know which was worse, Gladys or his son. Sometimes he felt as if he were carrying the world on his broad shoulders. He couldn't make enough to keep Gladys in gin and his son in drugs. The boy wouldn't work. He wasn't lucid enough to work.

Ward carefully changed a few key figures. With any luck at all, before the next quarter's figures went out, he'd have boosted them to this altered sum. It wasn't dishonest. He was only buying a little time.

"I need to ask a question, Ward," Dora said, interrupting his thoughts.

He looked up. She was so sweet, he thought. Pleasantly voluptuous, with a sweet smile and freckles and reddish-gold hair framing her very blue eyes. He wondered why she looked so sad. She had a successful husband, an educator, and two sons in grammar school.

"Ward?" she prompted, flushing a little at his pointed stare.

"Oh. Sorry." He smiled, his brown eyes twinkling. "What can I do for you, honey?"

The endearment made her flush even more, and he felt his chest swell. He still had an effect on her. Leaning back in his chair, he looked at her, a faint arrogance creeping over his face. He felt eighteen again, bristling with predatory masculine instincts. Although they'd never been really intimate in high school, they had spent a lot of time together.

"I wondered if you needed me for anything else?" Dora asked. "I only work mornings, you know." She smiled, seeing Ward as he had been at eighteen when he was captain of the football squad and she'd led the cheerleading team. In her eyes, he'd never aged.

He looked at the computer and grimaced. "I could certainly use some help with this," he said. "Can you operate a fax machine?"

"Why, yes," she said. "I did a little part-time work for an insurance company last year, and they had this same model," she added, moving toward the machine.

"Thank God," he said. "Amanda Todd always works this one, and she won't be back until Monday."

"Is she all right?" Dora asked. "I like Amanda. She's always been so nice to me."

"It's easy to be nice to you, Dora," he replied quietly. "Yes, she's fine. Sad, I imagine, but she's got the Lawsons to pamper her for a week and a luxury island in the Bahamas to lounge on. She'll manage."

"Mr. Lawson is very good to her," she remarked.

"Both Lawsons are," he mused. "The families go way back."

He sat up. "Well, I need to get back in there and finish making up the paper. I'll have to do a lot of this paperwork tonight. Would your family mind sacrificing you for an hour or two a couple of nights a week until I can catch up?"

"I'm sure they won't," she replied with a faintly nervous smile. "Edgar is taking a college course on his lunch hour this semester. He'll be home with the boys at night, grading papers or talking to students or tutoring," she said with more bitterness than she realized. "And all my boys do is play sports and talk about them. As long as everyone is fed and the house is clean, my time is pretty much my own," she added miserably.

Ward couldn't bear the thought of anyone as sweet and loving as Dora being taken for granted. "I'm sorry," he said gently. "I can't imagine any man grading papers when you're in the same room. If you don't mind my saying so," he added, careful not to offend her.

But she brightened and flushed a little. "No, of course not!"

He smiled. He grinned. She made him feel like a man again. "Okay, then," he said. "I'll see you later."

"Fine." She nodded. She started to speak, hesitated, and then plowed ahead. "How...how about your family?" she asked. "Don't they mind you working such late hours?"

He sighed wearily. "Gladys is...well, I'm sure you've heard

about her drinking. Everyone else here has. Half the time I don't think she knows if I'm there or not," he said. "And my son…" He let out a long breath. "He blames me for his mother's drinking. They'll both tell you I'm a total failure."

"That isn't the Ward Johnson I remember," she said gently. She smiled. "You could never be a failure."

He stared at her. "You really think so?"

She nodded. "I really think so. I'm sorry things are so bad for you."

The compassion in her blue eyes made him hungry and vulnerable. He wanted that caring for himself. He wanted someone to give a damn that his life was an unbearable mess. Dora appealed to everything masculine in him, and his body reacted suddenly, sharply, to her nearness.

"Can you come back about seven?" he asked.

She nodded. "Yes. Of course. I'll just paste up the rest of the personals." She went out quietly.

In the waiting room she hesitated, gnawing her full lower lip. She was going to get in over her head if she wasn't careful. She was a married woman with young sons, and Ward was a drowning man looking for someone to jump in and save him. The problem with trying to save drowning people was that if you weren't careful, they'd pull you down with them.

She couldn't possibly risk getting mixed up romantically with her boss. San Rio was a small community, despite being a cosmopolitan suburb of sprawling San Antonio. She and her husband went to the local Baptist church. He taught Sunday school. Her boys were involved in every sports activity they could find, which meant the family was very well known locally. She was a pillar of the community, as an educator's wife had to be, even in these permissive times. She couldn't afford any hint of scandal.

But she'd known Ward forever. He was a part of her happier, carefree past, and she cared about him. She felt sorry for him. Surely it wouldn't hurt to work late with him. She could listen to his problems and help him get home to his family quicker.

She passed by Lisa Marlowe, who was busily setting type on the computer, and spared the girl a faintly envious glance. Lisa was just eighteen. She had her whole life ahead of her. Right now all she talked about was boys and getting married. Dora wanted to catch her by the arms and warn her that there was no such thing as happily ever after, that romance was the stuff of novels. *Be careful*, she wanted to say. *There are no happy endings. If you choose the wrong man and you're too weak to break the chains of your relationship, you'll live to regret it.*

But even if she said it, Lisa wouldn't believe her; she was too full of youthful optimism. With a sad little laugh she went back into the composing room to finish her work.

Amanda had taken a cup of coffee with her down to the beach while Josh was making telephone calls. Harriet pointed him toward the direction she'd taken. He grinned at the jovial black woman and took his own cup of coffee along with him as he went in search of Amanda.

He found her perched on a sand dune, clad in jeans and a silky top in peacock blue, her long hair blowing around her in the wind.

"Avoiding me?" he asked pleasantly. He sat down beside her, stretching lazily. He was wearing tan slacks with a beige silk shirt, but he didn't mind the sand.

She had been trying to, yes. She'd hoped against hope the night before that he might kiss her, hold her, tell her that he couldn't live without her. But she was living on daydreams. The reality was that if Terri couldn't get a wedding band on his finger, *she* never would. She loved him, wanted him, would have been happy to live with him any way he liked.

But he wouldn't let her close enough. He'd told her that without saying a single word.

"I just wanted to watch the surf for a while," she said at last. She stared into her coffee cup. "Can you have the jet fly me back to San Antonio in the morning?"

He drew up his legs and rested his hands, with his own coffee cup, between his knees. "Certainly. Are you sure you're ready to go?"

"Work will be good for me," she replied. "It will help keep my mind busy. Too much free time can be uncomfortable."

He knew why. But he didn't say so.

She didn't look at him. Her coffee had gone cold. She let it trickle out onto the sand. "I've enjoyed being here," she said. She felt him beside her. Every cell in her body reacted to him. Her heartbeat was already faster than normal just from the sound of his deep voice, from his company. She loved him, an unrequited love that was only going to hurt her more every time she looked at him. He probably was trying to be kind, but she wanted him so!

His broad shoulders moved as he settled lazily on his side in the soft, warm sand. He sipped coffee. "I just spoke to Ward Johnson."

"Can you repeat anything he said about me?" she asked with a knowing smile.

"He thinks you're bright," he replied. He smiled back. "And 'inquisitive.'"

"I stick my nose in where it isn't wanted," she translated.

"He's going to fax me some figures on revenue."

"Voluntarily?"

"Amanda, I know how to read a spreadsheet," he reminded her gently. "He won't put anything past me."

"I know that." She put down her cup and twisted it into the white sand. "But unless you go there and look things over personally, you won't get the whole picture."

"I'm a busy man."

"Tell me about it," she murmured dryly.

His dark eyes searched hers. "Why is the job press so important?"

"It's a challenge," she said, her eyes kindling with excitement. "There are three other printers in San Antonio, but we're the only one in San Rio. Customers drive fifteen miles to get the same kind of service we could provide. It wouldn't even take a lot of new equipment. We've got the Heidelberg and the A. B. Dick and the Davidson presses. We can do hot type or offset. The problem is not with the equipment. It's the management and staff."

He pursed his lips. "That isn't what Johnson says."

"Ward Johnson has an alcoholic wife who's driving him batty," she replied. "He has a son who's been arrested three times for marijuana possession. The boy can't even hold down a job because he's stoned most of the time. Ward is trying to run two businesses and cope with a crumbling home life. You yourself would be hard-pressed to manage that situation."

"Like hell I would. I'd send her and the boy off to a clinic and dry them out."

"It only works if they want to be helped," she said. "You can't rehabilitate someone who refuses to admit that there's a problem."

He thought about his own brother and knew that she was right. He and Amanda didn't agree on the best treatment for Brad. She wanted to let him go on until he realized his situation, and Josh wanted to slam him into a wall. Perhaps they were both wrong. He pulled a cigar out of his pocket and clipped off the tip.

Amanda stared at his downbent blond head and ached all over. She was going home. He was letting her go. He wouldn't even touch her.

Well, she was going to give him something to remember,

she thought rebelliously. She was going to make him sorry that he didn't want her for keeps.

She touched his hand when he reached for his lighter. "Don't," she said softly.

He lifted an eyebrow. "It isn't a confined room," he reminded her.

"I know."

He dangled it in his fingers, searching her face. "Why not, then?" he asked huskily. Her eyes excited him. The loneliness of the beach, the memory of her soft mouth under his, made him ache.

She took the cigar out of his hand and dropped it beside him. She really had nothing left to lose. She was going home in the morning, and it might be months before she even saw him again. One memory, she thought. Just one, that's all she wanted.

"Be gentle," he cautioned.

She laughed as she put her hands on his shoulders and pushed him back against the sand. "Isn't that my line? *You're* not innocent."

He smiled faintly as her breasts eased down over his broad chest, her hip barely touching his, her legs to one side as she tasted the heady pleasure of seduction.

"Don't tell me this is the best you can do?" he muttered sardonically. "Schoolgirl stuff."

He smiled with tender indulgence as she propped herself up on his chest and stared down at him.

She smiled back. "I'm trying," she teased.

But he became somber, all at once. "Sex is addictive," he said simply. "I live in a goldfish bowl. It would destroy the company's conservative image if it got around that I'd seduced my business partner's daughter and was keeping her as my resident mistress."

"I won't be anyone's mistress. Not even yours."

"Any more than I'd ask you to," he agreed. He reached up and touched her lips gently. The feel of her soft, warm body made his own begin to throb. "You're much too intelligent to settle for being a man's toy. It would be a waste."

She sighed with soft contentment. Her fingers smoothed over his lean cheek and down to his square chin. He tensed when she slid her finger under one of the buttons on his shirt and touched his hair-roughened skin.

Her eyes lifted to his. "That arouses you, doesn't it?" she asked.

He nodded. "I meant it when I told you I don't want things to go that far. We can't make love. Not ever."

She grimaced, pain in her whole look. "Why?"

"How can I tell you?" He drew her down to him, his eyes solemn and sad and bleak. "Go back to San Antonio and use that mathematical brain of yours to save the job press. That should keep you occupied."

"You could keep me busy here," she suggested.

"We've had this discussion before," he pointed out.

It was harder than ever to breathe normally. She studied his hard face and remembered vividly how it had looked the night she'd seen him on the beach with Terri. Contorted, vulnerable, fiercely passionate. He never let go with Amanda. He was always in total control.

His dark eyes narrowed. "What are you thinking?"

"I was remembering how you looked that night I saw you with Terri," she said huskily. "Abandoned, carnal. You won't let yourself be that way with me."

"How do you think you'd react to a man's passion, Amanda?" he asked. "Because it's unmanageable. It requires a submission that I don't think you can give." His chest rose and fell heavily. "You aren't naive. You know exactly what I'd do to you. You saw me do it to Terri."

She shivered as the vivid picture imposed itself on her senses. "Yes," she said unsteadily. "I watched you."

He made a rough sound at the sensuality he read in her eyes, her face, her voice. Without one single thought of the future, he reached up suddenly and dragged her down to lie totally against him while his mouth ground up against hers in urgency and need.

It was immediately explosive. She moaned, and his body clenched. He parted her lips and caught her hair at the nape of her neck so he could grind her mouth against his.

She whimpered with the shock of pleasure it aroused. He caught his breath, but it was already too late to pull back. He was at the mercy of a need that knocked the breath out of him.

He whipped her over onto her back and drew her half under him, expertly guiding one long, powerful leg between both of hers.

She felt his arousal, was shocked and thrilled and intimidated by the intimacy of it. She stiffened uncertainly, and her nails curled into his muscular upper arms.

His breath sighed out roughly against her lips as his head lifted. He searched her turbulent eyes in a silence that magnified the sound of surf and heartbeats.

He scowled. There it was again, that unexpected fragility in her eyes. He tried to imagine seeing her like this with another man, and couldn't. He smoothed a big, lean hand against her soft cheek and watched her mouth turn to press tenderly against its palm.

That was when he knew. It would have been impossible not to. The infatuation she'd always felt for him was still there, but it was magnified by a sexual awakening. Her strengths were formidable in intelligence and independence and temper. But she would yield to him. The knowledge humbled him. He'd never felt this sort of protectiveness for any other human being.

"Here," he whispered, and a big hand dropped to ease her legs even farther apart so that he could press down to her. She gasped as his hand contracted, pulling her up rhythmically into the cradle of his hips. His own breath caught at the exquisite thrill of pleasure it gave him.

She'd wanted to be with him like this for so long that the joy of it almost made her faint. This was Josh, holding her, wanting her. She smelled the talc on his powerful body, the faint scent of his cologne, the whisper of coffee on his breath as his mouth poised over hers.

"And you want me...to leave!" she whimpered.

He shuddered. "The hell I do," he said huskily.

She moved. Barely, but enough to make him totally aware of her vulnerability, her complicity. She looked up at him unafraid.

"You could use something," she whispered. She lay trembling on the sand beneath the warm crush of his body, her black hair making a cloudy halo around her oval face. Her eyes were half-closed, misty. "Couldn't you?" she whispered.

His face hardened. His eyes darkened, and even though he didn't move, he withdrew from her. She could see it. Feel it.

Her eyes narrowed with hurt. She felt the passion go out of him, and it didn't surprise her when he suddenly rolled away and sat up. She bit her lip to stop the pain of his rejection. He was still in control, even now. He wanted her, but not enough.

She sat up, too, staring blankly at the bay. "Joshua, don't make me ashamed that I offered."

"*Shame* isn't a word that has any meaning between you and me," he said quietly. "Love is a very precious gift."

"Love?!" She panicked. He mustn't know, he couldn't! It would push him away. "Josh, it was only..."

His head turned, and he stared her down. "Only what? Puerile curiosity about intercourse? A whim? A sudden attack of animal passion?" He scowled at her.

She hesitated. Her shoulders rose and fell. She searched his face with eyes that grew dull with resigned acceptance. "You know."

"I always have," he replied. "No other woman has ever had the place in my life that you occupy."

"What kind of place is it?" she asked with an attempt at lightness. "That of a friend you can force yourself to kiss occasionally, but nothing more?"

He started to speak, but the effort failed. He averted his eyes to the sand and reached for the cigar she'd taken from him. He did light it this time. The pungent smoke drifted away in the breeze, and he didn't speak. Neither did she, for several tense, depressed seconds.

"There hasn't been anyone," she said dully. "I've saved it all up for you, for years, ever since I was in my teens. I don't know what it is to want anyone except you."

His eyes mirrored his anguish, but he didn't let her see them. Her words were like a knife through his body.

He lifted the cigar to his mouth with determination, and he didn't look at her.

She knew what he was saying with that deliberate silence. He was telling her that she was special to him, but not special enough. She could have his friendship, his support, his affection. But that was all. He had nothing else to offer her.

"You don't want to get married," she said after a minute.

He hesitated. "That's right," he said at last. "I don't. And you would."

His eyes closed, and all his muscles clenched. He could almost feel her, like that...

"It would be good," she said, tight-lipped.

"Too good," he rasped. His eyes opened, tormented. "Neither of us would ever get over it."

"Josh," she whispered, "I lo—"

His hand slid quickly, gently, over her mouth. "You and I will always have each other, even if it isn't in quite such a physical way," he said, cutting off the incriminating confession. "We'll forget what happened on the other island, and here," he added firmly. His eyes punctuated that determination. "It was my fault. The way things stand, I had no right to touch you."

"I don't understand."

"You will, one day," he promised.

She looped her arms around her updrawn knees. "Are you still my friend?"

"The best one you have," he replied quietly.

"Okay." She watched the progress of a sea gull across the sky. "I'll go home and back to work. Thank you for letting me stay."

"I think you know that I enjoyed it as much as you did. But it's past time to get back to reality. We've been dreaming, Amanda. Both of us. Dreams are like clouds. The first strong wind can scatter them."

She turned toward him, her expression one of subdued curiosity. "What do you dream of?" she asked.

His dark eyes dropped to hers, and in them was such pain that she caught her breath. "Don't ask," he said. "Don't ever ask."

He got up abruptly. "Bring the cups, will you? I've got to try to track down Brad. He's overstaying that business trip."

"All right." She picked up the cups and followed him back to the house. The memory she'd hoped to take away with her wasn't the one she would pack with her aspirations. It looked as if she might get her wish about the job press. The one about Josh, though, was as empty as the cups in her hand.

Josh flew to Jamaica. He didn't find Brad, who was off with some young woman, according to a clerk at the hotel desk.

He did find the group of businessmen with whom Brad had been hobnobbing, though. They were gathered in the lounge with their wives. When one of the women turned toward him, he recognized Terri.

There had been a time when the voluptuous brunette had made his pulses dance with a glance. Now, with the hunger for Amanda that he carried with him, Terri was not a threat to his senses any longer. She was just the wife of a business acquaintance. He laughed inwardly, considering how much he'd changed.

With a lazy smile, he took her outstretched hand when she approached him. "Look what the wind blew in," she mused gently as he bent to kiss her fingers with old-world courtesy. "What brings you to Jamaica?"

"I'm trying to find my brother," he replied easily. "He seems to have vanished."

"He's found a new conquest," she told him, smiling. "Leave it to Brad, right?" She turned and looked over her shoulder, motioning to a short, dark-haired man. "Josh," she said, sliding her arm around the newcomer, "you remember Nicos Mikapoulis, don't you? He's my husband now."

Josh shook hands and smiled. "Yes. I read about the wedding, along with the rest of the world. Congratulations."

"Thank you." Nicos gazed at his wife possessively. "I am a fortunate man. Your brother and I had a long talk last night," he added. "I am seriously considering his proposal."

Josh was impressed. It appeared that his little brother deserved his day off. He and Nicos discussed the details that Brad had already covered, then Nicos went to get another drink, leaving Josh alone with Terri momentarily.

Terri's dark head tilted to one side. "I understand Amanda's staying with you," she commented. "It was a shame about her father. Is she coping well?"

"I think so," he replied. He sipped his ginger ale. He never indulged in liquor at business meetings. "It's been rough on her."

"I don't doubt it. There was a lot of unfinished business between Amanda and her father. That always makes mourning more difficult." She searched his eyes and for a moment, hers were soft with memory. "Sort of like us. But now... Nicos and I...well, I think I'm pregnant," she said hesitantly.

His face showed no reaction at all, but his eyes darkened just faintly. "Are you? Congratulations. I'm sure Nicos is pleased."

"We both are. It's what I've always wanted." She was uncomfortable and looked it. "I really did care about you. It's just that I wanted something more."

"I know that. No hard feelings."

"Of course not," she said honestly, her eyes quiet and haunted. "I'll always want you," she murmured. "Perhaps that's my punishment." She gave him a smile that was a little too bright. "He's good to me, though. I'll never cheat on him."

"That will make him a very fortunate man," Josh said. "I saw enough raw, careless passion when I was a kid. If I'd married, I couldn't have lived like that. Fidelity should be part of marriage."

"Yes." She fingered her drink. "It's a waste," she added wistfully. "To look like you do and not want to get married and have a family."

"I am married," he reminded her. "To my business."

She sighed. "Yes. You always were. Are you going to stay for a day or so? Nicos and I have no plans for this evening..."

"I have to fly back to the cay," he replied. "Brad's done a good job here. I won't infringe on his territory. I just wanted to put in an appearance. If you see him, you might tell him that."

"I'll cover you," she said, chuckling. Then she smiled sadly and lifted her glass. "Here's to old times, my dear."

"And your forthcoming happy event," he said, meeting it with his. There was a soft tinkling sound.

As the other members of the group joined them, conversation became general. When Josh left, memories of his childhood returned to haunt him. His mother had been beautiful like Terri. But unlike her, she'd never been faithful to his father, or his father to her. It had made him sick to see how little real emotion existed between them.

He tried to imagine loving someone and being cuckolded. The memories he had of his parents had made him bitter and distrustful of emotion.

Then he thought about Amanda. He couldn't imagine her sleeping with anyone except her husband, if she married. Amanda loved him. And he...

His stride quickened. He mustn't let himself think about that.

On another beach, a few miles outside Montego Bay, Brad sprawled next to the blonde waitress on a private beach that belonged to the businessman he'd just closed a deal with for Josh. His sleek body was bare to the sun except for a tiny pair of white briefs that didn't reveal as much of him as his companion would have liked to see.

He was very nicely built, Barbara thought as she studied him. He was more man than she was used to, and devastating with that almost all-over tan. No body hair, either. Some women loved it, but she didn't.

She'd kept him at arm's length for two days. He'd taken her to the best restaurants when she was off from work, and he'd been kind to her. Really kind. She decided that it was time to pay him back for the respect and courtesy he'd shown her.

She stood up and untied her white robe. Under it she was nude except for her tiny thong bikini briefs. She let the robe drop on his chest.

His dark eyes opened. He smiled with surprise and lazy appreciation as he took in her bare breasts and the soft curves of her body. "Very, very nice," he said softly. "I was beginning to think you were wearing a habit under your uniform. Make yourself comfortable."

"Don't mind if I do." As she spoke, her fingers slowly undid the ties of her bikini briefs. She let them fall, watching his eyes slide over her with evident appreciation.

He arched his back sensuously, and his interest in her took a slow, physical form. "Ever made love underwater?" he asked huskily, because the pleasure of her lack of inhibition made him hungry.

"Not yet."

"We'll save that for another time. Lie down," he coaxed.

She spread her robe close beside him and stretched out on it, her blue eyes darting over him with blatant interest. "You're very experienced, aren't you?" she asked, remembering the way he'd kissed her good-night at her cottage in the wee hours.

"I get by." He turned his head and smiled at her.

"So do I." She rolled onto her side and slid her hand across his flat belly. "Want me to relax you?" she whispered huskily.

He lifted toward her with a pained smile. "Go ahead."

She teased him, toyed with him, until his face went rigid. This wasn't strange to her. She'd learned a lot about pleasuring men, even if she hadn't had much in return. She stroked him, smiling when he groaned.

"Damn!"

He stripped off his briefs and turned to her, his face as taut as his powerful, lean body. He hung there, waiting.

"Yes," she whispered.

He moved then, straddling her wide hips. "Wait," he said softly when she reached up for him. He retrieved his wallet from the folds of his towel and opened it. He removed something from it and put it in Barbara's hand before he tossed the wallet back onto the towel. "Do you know what to do with that?" he asked.

"Yes. I guess so. But I don't like them…"

"All the same, you'll use it with me," he said firmly. "I don't take those kinds of chances. Ever."

She made a protesting noise, but she wanted him enough to cooperate. She put it in place, making him pay for forcing her to use it as she teased him mercilessly.

He laughed softly. "Not bad," he murmured, shivering a little with pleasure. "Show me what else you've got."

She opened her legs and hooked them around his hips, watching him watch her. He bent and pressed his mouth down hard on her belly, working up to her breasts. He suckled them. While she gasped at the expertise of his movements, his hands learned her body as intimately as she'd learned his. He caught a hard nipple in his teeth and worried it with his tongue while his fingers invaded her in a slow, sensual arousal that quickly made a cry tear out of her throat.

He lifted his head. She was wanton now, her body shivering, her legs pulling at his hips. He laughed softly. "Do you want it?" he whispered.

"Yes! Yes, now now, now!"

Her voice broke as he thrust into her, his body fierce and merciless as he possessed her in one surge. She shuddered into completion almost at once, and he laughed while he taught her new sounds to make, new ways of moving, new rhythms. He kissed her roughly and then turned her under him, so that he was over her, behind her. Her hands clawed into the towel as she felt him.

"It's good. Yes, it's very, very good!" He moved, his hands lifting her hips up to him, and his rhythm grew more violent, deeper, slower. She cried out and pushed backward, weeping.

His movements shook her whole body as he increased the

pressure and the depth. His hands held the front of her thighs, and his teeth clenched. He heard a noise far away, but he didn't care now if the whole damned world saw and heard them, and neither did she.

"Quick," he jerked out. "Get it…get it now!"

He convulsed, a groan pulsing out of him in time with the savage throb of his loins. He felt her body shake uncontrollably under him, and he pushed her into the sand with the anguish of his need to get as deep as he could, to be physically complete with her.

She cried. It was the most violent climax she'd ever attained. Her body burned and throbbed and hurt with his possession, but when he began to lift away, she begged him not to.

"Barbara," he whispered into her ear.

"Not yet," she moaned. She turned under him, slid up, possessed him again, trembling, and her hips lifted. "Please. Please. Please." She repeated it with the rhythm of her body, satiated but still hungry, helpless, at the mercy of the uncontrollable need to experience again the savage satisfaction he'd given her.

"You're good. Angel, you're good, you're so good…" He kissed her, but tenderly this time. His hips moved again. She sobbed, and he felt whole again. It had been weeks since he'd had a woman, and he was willing to bet that she'd never had anyone with his expertise. Before he left the island, he was going to make her glad she'd invited this. He laughed softly as she began to shudder under him. His eyes closed. For a few achingly sweet minutes the world went away and left him alone.

He was sated when they went into the restaurant for dinner that evening.

The first people he saw were Nicos and Terri. She hailed him and stopped.

"You missed Josh," she told him.

His face went rigid. "My brother was here?"

"Just to say hello," Terri replied, clinging to Nicos's arm. "He said it would be impolite to let you close a deal while he sat on the cay and didn't even make contact."

Brad relaxed. "So that was it. He isn't still here?"

"It was just a brief visit. How nice to see him again."

Brad noticed the wistful look in her eye, but he didn't comment. She looked happy enough with her Greek millionaire.

"She's very pretty," Barbara remarked when they were seated and looking at menus. "Is she an old girlfriend?"

He laughed. "Not mine. My brother used to date her," he said, not revealing the intimate nature of Josh's relationship with Terri.

"Is that man her husband?"

"Yes. My brother was crazy about her, but he's a wild-eyed fanatic when someone mentions marriage."

"I don't know," she mused. "I don't really want to get married, either. Not for a long, long time."

"Honey," he said warmly, "you're a girl after my own heart!"

CHAPTER SEVEN

Josh had flown back to Opal Cay relieved to find that his brother had done more than his share of work. He worried that Brad might think he was being spied on, but he'd smooth that over later.

What really bothered Josh was some gossip he'd heard while he was having drinks with the business group in Montego Bay. One of Mikapoulis's associates who gambled had mentioned seeing Brad at Marc Donner's casino in Las Vegas recently.

Josh knew his brother. Once Brad started gambling, he wouldn't quit, and lately he was losing heavily. Josh knew Marc Donner all too well through one of his former executives. Donner always collected when someone owed him, and he was precise about his methods. Brad hadn't mentioned that he owed money or that he might be in trouble. But lots of odd little comments from Brad began to form an unpleasant picture in Josh's mind.

If he was right—if Brad had Donner breathing down his neck—it was amazing that his brother hadn't asked for help. Was it because he knew Josh wouldn't give it? Bailing out

Brad again would only send him right back into the casinos. He would have had to say no. But could he risk letting Brad get himself killed in the process?

He couldn't do much until he could get Brad to confess his situation, if he was really in one. So many complications, Josh thought wearily. He took another draw from his cigar. Before Harrison Todd's death, his big worry had been acquiring a new prospect in the Bahamas and closing the deal in the Middle East. Now he had the financial headache Harrison had left and the grief of losing his business partner, who was also a friend. Amanda's presence had stirred thoughts and feelings Josh preferred to keep buried, and Brad might be in danger of being destroyed by a gambling debt. He chuckled with black humor as he considered dropping himself into a shark's mouth. With his luck, he mused, the shark would throw him back up and complain that he tasted of tobacco—which was not a bad excuse for smoking, he thought. He'd have to try it out at his next executive meeting. Yet he was going to give up smoking. He'd asked Dina to enroll him in that seminar.

He wasn't really hooked, of course. It was just something to do with his hands. But it made a good impression with his board of directors, since many of them were also hooked.

He strolled outside and drank in the tropical atmosphere of the cay. All around, hibiscus and bougainvillea and jasmine bloomed in royal splendor. Ordinarily he enjoyed their perfumed beauty, but today he was much too preoccupied. He went back inside. Amanda hadn't come down for dinner yet, and he imagined she was packing for her trip back tomorrow. He would miss her, but he had no choice other than to let her go. Her job would help her cope.

The fax he'd just received from Ward Johnson was still lying on his desk. He pursed his lips as he studied it again. Everything looked solvent. But Amanda had said that although it might look solvent on paper, the production was far from efficient. He believed her. Johnson had every reason to stack the deck in his favor, and there were some dubious entries on the spreadsheet.

There was a tap on the door. Amanda stood just in the doorway, dressed in jeans and a yellow tank top, her hair in a bun. She looked young and defensive.

"Mima's putting supper on the table, if you're ready." She started to move away.

"Come in and close the door," he said unexpectedly.

She was reluctant to be alone with him after her boldness earlier in the day. Thinking it silly to show her fear, she closed the door and turned to him, her hands behind her as she leaned against the door. "What is it?" she asked.

He perched himself on the edge of the desk. "Johnson faxed me the lastest figures on the paper. It looks solvent."

She smiled wickedly, with a trace of her old humor. "From a distance, a white duck looks like a sea gull. He hasn't raised job work prices in two years."

"The figures indicate that he has."

She shifted. "Then it must be a recent change."

He nodded. "Very recent. Say, in the past few hours." He smiled at her stare. "I told you I could read a spreadsheet. I know padded figures when I see them."

He folded his arms over his chest. "You can try your luck at rearranging things, if you like," he told her. "If push comes to shove, and he threatens to kick you out, remind him who you are. There are ways to get around reactionaries, Amanda, if you use your brain. You don't have to confront him head-on."

She laughed gently. "Something I've learned from you," she agreed.

"Another thing," he said with narrowed, threatening eyes. "Has my brother said anything to you about being in hock up to his eyes to a Las Vegas casino owner?"

She frowned. "No. Is he?"

"I think so," he replied. "He hasn't asked me for anything. I'm not sure he will. But if he mentions it to you, I'd like to know. I still think he needs counseling, but I'm not going to throw him to the wolves. Whatever his weaknesses, he's my brother."

"I know that. So does he, I'm sure."

"Gambling is a disease," he said wearily. "If I bail him out, he'll go right back to it again. I wish I knew the answer."

"Brad is jealous of you sometimes," she told him. "He's smart and he can charm, but he's not you."

"We were raised very differently," he replied. His eyes fell to his cigar. "I had nothing of love. My mother was a gadfly, and my father was just as bad. They stuck me in military school and put Brad in the care of one governess after another."

"Most of whom he seduced when he was in his teens," she said dryly.

He didn't smile. His dark eyes were somber. "Then they sent him to high school. So he could only seduce girls his own age. How did you ever escape?"

"I was off-limits," she said. "Brad told me so once. I'm the only woman he can talk to about his other women," she said, laughing.

He stuck a hand in his slacks pocket and puffed on the cigar. The air-conditioned room had a huge, expensive filtering system that took out the pungent smell. Josh indulged his habit, but he was very careful not to subject anyone to secondhand smoke.

"Why do you smoke?" she asked abruptly.

"I don't know." He shrugged. "Maybe it's to keep from overeating."

"You'll never be fat. You're too busy."

"Wearing out from the inside, I think you said."

Her pale green eyes scanned his face. "I hope you won't

kill yourself with work. You don't have anyone around you who would sit up with you if you got sick or collapsed. Brad is very rarely here. Ted is kind, but he lets you intimidate him."

"Would you sit up with me?" he asked cynically. "Soothe my fevered brow and spoon-feed me?"

Her face closed up. "Isn't that what friends are for?" She turned and put her hand on the doorknob.

"I'd do it for you, too," he said curtly. His face hardened. "I'd do anything for you, Amanda."

Her eyes half-closed. "Anything except let me get close to you," she whispered.

With a rough sigh he turned back to his desk and braced his hands on it. They turned white. He didn't move. After a minute he heard the door open and close. The finality of it echoed in his ears.

Despite the way they'd parted, Amanda was gay and pleasant over the rather late dinner that Harriet prepared. Brad showed up midway through dessert, looking smug and weary.

Josh recognized the look, but he didn't say a word. Brad's private life, and the way he conducted it, was his own business. He'd been coddling his baby brother too long already. It was time to step back and see if Brad could handle life by himself.

"Want some dessert?" Amanda offered.

"No, thanks. I ate in Jamaica before I flew home. I saw Terri," he added, glancing at Josh and unaware of the stiffness of Amanda's face at the news Josh hadn't mentioned to her. "She said you'd been by to shake a few hands. How'd I do, boss?"

"I'll slip a bonus into next month's check," Josh said, chuckling. "I'm proud of you."

Brad tried not to look too pleased. "Thanks. I think I'll have coffee, anyway. Harriet!"

After they ate, Josh was called to the telephone, as was usual in the evenings. Brad and Amanda walked out onto the porch to sit on wicker chairs and listen to the sounds of the night. The surf was muffled here, but pleasant and calming.

"I gather that you closed the deal," she murmured.

"The original one, and another besides," he said smugly. "It feels pretty good to have my big brother proud of me once in a while. God knows I hardly ever please him." He glanced at her. "If you're still determined to go home tomorrow, I'll go with you. I can't leave my department hanging by Frederick Karlan's fingernails much longer, or he'll have my job! He's ambitious, that Karlan."

"You're irreplaceable. Ask anyone," she said glibly.

He stretched and yawned. He hadn't had much sleep. He'd promised to phone Barbara the next time he was in Jamaica, and he would. She was a pleasant little diversion.

"Brad, can I ask you something?"

"Sure. What?"

"Are you in some sort of trouble?"

He hesitated, but only for a minute. "Yes," he said. He folded his hands on his knees and leaned forward. "But that bonus Josh promised will help. And I'll turn up something," he added. "It's nothing I can talk about."

"You and Josh and your secrets," she mused sadly. "Everybody's got a secret."

"Even you?"

She had, but Josh knew it. He knew exactly how she felt. But he didn't want her to love him. Her inferiority complex told her that it was her lack of beauty, of sensuality, of talent, that kept him away. It might be the specter of Terri, too. He hadn't wanted to marry Terri, whatever he'd felt for her. Amanda couldn't help wondering if Josh had some dark secret that made him afraid of commitment. Perhaps it was something from his childhood.

"Was your father unkind to you and Josh?" she asked.

"He was distant," he replied. "Not very communicative

or very affectionate. Josh had less attention than I did. He was always alone. No one ever did anything for him unless he paid them."

She winced at the thought. At least he knew she'd never cared about his money.

"Women would love him anyway," he said dryly.

"He's very good-looking," she agreed.

"Terri and her new husband are coming to stay at the cay next week," he said absently. He'd invited them, and Terri had accepted. He hadn't told Josh yet, and he was totally unaware of what had happened between Josh and Amanda in his absence. "I hope to God Josh doesn't involve himself in a ménage à trois while they're here and kill a million-dollar deal with that Greek tycoon Terri married. I know he still aches for her, but Greeks are possessive and vengeful. Terri looks sad when she talks about him. Marriage or not, she hasn't stopped caring about Josh." He hoped he hadn't committed a real blunder by making the invitation without checking with Josh first. He'd have to mention it to his brother later.

Amanda's ego took a nosedive. Certainly Josh hadn't mentioned Terri or her husband or any visit to her. Perhaps that was why he didn't mind if she went back to San Antonio. Perhaps the reason he had rejected her had nothing to do with her appearance, but everything to do with Terri. Maybe he still loved Terri after all this time.

That would make sense. Amanda couldn't imagine letting anyone except Josh touch her. If he felt that way about Terri, then his withdrawal from Amanda was terribly understandable.

She felt sick.

"You're very quiet."

"I'm thinking about work Monday," she said, faking pleasure that she didn't feel. "I'm going to make a few little changes around the old place and see what happens. Brad, my boy, I think I have it in me to become the Lady Astor of the job press set."

"More power to you," he replied dryly. "Put me on the invitation list when you hold your first presidential primary. I can hardly wait."

"President Todd. That has a nice ring to it," she agreed. She leaned toward him. "But if I married, wouldn't my husband balk at having to wear an evening gown to receptions?"

He laughed lazily. Amanda could always cheer him up. "You have to get married first."

"Not me," she said. "Not even to get control of the *Gazette*."

"That's right," he said to himself. "You would get control immediately if you married, wouldn't you?"

"Forty-nine percent of it, anyway," she replied. "I'll be twenty-five in two years. If I can survive that long."

Brad didn't say a word. His eyes narrowed as he looked more closely at Amanda, the girl he had known forever. He had no doubt that she would somehow succeed and one day run the paper and job press more profitably than ever. Whoever married Amanda would not only win a devoted wife, but probably a small fortune as well.

Amanda was on her way up to bed the next time she saw Josh. He and Brad had been closeted in the study for a long time, and then Brad had gone to the living room to watch a movie on a satellite channel.

She paused at the staircase, her eyes fixed accusingly on Josh's. "You didn't tell me that Terri was coming here."

His eyes went cold. So Brad had told her. Why shouldn't he? Brad had no idea of the undercurrents at work here.

"I didn't think it concerned you," he said with quiet hauteur. "I only found out about it minutes ago, and besides, Terri is none of your business." He waited for the snub to register. When he saw the anger narrow her green eyes, he turned away. "I'll put the corporate jet at your disposal. You can leave when you like tomorrow."

That was a definite closed door. She knew that set of his broad shoulders. He was inflexible. He had Terri in his sights. That was why he didn't want Amanda. If only it didn't hurt so much to know it!

"I thought Terri was married," she said through tight lips.

He glanced at her with urbane amusement. "So?" he asked with forced indifference to her pain. His hands balled into fists in his pockets, and he even managed to smile mockingly. Her disgust and contempt at his morals showed on her face, but it got no reaction from him beyond a faint tautening of his jaw.

"I see."

He turned away with forced nonchalance. "I've got some phone calls to make. I'll see you in the morning."

"Certainly." She didn't see the steps as she climbed them. Her father's death had devastated her. Her father hadn't loved her or wanted her. Josh didn't want her. Would anybody ever want her? she wondered. She'd always been a leftover person in the world, but it had never hurt so much before.

He'd done it, he told himself. He'd made her think Terri was back in his life, and now she'd leave without a protest. Her pride would see to that. But he felt no triumph.

She'd go back to San Antonio, and he'd get a grip on himself. His life would go back to normal. So would hers. One day they'd regain their old relationship, and the world would settle back into place. He went into his office and closed the door. He was, he considered, lying through his teeth.

The next morning Amanda changed into a pale blue silk suit. Silk was wonderful for tropical climates, she mused. It kept you cool. But even in a cool climate it was warm, and it seemed to breathe, like skin. If only it didn't wrinkle so easily!

She put her hair up neatly and fixed her makeup before she took her purse and went downstairs.

"I'm ready to go," she told Josh.

He turned from where he was standing on the balcony. Brad was putting their bags in the launch. At least, he told himself, Brad would keep up her spirits. He had no one to keep his up. His heart was on the floor at her feet, if she only knew it.

"Have you enough money?" he asked her coldly.

She was puzzled by the ice in his voice. He sounded as if he hated her. "I have enough," she said. "I have a credit card, too." She clutched her purse. It felt like a life preserver. She smiled at him forcibly. "Thanks again…"

"It was no hardship," he replied curtly. He glanced at the door as Brad stuck his head inside for a minute.

"The Learjet's gassed up and waiting. Get a move on, chicken!" he teased.

"I'll be right there," she called.

"See you back home, Josh," Brad added, and vanished.

Josh didn't speak to him. He'd tried to get his brother to talk to him the night before, but Brad had just smiled and said there was nothing to talk about. Josh felt as if everyone were deserting him. It was his choice. But it was no choice.

He stared at Amanda, so quiet and withdrawn. It was like saying goodbye forever. He felt it, as she must, and saw the suggestion of pain in her soft green eyes as they searched his with visible, aching need.

"Do you have to look at me like that?" he asked harshly.

"Like what, Josh?" she asked innocently, although she hoped that it would disturb him,.

His chest rose and fell quickly. His lips thinned. "Damn it all, Amanda!" he said under his breath.

His willpower was no match for those eyes. In one smooth motion he caught her arm, pulled her unceremoniously into his study, and slammed the door, his dark eyes blazing with emotion he couldn't control. She gasped, her eyes helplessly mirroring her own hunger, and his good intentions vanished like smoke.

He pushed her back into the mahogany panels of the huge door with the weight of his steely body, and while she was thinking that her suit would be wrinkled beyond repair, he bent and his mouth opened on her lips.

The surge of pleasure was instantaneous, incandescent. She moaned with aching abandon and began to move under the aroused crush of him, her hips undulating softly, her breasts flattened under the pressure of his chest.

"Yes, you want me," she whispered, clinging to his neck. "You know you do!"

His mouth bit into hers again and probed it with expert skill until she was moaning and trembling, her legs barely able to support her. He had her hips in his hands, and he was tugging her into him rhythmically, making her feel the power and heat of his arousal.

She met him halfway, and time stood still until at last he lifted his head and looked into her dazed eyes. He cursed his own weakness for her. He couldn't do this. He had no right. His face hardened.

"Can you tell me that you still want Terri, after that?" she asked through swollen lips. "What can you have with her that you couldn't with me?"

Terri. The name brought him back to cold sanity.

He pulled away from Amanda, and his features froze as he looked down into faintly triumphant green eyes. "Freedom," he returned. Her eyelids flickered. "Terri won't expect to marry me for a few heated hours in bed."

"I'd give you more than that," she said huskily.

His eyes narrowed. "Bargaining with me, Amanda?" he asked. "Sex in exchange for a wedding band? Or maybe," he added mockingly, "for control of a newspaper?"

She flushed angrily. "That was low, Josh."

He ran his hand through his thick blond hair. "Go ahead. Tell me you're not like that," he challenged. "Tell me that it's my heart you want, not the power and money and prestige that go with it. Tell me you wouldn't do anything to get control of your mother's newspaper."

She threw up her hands. For just a minute she'd thought she was winning. But he was the iron man again. "Oh, for God's sake, have you gone daft?" she muttered. "You know I'm not mercenary!"

"Women have bargained their bodies with me for years," he said with blunt cynicism. "Most of them got diamonds and fur for their favors. But Terri," he added, lying deliberately, "will settle for my body, since she's got Mikapoulis's millions."

Her eyes flashed. She wanted to swing at him, but that wouldn't do. "I wish you joy of her," she said through clenched teeth.

"I've already had it," he mused. "And I will again. She and I have no business dealings together."

It took every shred of dignity and control she had not to slap that mocking smile off his handsome face.

"And you and I do," she said.

"That's right," he said unpleasantly. "Now we're business partners, which puts you in a totally different bracket. In two years you'll have forty-nine percent of the paper. By then you'll have earned it. Until then," he added, "Ward Johnson is the man in charge."

"It isn't Ward Johnson's paper, it's mine! My legacy from my mother!" she raged at him. She realized that her outburst was going to go against her, and she controlled herself. "I don't know what Johnson told you, but he's losing money hand over fist. I'll prove it to you if it's the last thing I do!"

"You do that," he agreed.

She drew herself up to her full height. "I will!" she said with mangled pride. "And from now on, as you said, it will be business between us. Just business. No personal remarks, no personal contact. I'll take that newspaper right out from under you, if you aren't careful."

His eyes went black and cold as ice. "Don't make an enemy of me if you don't have to," he said with soft menace.

She felt chills at the thought. "I wouldn't dare." She laughed hollowly. "After all, I have to depend on you to keep my inheritance solvent until I inherit it, don't I?"

He didn't say anything. After a minute he turned away. "Goodbye, Amanda," he said, barely trusting his voice through a red rage of anger, frustration and passion.

She jerked open the door, her hand trembling on the knob.

"Amanda!"

She almost jumped at the curt tone. "What?" she asked without looking.

There was a faint pause. "Phone the house when you get to San Antonio. I want to know that you got home safely."

"Do you care?" she asked haughtily.

"Care!" He looked violent for an instant, and there was something unfamiliar in his eyes, his face. But she couldn't register what it was, and he turned away before she could analyze it.

She took one last look at his back and closed her eyes for an instant as she turned away. "Goodbye, Josh," she said.

He didn't say another word.

The walk to the launch was the longest she'd ever taken. It was another milestone of disappointment in a recent past filled with them.

At least she still had a job to go to and the hope of a little money to inherit. Many people had less.

She forced herself not to think about Terri, probably even now waiting to rush into Josh's bed despite her marriage. If she did, she'd cry. She couldn't do that. She couldn't afford to show any weakness now. She had to be strong.

Josh waited until he heard the launch crank up and pull away before he went to the curtains and peered through them. His big hand contracted on the soft, sheer fabric as he watched the launch grow smaller and smaller in the distance. He felt a wave of pure anguish.

"Amanda!" he whispered. His voice would have sounded no less anguished if he'd suffered a knife twisting through the heart. She was gone. He was alone as he'd never been before. Unless it turned out that his suspicions were unfounded, he'd be alone for the rest of his life.

CHAPTER EIGHT

San antonio was muggy and wet when Amanda emerged from the private jet. She was wearing the same blue silk suit she'd started out in that morning, but it was more wrinkled now after having been confined to a seat in the plane for several hours. Josh's inexplicable surge of passion before she'd left the house had added to her dishabille. She couldn't quite equate that desperate hunger with the antagonism that had followed it or the deliberate reference to Terri. It wasn't like Josh to be hurtful. She felt a deep sense of loss.

After she said goodbye to Brad, she walked into the lobby of the airport. Mirri met her there, rising from her seat on the aisle to hug her friend enthusiastically in welcome.

"It's been dead here without you!" she exclaimed as they walked out into the dreary parking lot, palm trees shimmering in the heat beside them. "I parked just over there. Come on, before the rain starts again. It's hardly stopped this week, and we've had flooding...not where you live," she added, smiling at Amanda's worried look.

"I couldn't care less. I'm worn to the bone," Amanda said

wearily. "I'm going to have to fight Josh for every inch of that job press. He still retains control, and I can't think of a way around him. There are no outstanding shares—everything is split between Josh and me. The only chance I have at control before my twenty-fifth birthday is to marry or prove that my father was crazy." She sighed. "He wasn't crazy. And I don't want to get married."

Mirri whistled. "Did you and Josh fight the whole time you were on Opal Cay?"

"Not quite, but we parted swinging," Amanda muttered. She took a deep breath. "How are you?"

"Same as always. Beautiful and unappreciated. How was Opal Cay?"

"Relaxing, at times," Amanda said, hoping her face didn't give the show away. "Business as usual for Josh, of course, but Brad kept me company for a few days. He flew in with me on the jet, but he had some stops to make on the way to his house. That's why I phoned you in Nassau and asked you to meet me. I hope you won't get into trouble with your boss."

"Not me. He worships the ground I walk on," Mirri said with dry humor. "Any day now he's going to collapse at my feet and beg me to notice him."

"What an interesting prospect," Amanda murmured. "So you and the taciturn Nelson Stuart are still getting along?"

Mirri shrugged. "If they burned me at the stake, he'd be the last person to do a rain dance."

"Maybe he's hiding a secret passion for you," Amanda ventured as she got into the car. "He doesn't date anybody, does he?"

"Not since I've been working in the office," Mirri replied. "Some of the other operatives give him strange looks, but he doesn't cast wandering eyes at any men, either, so I know he's straight. Maybe he has a broken heart."

"That's possible."

"If he has a heart," Mirri added.

She might have been surprised to see the redoubtable Nelson Stuart standing near his car at the airport, watching her. He'd driven in to pick up a visiting agent, not having realized that Mirri had lied about wanting to sit with her sick grandmother in the hospital. His brows drew together. She'd catch hell for lying to him. He hated lies and subterfuge, especially from women. Besides, she could have saved him some badly needed time by picking up his visitor here.

On the other hand, the visiting agent, Fletcher Cobb, was a single man with a reputation for being a veteran womanizer, and throwing Mirri at him would be unforgivable. He watched her curiously, his dark eyes never leaving her as she got into the car. She was so flighty that sometimes she made him think of rainbows and butterflies. Imagine that, he mused, with his no-nonsense approach to life.

He had no time for rainbows, butterflies, or women. His job saw to that.

But every once in a while he permitted himself to think about Mirri. It was stupid. He laughed silently at his own folly. His redheaded coworker probably had more notches on her bedpost than all the men in the office combined. He despised that kind of woman. Which made it even harder to understand why he couldn't stop looking at her sometimes.

He turned to walk into the airport. To a casual observer, he looked like a man who didn't know what tenderness was. The truth was that he'd never had the opportunity to find out. Nelson Stuart was not a frivolous man.

In the car, Mirri was chatting easily to Amanda about work and a new concert at the civic center while Amanda's mind was on Josh and the way they'd parted.

"When do you go back to work?" Mirri asked.

"Monday. Which reminds me," Amanda said, frowning,

"how is it that you managed the time to meet me? Did you bribe someone at your office to let you off?"

"Bribe a special agent? I'm shocked!"

"Come on!"

"I told Mr. Stuart that I had to visit my sick grandmother in the hospital."

"Your grandmother has been dead for fifteen years."

"He doesn't know that. He knows nothing at all about me."

"You should have told him the truth."

"If I had, I'd still be in the office answering the phone and typing out arrest records and reports."

"I could have gotten a cab."

"Don't be silly," Mirri said gently, and smiled. "You've had a bad time of it, and you needed me. God knows Nelson never will. Anyway, it's no big deal. He'll never find out."

That blissful ignorance lasted until Mirri deposited Amanda at the small two-bedroom cottage behind the two-story red-brick house where Amanda had grown up. Leaving with a promise to meet her friend for supper at six, Mirri drove back to work and found an angry Nelson Stuart perched on the edge of her desk, waiting for her.

Amazing, she thought, watching him, that such a cold, broody, melancholy man could also be physically attractive. She'd never found any man appealing in that way before. In fact, her single experience with men had been traumatic and had left her afraid of all of them. But Nelson Stuart was tall and powerfully built, with the face of a plainsman and the carriage of a king. He had a regal elegance that sat well with his natural reticence of character.

Mirri would have loved to climb into his arms and tell him the sad story of her life. But that was laughable. He looked at her with eyes that spoke volumes about his opinion of her character. Apparently he approved of nothing about her. That blind condemnation was what put her back up and made her so antagonistic toward him. It was self-defense, faking him out, so that he'd believe she found him amusing when the truth was she found him devastating.

"I hope your sick grandmother is better," he said as she approached the desk, holding her purse to her breasts like a shield.

"She's, uh, much better, thanks," she said warily.

"Yes, so I noticed."

Her face stilled. "I beg your pardon?"

"She bears an amazing resemblance to Amanda Todd, don't you think?"

"Caught in the act," Mirri said with irrepressible humor. "Okay, boss, you found me out. I went to the airport to get Amanda and drop her off at the cottage. If you want to shoot me, I'll get you some bullets for your gun."

He cocked an eyebrow. "It isn't funny."

"Of course not." She composed her features and struck a serious pose.

His eyes twinkled for an instant with kindling humor before he got up and turned his back to her. "Next time tell the truth," he said curtly. "I'd have given you permission."

"Why do you do that?" she asked impulsively.

He scowled at her. "Do what?"

She moved a little closer, peering up at him like a curious cat. "Try to blank it out when something amuses you," she explained. "I don't think I've ever seen you smile, really."

The personal bent of the conversation made him nervous. He glared at her. "My reactions are none of your business. Get back to work, please."

She reached out without knowing why and put her hand on his arm to delay him. The reaction she got was immediate, decisive and a little intimidating. His hand came up and deflected her fingers just as they made contact, wrapping tautly around her wrist in a warm, firm grasp.

"Don't ever do that," he cautioned in a voice soft enough to be menacing. "I don't like to be touched."

She flushed. "I... I'm sorry, I didn't mean..."

He dropped her wrist, his eyes glittering darkly. "Your kind of woman disgusts me," he said through his teeth. "Blatant, wanton, purely pleasure-centered. I can't imagine why you think I'd want any part of you, even if I was desperate for a woman!"

Her face went pale. "You're wrong about me," she began. "Dead wrong. I'm not—"

"You couldn't tell the truth in a pinch," he replied, and walked away from her, calmly lighting a cigarette as if he hadn't a care in the world.

Mirri stared after him in shock. She'd always known that he didn't like her, but his cold contempt really shook her up. She did dress in a blatant fashion, but it was all camouflage, an act. But he didn't, or wouldn't, see beneath the mask she presented. Perhaps he'd been in love with a woman who was like her adopted persona and was taking out his wounds on her. He couldn't have known how deeply he'd hurt her. She was anything but a playgirl.

Nelson went back to his office, forcing himself not to look back. He'd been shocked at the look on Mirri's face, at its unnatural whiteness. He didn't try to hurt people. But she got under his skin. One flamboyant woman had already taken him for a ride and crushed his pride. Mirri's touch had inflamed him, made his knees go weak. He'd had to make her back off before he did something really stupid, like making a grab for her. He closed his office door and leaned against it, taking a deep, steadying breath. God, he wanted her! He was going to have to get her out of this office before he caved in. Every day she wore on his nerves more and more.

Later, while she was having dinner with Amanda, in a small Italian bistro, Mirri blurted out the whole story.

Amanda had known that something was wrong. Her friend was wearing a very simple beige dress, with her long hair in a neat bun and very little makeup. She looked like a shadow of her usual self.

"So that's it," she said gently. She smiled. "Love rears its ugly head, I gather?"

Mirri actually blushed. "Not for the iceman, it doesn't," she said with resignation. She fingered her coffee cup, watching the ripples move across its silvery surface. "He hates me. What am I going to do? I hate to leave my job because my boss thinks I'm a tramp."

"Listen," Amanda said gently, "why don't you go to him and tell him everything."

Mirri's eyes widened into saucers. "Are you nuts!"

"He isn't what he seems, any more than you are," Amanda told her. "Can't you look deep enough to see that he's been hurt, too?"

"I wondered…" She lifted her eyes. "But it isn't something I can just blurt out."

"Then invite him out for a meal, or just a cup of coffee. Somewhere away from the office, so that you can talk to him."

Mirri tingled all over. "He wouldn't go with me," she said after a minute, grimacing.

"Try it."

The other girl sighed and then smiled wistfully. "Well, nothing ventured, I suppose. But he'll just slap me down, you know."

"I don't know. Neither do you. Give it a try."

Mirri gave her a toothy smile. "Can I quit first, and then ask him out?"

"Chicken."

"Shades of Stephen Austin Elementary!" Mirri laughed. "Is that a double-dog dare?"

"You bet."

"In that case—" she lifted her cup in a mock toast "—here's to success. If I lose, you have to find me a new job."

"No problem there. I own half a newspaper, if I can ever convince my nemesis that I'm capable of running it."

"You've got a marvelous head for business. Of course you can run it."

"I know that. I wish I could convince Josh," Amanda said bitterly.

"You can't tell Josh anything. You have to show him," Mirri mused. She studied her friend closely and then crossed her hands over each other. "What went on down on Opal Cay? You look different. Did Josh finally get around to making a pass?" She knew how Amanda felt about Josh.

Amanda averted her face, but not quickly enough. She saw Mirri's knowing smile and grimaced. "Well, yes. But Terri's back in his life. He decided that I was dying to exchange my body for a wedding ring or control of the newspaper. He said so," she added when Mirri looked incredulous.

"My gosh!" Mirri gasped. "Has he finally gone off the deep end after years of living on the edge of pandemonium?"

"I don't know. He was furious with me. I've never seen him like that."

"That doesn't sound like Josh."

She frowned. "Yes, I know. Perhaps this whole financial mess Dad left has affected him. He's worried about Brad, too." She put her head in her hands. "Terri is married, but Josh doesn't seem to mind."

"That *really* doesn't sound like Josh! He wrote the book on moral behavior. I mean, he even chews out executives who cheat on their wives, doesn't he?"

"He used to. He's changed," Amanda said sadly. "When I left he sounded as though he almost hated me."

"You've always been precious to him," Mirri said worriedly. "He was always on your side, at any cost. Why would he savage you for no reason, and even mention entertaining one of his ex-mistresses when you're just getting over your father's death? That's not like Josh."

Amanda knew that it wasn't. His tenderness with her had raised the eyebrows of outsiders for years. "I don't understand, either. But we've both agreed that it's going to be strictly business from now on. I'm going to keep that job press running," she said, lifting her chin and looking so much like her late father in a temper that Mirri almost grinned. "Nobody's closing it down without giving me a fighting chance to save it. I've heard rumors about a shopper starting up in San Rio. I didn't mention it to Josh, but it could be true. If it is, the job press may be the only way to save the *Gazette* from going under. I have to save it."

"Good for you!" Mirri cheered.

"Then," Amanda added, "I'm going to buy a lacy black negligee, have myself photographed in the most seductive pose I can manage, have a life-size enlargement made, and ship it to Joshua Cabe Lawson!"

The other woman pursed her lips and whistled. "Is this really you? I mean, until a week or so ago, you were pretty much the type of woman who thought that kind of behavior was debasing."

"I didn't mean it like that." Amanda sighed. "I don't know how I did mean it. Men are the very devil, Mirri!"

She nodded and smiled. "Yes."

"If he'd only listened to me about Ward Johnson and the mess he's making of the paper. I can't prove it, but I know Ward's juggled the figures in his favor. Josh didn't believe me."

"Now that *is* sad," Mirri replied. "I put trust at the top of any relationship that works."

"So do I. But then Josh closed the door on any kind of intimate relationship with me. He's acting strangely lately, very broody and preoccupied. Brad said as much."

"You watch brother Brad," Mirri cautioned seriously. "He's a sweet man, but he can be devious and selfish. I don't trust him at all."

"I do," Amanda said, smiling. "Brad's my favorite man at the moment. At least he's on my side."

"So am I."

"You always were," Amanda replied. "You've been more like a sister than a friend all these years. I don't know what I'd have done without you."

"Double that for me," Mirri told her affectionately. "I think you're an angel."

"No hope of that, not while I'm harboring such evil thoughts about Josh and Mr. Johnson." She glanced at her watch. "I'd better go. I have to be back at work Monday, and the cottage is in ruins from lack of clean dishes and clothes. Imagine, I get to convince Mr. Johnson that he needs to manage my mother's paper in a more responsible manner."

"It wasn't fair of your father to tie up the paper this way," Mirri said angrily. "It was your mother's legacy to you."

"Well, these days it's the prize in a tug-of-war. But I'm going to win this one," she promised. "I swear I am. It's mine, and I won't give it up without a fight. If Mr. Johnson wants to be underhanded and play dirty, so can I. Josh is going to see that I can take care of my own business."

Mirri laughed. "Now that," she said, "sounds more like the Amanda I used to know!"

Amanda went in to the office with all flags flying, wearing a natty gray suit with a white blouse and a discreet amount of makeup. Dora, the new part-time employee, scrutinized her while they took a quick coffee break. Both women were breaking later than the others because Dora had been sent to pick up an ad and Amanda had been sidetracked trying to find a lost subscription for an out-of-state customer who insisted on holding on the telephone while she did it.

The *Gazette* was a small, intimate office with no social structure. The full-time employees included Ward; Amanda; the typesetter, Lisa Marlowe; and pressman Tim Wilson, who doubled as staff photographer in between his duties for the print shop. Dora, who primarily helped make up the paper, and two college students, Jenny Creigh and Vic Martin, who did a little reporting and a lot of proofreading, pasting, and random work, worked part-time. But regardless of their status, everybody took their coffee break at the same time. It was one of the few things Amanda did admire about the way the paper was run.

Ward Johnson, after a quiet greeting to Amanda, had gone out to see a potential advertiser. Amanda had started to ask him about the figures he'd sent Josh, but he was out the door and gone, as if he anticipated that she was going to be asking him some more irritating questions. He had tended to avoid her recently.

Still fuming, Amanda put more sugar in her coffee than she could drink and made a face at it.

"You look very elegant this morning," Dora began nervously, and forced a smile. "I always feel inadequate when you walk into a room. You're every inch the executive."

Amanda grinned at her. She hadn't thought she presented any image at all. "Please, would you sign an affidavit to that effect and let me send it to Josh Lawson? He thinks I need my hand held in business."

"Oh, I'm sure that's not true." She peered at Amanda over her coffee cup and flushed a little. "Is that South American woman really his latest mistress?" she blurted out. "I saw their photograph in one of the supermarket tabloids. He's so handsome! And she's a knockout, isn't she?"

"Yes." Amanda hated the Latin woman, and she'd never

even met her. She hadn't asked Josh about her, because she hadn't wanted to know. Now Terri was back in his life like a persistent ghost from the past. Josh and his women. Amanda felt she wouldn't ever escape them.

"How are things going with you?" she asked, changing the subject. "Do you still like it here?"

"Very much." Dora laughed a little uneasily. "I've known Ward since we were in school together. He was always nice to me. I liked staying at home with my boys, but we needed the extra money so that Edgar, my husband, could take a couple of college courses to keep his teaching certificate current." She hesitated. "I suppose you young women wouldn't want that kind of life, you're all so independent and business-minded. I don't guess most of you want children until you're settled in your careers."

Amanda thought about rocking a baby in her arms on Opal Cay. Josh's baby. Business and independence were less pleasurable to her mind than living with Josh and loving him night after endless night and raising his children.

She cleared her throat. "It's a new world," she told Dora.

"Yes." The older woman sighed. "I don't like it very much," she confessed quietly. "Maybe there are advantages, but in my day a woman was the center of the family. She kept everything organized and got the men and children to church on Sunday and made sure that everyone had nice manners and clean clothes. She cooked and kept a nice house and worked in the garden when she wasn't helping out at church socials or looking after people who needed it." She put down her coffee cup. "Forgive me, but it seems to me that these days it's very much a selfish kind of society, with people doing only what benefits them. Self-sacrifice, family honor, ethics, compassion—those things don't even exist anymore."

"Yes, they do," Amanda said with a quiet smile. "Don't believe everything you see in the movies and on TV about modern lifestyles. In the fifties, television portrayed housewives like Donna Reed, doing dishes in high heels and a Sunday dress. Do you know, some of this modern generation actually believe women lived like that?"

Dora giggled. "You're kidding!"

"No, I'm not." She shook her head. "True history never gets a fair shake. A friend of mine used to say that history was the story of mankind written by the winners."

"Distortions," Dora agreed. "Yes. I see what you mean."

"I like my independence," Amanda continued, "but that doesn't make me a crazy woman with a seething man hatred. I'm a professional with a lot of hard-bought education and a mind that I want to use. Did you know that there was a woman named Hatshepsut who was pharaoh of Egypt for twenty years?" she added. "Or that the Amazons really existed, hunting and going to war alongside their men? Or that most Native American women in this country really owned all the property in their villages, and men came to power through their mother's lineage, not their father's?"

"You're joking!"

"No, I'm not. Interesting, isn't it, how history has written the story of women?" She chuckled. "Now we're finally getting it straight."

Amanda watched her colleague turn away to finish pasting up ads, and she wondered at how much alike they were, for all that they were a generation apart.

She went back to her computer to go over the figures that Ward Johnson had given Josh. She wasn't surprised to find inaccuracies; in fact, she found them quite easily. But she saw the books every day and knew what the figures actually were. Her pulse raced when she realized what a false picture Ward had given Josh.

But she couldn't call him on it. If she dared, she'd be giving him just the weapon he needed to get her out on her ear.

Josh had said that he wouldn't let that happen, but he was in a volatile mood lately. Having her call Ward a liar and make accusations could be construed as sour grapes, after she'd complained that she had no real control of her family's enterprise. Josh wasn't on her side anymore. He'd be more than likely to take Ward's.

Her temper cooled as she realized what she was going to have to do. She had to lie low and jockey for a position of power. It would take cunning and guile, but if she worked at it, she could pull it off.

She began to hum softly to herself as she bypassed Ward's figures and started on the current accounts. He thought he'd outfoxed her, but he had some surprises coming. She was Harrison Todd's daughter, with all his genes and, God willing, his shrewd business head as well. If she was careful, she could still win out over Ward. And over Josh as well.

CHAPTER NINE

Josh flew back to San Antonio a few days after Brad and Amanda, putting in an appearance that dispelled the relaxed atmosphere at the Lawson Company. Everyone jumped when Josh was in his office just on normal days, but he was more demanding than ever now, impatient and living on his nerves. Even his usual dry humor had gone into eclipse. He spent long hours at his desk. He didn't seem to sleep.

"I know you don't like talking about what bothers you," Brad said the second day he was at work, "but you're my brother, and I am concerned about you now and then. Can I help?"

Josh glanced at him over a page of figures, dark shadows under his black eyes, new lines in his lean, handsome face. "No. When are you going to talk to Holmes about the shipping holdup on his computer software? Have you contacted the consultant who's supposed to reengineer the database for him?"

Brad laughed with cold humor. "So much for that approach. No, I haven't, but I will. My God, don't you ever get tired of the stone-man facade?"

"I've got several appointments to get through."

"Why not talk about what's bothering you, Josh?" Brad complained. "Why is it always business with you?"

"When you get to the top, that's what's left," his brother replied. "Business and solitude."

"Well, you know all about that. All our lives your only direction has been to make more money and get more power. You've sacrificed everything for it." He rammed his hands into his pockets. "Why don't you get married and start producing heirs to inherit all this?"

Josh stood up, his dark eyes narrowing with anger. "Don't you have something to do, little brother?" he asked menacingly. Even his posture was threatening.

"What did I say?" Brad cried, exasperated. "You won't even talk about a family life—"

"I don't want it!" Josh said harshly. "I like my life as it is, without complications."

"And without women?" Brad eyed him curiously. "Terri was supposed to show up at the cay with her husband. Did she?"

"I canceled the visit," Josh said. His chest rose and fell heavily. "I told you, I don't need complications."

"Okay, okay. I'll change the subject. I've had my yearly physical. You're still going in for yours, right?" he prodded. "The insurance company called again about it."

"Yes, dammit!" He glared at the younger man. "No one is going to find a brain tumor or anything fatal."

"I never thought they would."

"When are you leaving?" Josh asked with casual pleasantness, the anger gone now. He even smiled.

"Tonight. Does that make you happy?" Brad replied, stung.

"It does indeed."

"I suppose you already know about the jam I'm in?"

There was the slightest hesitation. Josh didn't like people knowing that he had spies and used them. "Yes," he said.

"Leave it to you to dig deep." He rocked back on his heels, his hands in his pockets. "I'm overextended. I can't borrow any more. I don't suppose you'd bail me out one more time if I promised to stay away from the gambling tables and get help?"

"You promised the same thing last time I pulled your irons out of the fire. I believed it then." Josh shook his head. "I don't now. You'll have to get yourself out of trouble this time."

"Thanks. Nice to know I can count on you when I'm in over my head."

"The only person any of us can count on in this life is ourselves. You're overdue learning that." Josh's eyes narrowed. "I've sheltered you too much already. I felt that you got a bad shake because of Mother's ongoing marriages, and Dad's neglect and endless affairs. When I got old enough, I took you out of boarding school and tried to make it all up to you. But I've done you no favors. Now I have to do right by you. You have to learn to solve your own problems, avoid your own mistakes, pay your debts without a safety net. It's time to grow up, Brad."

"I'll grow under if you don't help me," he said in exasperation. "Don't you understand that they'll kill me?"

"No, they won't. Marc Donner may have mob ties, but he's no killer. You're a con man at heart, brother," Josh said imperturbably. "Con them. After all, you got yourself into this mess."

"Get myself out," Brad finished for him. "Sure." He rammed his hands into his pockets. "Somebody will let you know when to send flowers and pretend to grieve for me."

"I would," Josh said honestly. "But if I get you out of it again, I'll spend the rest of our lives doing it. This time you have to do it alone."

"Thanks for nothing."

He should be used to it, Brad thought on his way out. He never won an argument, he never got his way. Josh would let the gambling syndicate assassinate him without blinking an eye. They said brotherly love was sacred, but here was Josh dropping him into boiling oil. He was too stubborn to admit that his brother was right. He didn't want complications, either. He wanted to enjoy his life. Gambling had always been part of it. He loved the risks. Why did he have to give them up? Surely, if he worked at it, he could find a way out. He had to, now, if only to show Josh that he could.

Ward Johnson watched Dora finish up the work on the computer and shut it down, his eyes thoughtful and more wistful than he knew.

"Why didn't I marry you?" he mused aloud.

She flushed, smiling like a girl as she glanced at him. "You never noticed me," she reminded him. "I was always the wall-flower, hiding in the back of the class and never raising my hand all through school. I was too shy to even smile at you."

"Gladys wasn't," he said with a bitter laugh. "She seduced me in the gym after class one day, on the floor behind the lockers. Two months later she said she was pregnant by me, and I married her. What a mistake. She wanted a rich man. She tried to make me into one by pushing me and pushing me, but I didn't have the ambition or the talent." He rubbed the back of his neck and shook his head. "When she couldn't force me into brown-nosing for an executive job, she hit the bottle. She's still hitting it."

"I'm sorry."

"So am I. It's affected our son all his life. These days, he's forever in trouble with the law," he added heavily. "When I try to make him stop drinking and smoking pot, he laughs and says I never try to stop Mom, and isn't alcohol a drug? What do I say to that? Of course it's a drug, but she won't stop. She knows I hate it. That's why she does it, to punish me."

Dora smiled a little nervously. "Some women don't seem to take well to marriage, I suppose. Your wife…perhaps she's very ambitious and smart. If she'd gone out for a career, she'd probably have made it to the top and have all that money she wanted."

"She'd have been happy," he agreed. "But she thought she wanted me and kids." He shrugged. "Do any of us know what we really want?" He stared at her. "How about you?"

"Oh, Edgar and I are happy, I suppose. The boys will both be in junior high next year. Edgar is a deacon in church, and I teach Sunday school." She stared into her lap. "He teaches, so we have to be so circumspect and above reproach." She smiled wistfully. "Just once I'd love to go to some swank party and throw off my clothes and swim naked in someone's swimming pool." She laughed at her own fancy. "Can you imagine my doing something like that, at my age?"

He frowned. "Why not? You have a beautiful figure, Dora."

Her face changed, became radiant. She flushed and looked at him. "Do you…really think so?"

He felt young again. Free again. He stared at her and saw the shy sixteen-year-old he'd gone to school with, just as she must have seen the slim boy who was just as shy around her.

"Come here, honey," he said softly, standing in front of her. He opened his hands and held them out to her.

The look on his face was explicit. Dora hesitated. "Ward, I can't… "

"Yes, you can," he said huskily, his face hardening. He reached down and pulled her up, into his arms. They went around her, staying her against the length of his body. "I have nothing! Nothing! Neither do you. We're both trapped, like mice in a maze. My God, doesn't life owe us a little happiness?"

"I'm married," she moaned.

But his mouth covered the frantic words and pushed them

back against her teeth. He tasted of coffee and passion, nothing like her very proper Edgar, who hadn't touched her in two years. She was a voluptuous woman with a passionate core that had barely been touched in sixteen years of marriage. Often she thought she'd only married Edgar because no other man wanted her. But Ward did. She could feel that he wanted her, feel his desire like a brand against her belly.

She moaned and opened her mouth, trembling a little when his hands went to the skirt of her dress and began to push it up.

The office was closed and locked. The window shades were drawn. No one could see in. They were alone.

Dora felt Ward's hands on her breasts, her belly. He touched her with desperate need, and she gave in without a protest. She forgot Edgar and all her principles in the heat of what Ward was doing to her starving body.

"Here," he choked, moving her so that she was sitting on the edge of the desk. He kissed her again and again, drowning her in his need. All the while his hands were working, pushing aside her clothing. There was a metallic rasp.

His mouth grew insistent. She felt his big hands shift her on the desk, and then she felt him in stark intimacy, probing at her. There was a muffled groan, then his body seemed to clench as he pulled roughly at her hips and went into her.

She cried out at the intimacy and the pleasure. Edgar was all but impotent, but Ward wasn't. She clung to him while he buffeted her, his mouth against her, his gruff moans of pleasure vibrating in his throat. Her last conscious thought as he increased the rhythm was that she was going to have bruises on her hips because his grip was strong and painful. Then a wave of pleasure spread all over her in a shock of heat. She shuddered just as she heard Ward cry out hoarsely and go rigid in her arms.

For a few seconds she was submerged in the drowsy aftermath of pleasure. Then came reality and shame and self-contempt.

They hadn't even undressed. She'd given herself to a man to whom she wasn't married. She'd committed adultery.

She began to cry.

Ward righted their clothing, murmuring soft words of apology the whole time. "God, I'm sorry, Dora," he said miserably, holding her close. "I'm so sorry! It's been years since I had a woman…"

She swallowed, dabbing at her wet eyes with the back of her hand. "Doesn't your wife sleep with you?" she asked through her tears.

"No," he replied. "Not for years and years." He lifted her face to his eyes and grimaced. "I'm sorry. You're so sweet, Dora, so much a woman. I've watched you and wanted you… but I shouldn't have let it happen."

She gnawed her lower lip. "Edgar," she began, stopped, and tried again. "Edgar can't…in bed," she whispered.

"For years and years?" he asked softly.

She hesitated. Then she nodded and lowered her head to his chest. His shirt was damp with perspiration, but he felt comfortable and familiar. "I enjoyed it. I'm so ashamed!" she wept.

His hands were hesitant as he patted her on the back and then began to caress her. "I enjoyed it, too." He groaned and bent to kiss her, softly. "Will it really hurt anyone if we make each other happy?" he asked miserably. "They don't want us, and we do want each other. It would just be that, you know. I wouldn't make any trouble for you or try to break up your marriage. And no one would ever know. Only the two of us. Who would it hurt?"

"No one, I guess," she said, rationalizing it because she wanted him, too. She wanted to be loved, needed, adored. She wanted to feel like a desirable woman. She wanted to experience sex as a delightful form of communication instead of as an unpleasant duty.

Ward hugged her close, his eyes closed, trembling at his good fortune. He had Dora, for a little while, at least. He had a woman who enjoyed him, who didn't rage at him in a drunken frenzy or deny him her bed. It was such a pleasure to hold a woman who smelled of perfume and flowers instead of a bony shadow of a woman who reeked of sour whiskey.

"It will be all right," he said, clinging to her. He felt the cold chill of desperation as he formulated how they could keep their secret from their spouses, hold on to their little oasis of hope in a desert of despair and hopelessness. "We'll manage."

Dora hoped they would. Guilt was riding her, but surely she deserved something besides work and duty and service!

Later Ward walked her to the parking lot, very correct in the distance he kept between them. He didn't pretend that what they were doing was either all right or noble. He knew that it could easily lead to shame and public disgrace and even tragedy. But he was too weak to fight it. Apparently so was she. He remembered lines from a song or poem, about people leading lives of quiet desperation. He understood now what they meant. He was stealing a few hours' pleasure to escape his hopeless loneliness. He hoped the price he and Dora would ultimately have to pay wouldn't be too high.

Amanda sensed a different atmosphere in the office the next day. It wasn't something tangible, but there was a strained, almost forced reserve between Ward and Dora. In fact, they seemed to have trouble not looking at each other.

When they went out to lunch, Amanda pretended not to notice that they got into the same car, but immediately she figured everything out. She didn't approve, and she knew Josh wouldn't. But she could hardly tell him something that was only a suspicion. After the way they'd parted, perhaps he wouldn't even speak to her. She couldn't remember ever having a serious argument with Josh before. She didn't like being at odds with him.

She stared at the computer screen, determined to concentrate on the matter at hand. She noted with an accountant's keen accuracy the changes Ward had made in the sheets he'd faxed to Josh. These reflected a wholesale percentage rise in classified ad prices and display ad prices, and even job press prices, in increments that were barely noticeable unless someone saw the books on a daily basis and recognized the bulk rates for the ads and various printing jobs. But she did. She glared at the spreadsheet, wondering if Ward Johnson really expected to pull off the deception.

If he planned to raise those prices to correspond with his figures, he might actually manage it.

The price increase had been Amanda's idea, but Ward had made Josh think it was his own. She wanted to throw things and scream. Ward had outfoxed her. She could go running to Josh yelling foul, but that wasn't her way.

She'd have a better chance if she slowly initiated other changes to improve revenues at the *Gazette*. And Josh would believe her when she finally told him whose idea it had been. He knew, if nothing else, that she never lied.

Amanda wished she'd never known what it was like to kiss him, to be held by him, wanted by him. Her nights were tormented, and her days were full of thoughts of what their nights could be like. But she couldn't continue to brood, or her mother's family's newspaper enterprise would go down the tube. There was no way Amanda would let her inheritance slip by her as easily as Josh had. At least the newspaper held the promise of a secure future.

She went to the back, where Tim Wilson was running the big Heidelberg press, its hydraulic action sounding like a jazz rhythm as it lifted each printed sheet into a neat pile. They used the offset press for most jobs, but there were still some that demanded the accuracy and precision of the Heidelberg.

"I want to talk to you about something," she said, perching herself on a stool beside him.

"Sure," he said, grinning. He was in his thirties, tall and slightly balding, and happily married with a brand-new son. Everyone liked him. "What is it?"

"When you set up a job, it's before we've had the customer come in and read the proofs, isn't it?"

"Well, yes," he confessed. "I don't like it, but Mr. Johnson says we've done it that way for fifteen years and he doesn't want to make anybody mad."

"The way we're doing this isn't cost-effective," she said. "The cost of setting up the job is offset by having to do it all over again because it wasn't proofread first. The same thing is happening with jobs we do on the offset press. Negatives and plates are expensive to make. We're throwing away money."

"That we are."

"I want the customers to read proofs before we print jobs from now on. You or I can call and ask them to come in and look over the proofs and sign a paper attesting to that."

Tim whistled softly. "Ward won't like it."

She lifted her eyebrows. "Ward doesn't have to know, if we're careful," she told him. "He's always out of the office on Thursdays, and sometimes on Fridays. He involves himself with the newspaper, yes, but he leaves most of the printing decisions to you."

"That's true." Tim smiled apologetically. "Stings, doesn't it?" he asked gently. "This whole operation belongs to your family, and you don't have any say in how it's run."

"That's going to change," she assured him. "If I have to fight Ward and Josh Lawson both."

He chuckled. "You're like your dad, aren't you?"

"I never thought so before. Maybe I am, a bit. Will you do it?"

"If I get fired..." he began slowly.

"I know. You have a family to support. Tim, I can always appeal to Josh if I have to. Believe me, you won't lose your job, even if I do."

She looked and sounded sincere. He knew already that she never made promises she couldn't keep. "Okay," he said finally. "We'll give it a try."

"I want to do an inventory, too," she added. He groaned, and she smiled. "Don't panic. I'll make sure we have help. But it's overdue. I want to see what we have. Then we can decide what we need."

"You're actually planning to run this business to do more than break even, aren't you?" he asked with pure delighted sarcasm. "Damn. There go my four-hour coffee breaks."

She laughed. "There's a first time for everything."

"So they say. I'll do my part. But it's your funeral."

"Then I'll take my chances."

As it happened, the implementing of the new system was done pretty much with Ward's nebulous approval. Amanda caught him one day just after a very long lunch with a radiant Dora, and he agreed without any argument to Amanda's casual suggestion that clients proof job work before it was printed. His involvement with Dora, which was becoming pretty obvious to his coworkers, might very well work to her advantage, Amanda mused. While Ward was indulging his libido, she had the time and opportunity to indulge her business sense and get the press back on its financial feet.

It would take a little stealth, but she was more than capable of that. Besides, she thought wistfully, it would keep her from brooding over Josh. He hadn't called or written. Brad, however, was back in town, and he had called her. Neither of them had mentioned Josh, although he sounded belligerent. Amanda wondered if he'd argued again with his brother. They hardly did anything else lately, he said. She'd accepted Brad's offer of lunch because she needed to hear about Josh, even if it was secondhand. She was dying to know if Terri had shown up, if Josh was falling into Terri's arms again. She had no pride when it came to that question. She *had* to know.

They went out to lunch that Friday. He was less animated than usual, something she noticed immediately.

"Josh is in town, isn't he?" she asked, trying to sound nonchalant. They'd just finished their salads and were waiting for the main course to be served.

"Does it show?" he mused.

"I'm afraid so. You look absolutely driven."

"I am driven." He propped his head on his hands and stared at her across the table. "You might as well know that I'm in debt up to my neck because I went a little overboard one night in a Las Vegas casino. The owner wants his money yesterday, but I can't raise it."

"Did you tell Josh?"

"Yes," he said tersely. "I told Josh. He said that if he bailed me out again, I'd never stop gambling."

She shook her head. "I'm sorry."

"But you agree with him, don't you?"

"It isn't what I think that matters," she replied. Her green eyes were compassionate. "What will you do?"

"I don't know. I can't raise twenty thousand dollars on my own within a month's time. I certainly can't borrow that much, considering how far I'm overdrawn. I can't even mortgage my house—I'm still paying off the interest on the loan." He smiled at her with a whimsical expression on his handsome face. "I don't suppose you'd like to shoot me? That would solve my problems. Then at least I won't get dropped in some river with lead shoes on."

She chuckled. "I wouldn't call getting shot solving a problem. I wish I could loan you the money," she said, smiling at him gently. "I'd do it in a minute if Ward Johnson wasn't in the picture. But, if I staked you, I'd stand to lose the paper. That's what I'm fighting for right now."

"I know." It touched him that she was willing even to think about such a strategy. They had a long history, and she cared about him, even if it wasn't with the same passion he knew she felt for his brother. He suddenly hated Josh. He didn't deserve someone like Amanda. He wasn't as concerned about her as Brad was. Brad would have loved her and cherished her and treated her like a queen. His eyes narrowed. Hold that thought, he mused, watching her lovely face intently. If he could straighten out his life and pull himself together, mightn't she turn to him after all? He had overheard their last conversation and knew his brother had rejected her.

"You're plotting something," Amanda accused lightly.

"Oh, yes, I am," he said softly. "I am indeed."

"Well, stop," she said. "We have to find a way out of your predicament. Don't you have any assets that you could liquidate?"

He wasn't really hearing her. He'd always liked Amanda, and it seemed to him that the more she blossomed in that job, the prettier she got. She was an exciting and interesting woman. Josh was a fool for not seeing it.

"Liquifiable assets?" she prompted.

"Oh. Yes." He thought for a moment. "Nothing except some old stocks packed away at my late great-uncle's house. I doubt they're worth the paper they're printed on. The company they backed went broke. When I saw them in the safe, I didn't even have them checked out. I recognized the name of the bankrupt agency that issued them."

"How about your Ferrari?"

He laughed bitterly. "Want to see the coupon book? I've only paid on it for two years. And the business belongs to

Josh. I just work for it. I have stock in it, sure, but if I sell it, the family will lose control of the company. Josh would never let me sacrifice it to save myself."

"Josh loves you."

"He has one hell of a way of showing it," he said brutally.

"Go home and get some sleep, why don't you?" she said. "Tomorrow's Saturday. Sleep late. Maybe you'll come up with something."

"I wish I could be that confident."

"You really do need help, Brad," she said seriously. "I care about you. You know that. I wouldn't say it if I weren't concerned. Gambling is just like alcoholism, they say. You get to a point where you can't stop by yourself."

"I can when I want to."

He sounded so much like Josh that she smiled wistfully. "All right. Be stubborn. I have to get home."

"I'll drop you off at your office to pick up your car."

She touched his hand. "It will be all right," she told him.

"Sure. Let's go."

Amanda felt guilty that she couldn't do anything to help him. The sad fact of it was that he'd yielded to his own weakness, and he was having to pay the price. It wasn't bad luck, as he thought. It was just the way life was. Brad would learn a hard lesson, but it would ultimately save him some money. Or even his life.

CHAPTER TEN

Mirri had been trying all day to work up enough nerve to approach Nelson Stuart and ask him to have coffee or a sandwich with her one evening after work. The situation between them had become so tense and explosive that he bit her head off for asking the simplest question. The other agents were beginning to murmur among themselves. It couldn't continue. Mirri was going to have to gain his friendship or quit. There wasn't any other course open now.

Nelson noticed her discomfort. He encouraged it. He was trying to make her leave the agency. His interest in her was becoming disruptive. She was efficient and skilled, but she had to go.

This day, though, she was more disorganized than usual, in a flushed frenzy of nerves. He got tired of asking for the same piece of information twice and having to answer his own telephone because she was too rattled to type and do that at the same time.

He called her into his office and pushed the door shut with

such unusual force that heads turned toward his hard face before the door closed.

"Sit down," he told her curtly.

She did, almost shaking with uncharacteristic shyness. She looked at him and colored, her fiery hair all disheveled, her blue eyes darker than usual and huge as she averted them from his angry face.

He perched on the edge of his desk, very attractive in a neat gray suit with a spotless white shirt and a neat gray-striped tie. His thick black hair was pulled back from his lean face, emphasizing the rawboned look of it and his high cheekbones. His equally dark eyes narrowed on her face. "What the hell is wrong with you today?" he asked without preamble.

She clenched her small hands in her lap and went for broke. "I'm trying to get up enough nerve to ask you to have coffee with me after work."

He looked at the door and then at the carpet, to make sure he was awake. He was glad he was sitting down. He stared at her. "I beg your pardon?" he asked slowly.

She looked up at his rigid features. The almost whimsical expression on his face lessened her inhibitions. She sat forward on the chair. "I know you don't like me," she said quickly, "but could we... I mean, could we have coffee or something and just...could we just talk? Away from here," she added.

He'd never dreamed of seeing her so unsettled that she had to work to make a coherent statement. One dark eyebrow went up. Her nervousness made him calm. He actually smiled. "Where?" he asked, his deep drawl oddly sensuous.

Her eyes brightened with hope. "There's a cafe down the street from me," she said. "It's not fancy or anything, but they make the best spaghetti in town."

"Where?"

Her heart ran wild. She'd never dreamed that he'd actually accept. Her lips parted on a rushed breath, and her face became incredibly radiant.

Nelson, watching her, was amazed at the change, at the softening of her features, the blaze of delight in her eyes. His body stiffened, and he almost laughed out loud at his head-long response to her. Unless he was badly mistaken, she was attracted to him! The thought went to his head and made him dizzy.

"I live on Ivy Street," she said after a minute. "Number two fourteen. It's an apartment house."

"I'll find it."

She stood up. "I'm sorry about all the foul-ups today. I'll do better. Scout's honor." She raised four fingers.

"*Four* fingers?" he queried.

"Martian scouts, sir," she assured him. "I'll look for you at seven, then." She hesitated at the door. "It's a sort of old-fashioned cafe," she began. "They don't serve beer or wine…"

"I don't drink."

"Neither do I," she said, feeling a wave of relief spread through her. If Nelson had wanted even a glass of wine, she would have felt uncomfortable. That had been the one worry in her mind. Mirri had not been able to tolerate alcohol at even the most moderate level for years because of what had been done to her. She had never discussed her fears with any-one but Amanda, and now it seemed the matter wouldn't even come up with Nelson.

He was even more distracted than before for the rest of the day.

At seven o'clock sharp he pressed the buzzer downstairs in the lobby. She buzzed him in the front door and then stood at her own door waiting, all nerves.

It was the first time in two years that she'd opened her door to a man. Her last date had been a quiet, unassuming young man who'd wanted to talk about bugs. Mr. Stuart might, too, of course. But it would be an electronic one, if he did.

She had on slacks and a brown silk blouse with a pull-over cream sweater. She'd purposely underdressed so that she wouldn't emphasize the flamboyant mode of dress that her boss disliked. Tonight she didn't want to antagonize him.

He had on slacks and a sports coat. He looked as tense and reluctant about this as she did, but at least he'd shown up.

"Are you ready?" he asked. "I brought the car, unless it's within walking distance."

"It is," she said. "Good exercise, too. It's a safe neighbor-hood."

"Everybody says that," he murmured cynically. "But it never is. Statistically—"

"Wouldn't you like to talk about bugs?" she interrupted politely.

He scowled. "I beg your pardon?"

"I'll just get my purse!"

It's going to be a disaster, she told herself silently, *it's going to be a disaster, and he'll fire me sure as the world if he can find an excuse. I must have been out of my mind!*

She grabbed her small shoulder bag and rushed out to join him, pausing to lock her door before they left.

The street was a quiet one, almost like a residential area. Most of the shopkeepers were elderly people who'd been there for decades. There was talk of a complex going up to replace these old shops, and Mirri had hated to hear it. A modern high-rise was no suitable substitute for a tiny grocery store where the proprietor knew your name and your food preferences.

"You're very quiet for a woman who wanted to talk." He'd lit a cigarette and was smoking it leisurely as they walked down the sidewalk, a little apart.

"I'm thinking up safe subjects," she replied, smiling at him.

He laughed faintly. "Are there any?"

"How long have you been with the agency?" she asked curiously.

He shrugged. "Fifteen years."

She hadn't known that. He didn't seem old enough.

He looked down at her, and she looked at him—really looked at him. He was older than she'd realized. There was a sprinkling of gray in the hair at his temples, and his lean, hard face had lines she'd never noticed.

The soft scrutiny made him more aware of her than he'd ever been. He should have followed his survival instincts and stayed home, he thought irritably.

"I'm staring. I'm sorry." She motioned toward the cafe. "There it is, Mama's Place."

"Nice name."

"She's like everyone's mama," Mirri explained. "Her husband died last year, and she's managed to keep the doors open with some help from her son. But it's been hard for her."

She had a heart. He'd known that she was compassionate, but he tried not to notice it. The way she looked stirred him up enough without the added complication of admirable personality traits to magnify his interest.

Mama Scarlatti was in her fifties, a small buxom woman with a ready smile and an affectionate personality that won over even the icy Mr. Stuart. She seated him with Mirri at a window table and left them with hot coffee and a menu.

Mirri noticed that Nelson Stuart drank his coffee with cream and no sugar. She liked her own black and strong, with nothing added.

"All right," he said, leaning back in the chair. The action opened his jacket and hinted forcibly at the .45 automatic he carried always, in a holster under his arm. "Spill it."

"Sir?"

"What do you want to talk to me about that can't be discussed at the office?"

"That's not going to be easy."

"Why?"

She looked at him over her coffee cup. She'd barely touched makeup to her face. Her red hair fell in springy curls down to her shoulders, but it was the only colorful thing about her tonight. She was pale, and her freckles stood out vividly.

"I thought we might manage a compromise," she said finally.

He just stared at her, without speaking.

"Could we talk honestly?" she asked. She rested her hands around her coffee cup to warm them. "Mr. Stuart, I know you think I'm an unwarranted pest. You don't like the way I dress or the way I look or the way I act. You'd like to fire me, but you can't find a reason that would stand up in court. Am I right?"

"Yes," he said frankly.

The word was painful. She'd suspected that, but she'd wanted him to make at least a pretense of denying it. He wouldn't. It was like him not to pull his punches.

"I like my job. I enjoy working for you. If I dress a little less dramatically," she began earnestly, "do you think you might be a little less obvious about your distaste for me?"

He crossed one long leg over the other and pursed his lips to study her. "That's honest. I'll be as blunt with you. I think a business office should be run in a businesslike way. We reflect the agency we represent. We should present a suitable image to the public, one that inspires confidence and respect."

"I've never been disrespectful to anyone," she reminded him.

"That's true," he had to admit. "But having you swan around dressed like a rainbow isn't doing a lot for our reputation or my temper."

"I noticed."

"What you're wearing tonight is perfectly suitable for a working office," he told her. "Why can't you dress like that on the job?"

"Because I should have the right to dress in a way that matches my own concept of who I am," she replied. "I have that right."

"Not in an office where your manner of dress compromises the integrity of the staff," he returned.

"What is wrong with a colorful skirt?"

His dark eyes narrowed coldly. "You dress to attract attention. It's wanton."

"You don't understand," she began.

Mama Scarlatti came back with a tray and interrupted cheerfully as she put plates of spaghetti and garlic bread on the table. She indicated the condiments in their pretty little jars, ignored the set faces of her guests, and went about her business before she could get caught in any crossfire.

"It's good spaghetti," she said defiantly. "Of course, if you don't think so, you can always pull out that cannon you carry around with you and shoot it."

He muffled a laugh. She was incorrigible even when she was angry. He picked up his fork and sampled the fare, surprised to find that it was the best spaghetti he'd ever had.

They ate in a strained silence. He felt uncomfortable after the heated argument. She did have a right to dress as she pleased, but he had the right to make sure she didn't turn the atmosphere of the office into a nightclub.

"Look," he said when he was through with his meal and polishing off his second cup of coffee, "how would people react if I came to work wearing cutoffs and a tank top?"

"Everyone who worked there would faint," she observed, "and the janitor would stop drinking."

He glowered at her. "Don't be sarcastic. You know what I mean."

"I'll bet you don't own cutoffs and a tank top, but I get the message. I'll buy a funeral suit and a couple of mix-and-match black blouses to wear with it. Will that do, or would you like me to get some black hose, too?"

"Are you always this unreasonable?"

"You ought to know."

"You're not a bad typist, and you're intelligent," he said. "I admire intelligence in a woman."

That surprised her into looking up at him.

He searched her quiet eyes for a long, static moment while the sounds around them suddenly disappeared and the world shifted five degrees.

Mirri's lips parted as she registered the heat and power of that pair of eyes. Her heartbeat set out to break records.

Nelson Stuart felt something similar. His body burned with the sensuality she kindled in him. He'd given up women in recent years, but this one was getting to him. She had a figure that made him dream unspeakable things, and he wanted her. Until now he'd never thought that she might feel that way about someone as ordinary-looking as he was. But that look in her eyes was sultry, and he had a feeling she was pretty experienced about men.

That put him off, but not for long. His hunger, once unleashed, refused to be put back into its compartment. He felt achy all over as he paid the bill, ignoring her protests, and left her to follow him out onto the street.

"See here, I invited you to supper!" she muttered.

"So you did."

"I was going to treat you."

He stopped to light a cigarette. He didn't smoke much, only occasionally. But this was one time when he needed its relaxing effect.

"It wasn't much of a meal," he said, towering over her. "I shouldn't have come down on you so hard," he admitted. "The job means a lot to me. I forget sometimes that other people might feel differently about it."

"I like my job," she protested. "Really, I do, I just hate being told how to dress and act."

"All right. I'll stop riding you. But you could play down the bangle bracelets and hanging earrings of Babylon, couldn't you?"

She smiled. "I guess. If you'll stop insinuating that I dress like a madam."

"I've never done that," he shot back. "Look, there's a hell of a difference between describing the way you dress and the way you live," he said irritably. He'd let that slip out. He shouldn't have used the terminology, even if he did think she was promiscuous.

"You're cursing."

"Damn it!"

She grinned. He looked really ruffled. It delighted her to do that to him. She didn't understand why, but she liked seeing him vulnerable. He so rarely was, and never with men or other women. Only with her.

His thin mouth flattened with frustrated anger. She made him want things he'd denied himself for years. She made him vulnerable. He could hate her for that.

If only he could get her out of his system!

He started walking, and she strolled along beside him. Amazing how safe she felt, she thought.

"I'll try to reform. Really, I will," she promised.

"That would be nice."

They were at her apartment house now. She didn't want him to go. She wanted to find out about him, to get to know him. That was one reason she'd invited him out to eat, but all they'd done was argue.

"Thank you for supper," she said graciously.

"My pleasure."

"I can cook," she added.

He didn't speak. She was moving from side to side as she stared up at him, her body sensuous in its covering, her eyes flirting with his.

"Can you?" he asked after a minute. His voice sounded strained. It felt that way, too.

"You bought my supper tonight. Another time, I could make yours."

He knew very little about women. But unless he missed his guess, that was a come-on. Why else would a woman invite him to her apartment alone at night? Sex was probably like an aperitif to her.

He considered how it would affect the job and decided that it might yet give him a wedge to use to get her out of the agency once and for all. He smiled with faint triumph as he thought about how the evening might end, and his body throbbed with anticipated delight.

"When?" he asked.

"Saturday," she said. "Saturday night, about six. I could make Stroganoff, if you like it."

"I like anything with beef," he replied.

She felt her heart lift. He had to like her, or he wouldn't have accepted. She grinned. "Saturday, then."

He nodded.

She hesitated, thinking that he might come closer, he might kiss her. Her heart raced. But he only stood where he was as she started toward the steps, smoking his cigarette as casually as if he had all night.

"Good night," she called.

"Good night."

He walked back to his car without a backward glance. Mirri drew in a disappointed breath and went up to her apartment.

She wondered if he was ever going to let her get close enough to find out anything about him that wasn't job-related.

Amanda was on her lunch hour. She'd already spent forty-five minutes of it at her desk, reading the instruction manual for the copying machine. When she finished she called Lisa into her office and shut the door. Everyone else was out to lunch, but she didn't want any returning part-timers to hear her.

"Have you ever read this thing?" she asked the girl.

Lisa shook her head. "There's no time," she began. "Ward does everything out of sequence. The correction lines are always messed up because I can't read his scribbling, and there's nobody to answer the phone except me."

"It will change. Trust me. Suppose we try doing things just a little differently."

Lisa's eyes widened. "How?"

"First, I want to get Jenny to come in on Tuesdays after her morning classes in college, just to answer the telephone, take subscriptions and job press orders, and refuse ads that come in after the deadline. That will leave you free to write cutlines and do correction lines and set copy uninterrupted. I want to teach Tim to use the copier the right way, so that we can start getting back some of those customers who are rushing off to San Antonio to get their printing done."

"Does Mr. Johnson know about this?"

"He will. Ultimately, too, I'd like to send you out a day or two a week to sell ads for the paper and get new customers for the print shop."

"But he'll never agree!"

"Yes, he will. Trust me. Are you game, if I can convince him?"

Lisa's whole face changed. "It's what I've dreamed of doing!" she exclaimed. "Public relations. Sales. I took a cou-

ple of college courses in marketing, and I love meeting people. I'm not a very good typist," she confessed, something
Amanda knew but had tactfully not mentioned. "But Mr.
Johnson would never let me do anything else. Tim's so dis-
gusted with the print shop that he's ready to quit, too."

"He can't. I have plans for him as well," Amanda mused.
"We are going to turn this place around, if I can get some
volunteers to work overtime and help me do it."

"I'm all for it," Lisa said. "What can I do?"

"Leave it to me," Amanda replied thoughtfully. "It will take
a little work, but I think I have a way figured out."

She cornered Tim later that afternoon, when Ward had
driven off to take the paper to the community press in San
Antonio to be printed. The *Gazette* was set up for small print
jobs, but it didn't have the facilities or equipment to print its
own paper. That had always been done elsewhere.

Amanda explained what she wanted to do, to upgrade the
printing enterprise. Tim listened, his eyes growing brighter
and bigger as she talked.

"Give me just a little time to get a plan of attack organized,"
she pleaded. "Don't quit yet. You're terrific at what you do.
I don't want to lose you."

"Johnson said they're going to close down the print shop."

"Josh Lawson hasn't said we are," she replied. "Until he
does, it's got a chance. Tim, there's some gossip about a throwaway being published. The print shop might be our last hope
to keep the doors open."

"I'm not arguing with that," he said. "But Mr. Johnson is
not going to cooperate, and he has the last word. I've tried
to steer him toward higher prices and better quality before.
He's only interested in news and newspaper. He's been trying
to kill off the job press ever since I came here five years ago."

"He isn't going to do it." She grinned. "There are ways

around any obstacle. Next week we're going for broke, if you're with me."

"How can I refuse?" He chuckled. "I was ready to quit and go to work down at El Mercado selling straw hats. I've got nothing to lose."

"All right," she said. "We'll see what we can do with this place before Mr. Johnson catches us."

"Go for it," he said, chuckling. "He can kill us, but he can't eat us."

Amanda thought the very same thing. She only hoped that she could pull off her implementation while Mr. Johnson's thoughts were tangled up in his own personal life. If he got wind of her interference too soon, even Josh's intervention might not save her job.

CHAPTER ELEVEN

The loud knock on the door surprised Amanda. It wasn't likely to be Mirri, and she never had other visitors.

She went to open the door, uncomfortably aware of her stained old jeans, which she wore to do housework, and the short-sleeved blouse with its laced front that really wasn't appropriate for company. Perhaps it was just a salesman.

"Yes?" she asked automatically when she pulled the door open. But the word just hung there in midair, like her heart.

Josh looked worn. There were deep lines in his face, shadows under his dark eyes. He was wearing a charcoal-gray suit with a pristine white shirt and a red tie. He looked much too elegant for a casual visit.

"Hello," she said jerkily. Remembering the way they'd parted on Opal Cay didn't elicit an attitude of good fellowship.

He had one hand in his pocket. The other was holding a cigar, which he dropped and ground out under his heel. "Am I going to be invited inside, or do you want to talk out here?" he asked quietly.

She could have refused to talk to him. But the past always

spared him any continuing grudges on her part. It was easy to remember how kind he had been to her when her father was still alive. That memory always defeated her when she tried to hate him.

"Come in," she said, opening the door for him. "Do you want some coffee?"

"That would be nice," he agreed. "I've been on the move for fourteen hours."

"Business trip?" she asked as she led the way into her kitchen.

His broad shoulders rose and fell. "What else? I had to fly to California and back with delays everywhere."

He sat down at her small kitchen table. The cloth was white and ruffled, like the curtains at the windows. The room had yellow highlights and white appliances. It was bright and cheery.

"I like the way you decorate," he remarked. "I haven't been here since you moved in."

"You haven't been anywhere except to your office and other offices in a long time," she remarked as she filled the automatic drip coffeemaker and turned it on.

He traced the pattern of a leaf on the tablecloth. "No, I haven't."

She got down cups and saucers and filled a cream pitcher. She put that and the sugar bowl on the table, because he took his coffee black but she didn't. She laid napkins and silver at two places. Then, strapped for anything else to do, she reluctantly sat down across from him. Her heart was beating her half to death already, and he'd barely been in the house five minutes.

"Is this a friendly visit, or do you want to hear about the *Gazette*?" she asked.

He searched her face. He wasn't the only one who was working hard. There were traces of fatigue there.

"Tell me about the *Gazette*," he said noncommittally.

"I'm going to make some minor changes that I hope your Mr. Johnson will be too preoccupied to notice," she said, smiling faintly. "He'll get around to it, and I'll probably be in trouble. But I'm going to make that job press pay. If you close it down now," she added, "you'll lose money."

"I haven't made a decision to close it down," he replied. His eyes fell to her hands, bare of jewelry, noticing their nervous clenching. He was just as unsettled by her, and trying not to show it. He hadn't meant to come here. But he was lonely.

He leaned back, his face taut as he stared across the table at her. "Life doesn't get any easier," he remarked absently.

"I know what you mean."

"Has Brad said anything to you about his finances?" he asked abruptly.

So that was why he was here. Her eyes fell. "I know about the gambling debt. But I can't discuss Brad's private business even with you. Whatever he tells me, I keep in confidence."

"Fair enough," he said. "But if he goes in headfirst, I'd like to know. You can tell him that."

"He already knows it. He's trying to take care of his own liabilities, though. I tried to point him in the right direction…"

"What an interesting idea," he said, annoyed that Brad had approached Amanda for advice. He didn't like to think of Brad getting too close to Amanda. "You aren't solvent yourself and you're advising my brother?"

His question made her angry. She had had enough of his patronizing manner. She smiled coldly. "Well, he could always solve his problems and mine just by marrying me," she said just to antagonize him. It worked, too. His face tautened to steely hardness. "I would inherit my share of the newspaper immediately, then I could loan him enough to bail him out," she added, turning the knife.

Josh went dead inside. His face, livid with surprise and distaste, was naked for the first time in memory.

She was surprised by his expression. She'd only been joking. Why was he taking it so seriously? "Josh, I'm not going to marry Brad," she said, forcing a laugh. "Why, he's like a brother!"

He was all but vibrating with rage. It had never occurred to him, God knew why, that if he found Amanda attractive, Brad might, too. His womanizing brother and Amanda! Brad needed money, she had some, they were old friends, and she liked Brad. The thought, just the thought of it, drove him crazy. He couldn't let that happen!

"Will you listen... Josh!"

He was on his feet beside her in seconds, and with one smooth motion he had her up in his arms and was carrying her toward the living room.

She didn't fight. The action was such a shock that she just lay against his chest trying to catch her breath. And then the familiarity of him began to work on her like a drug as she savored the warm strength of him against her.

"What are you doing?" she asked.

"God knows." He sat down on a big armchair with Amanda in his lap. His dark eyes slid over her face and shoulders, to the deep expanse of bare skin where the black laces held the bodice of her white blouse together. "I knew you'd been seeing Brad," he said, his voice choked with anger. "I didn't know things had gone that far."

"They haven't," she assured him. She let out a long, weary breath, and her green eyes were as cynical as his had ever been.

He made a rough sound deep in his throat and pulled her into a warm, close embrace. He sat with his face in her hair, just holding her, for a long time. It was like coming home.

"Can't you tell me what's upsetting you?" she whispered at his ear.

"Not yet." In that moment he wanted to tell her his deepest fear, but he couldn't. Amanda didn't deserve to shoulder that burden.

She smoothed his thick blond hair. He smelled of expensive cologne and clean cotton. She loved being held by him.

His cheek slid against hers, and he found her mouth with tender deliberation, parting it with his so that he could savor the delicate intimacy with his tongue.

He hadn't kissed her like this before. Not this deeply. She liked it. She loved it. Her mouth opened for him, and she shifted in his arms so that she could press her hands under his jacket, against the warm, hard muscles of his chest through the thin shirt.

He lifted his head and looked down at her hands. Under them, his heart raced. His gaze shifted to her bodice, and his body began to stir.

With a long, resigned sigh, he reached out and began to unlace the blouse, his dark eyes almost apologetic as they searched hers.

If he was looking for a protest, he wasn't going to find one. She lay with her lips parted, trembling a little. He'd never seen her without her blouse. Or touched her under it. They'd shared nothing more intimate than kisses. Until now.

"Is it because you're missing Terri?" she asked in a whisper.

His hand didn't still. He shook his head. "It's because my eyes ache for you," he said softly.

Her head rested against his broad shoulder. She watched his eyes, her body tensing as he drew the laces down and slowly, so slowly, pulled away the fabric that covered her high, tip-tilted breasts.

His breath expelled in a soft rush. He hadn't known that she'd be so exquisite. Her nipples were dusky pink, very hard. The shape and firmness of her soft breasts awed him, aroused him.

He bent, hesitating only for a second before his mouth fastened with delicate tenderness over a hard nipple and worked its way down in a blistering silence to the firm, sweet skin below it. His big hands slid around her, faintly rough but very gentle on the bareness of her back, as he lifted her closer to his mouth and fed on her.

She heard the sound he made, a harsh groan of pleasure. Her hands cradled his head and she closed her eyes, shivering with the heady newness of this sweet intimacy. She'd never imagined that it would feel like this to have his mouth on her skin. It was like sinking into heated velvet. Her whole body rippled with delight, and she tried to lift closer, to make it last. She moaned as the seductive tracing of his tongue and lips increased the tension explosively.

When the need was unbearable, he turned his cheek against her and enveloped her in his arms. There was a faint tremor in them, in his breathing. She felt it through her own aching quiver.

Time seemed to hang by a thread in the silence of the room. She was aware on some level of the sound of the coffeemaker *whishing* as it finished its cycle, of cars far away on the highway. But closer, there was the hard, quick beat of her heart in Josh's ear and the scent and feel of him. Years ago she hadn't thought him capable of this kind of tenderness. It seemed oddly contradictory for a confessed womanizer who kept pushing her away.

She said so, her voice unsteady above his head.

"Yes," he whispered. "Isn't it?"

She kissed his forehead, his closed eyes, with her heart in her lips. "Why did you come today, really?"

"I think you know."

She was afraid to say what she suspected. Afraid that, like a secret dream, if she said it aloud, it would turn to ashes.

He lifted his head and studied her rapt, abandoned face.

Her cheeks were flushed. Her green eyes were soft and half-closed and misty with pleasure. Her mouth was red and swollen from his kisses.

He drew his hand softly over the curve of one firm breast, tracing the mark his hungry mouth had made just below the nipple. "Did I hurt you when I did this?"

She smiled. "I didn't notice." She arched a little, still in thrall to the addictive sensations he'd aroused. "Wouldn't you like to do it again, so that I could tell if it hurts?"

He smiled back. He touched the hard tip, watching her eyes dilate. Gently he took it between his thumb and forefinger and caressed it. She made a sharp little sound in her throat, and her lips parted.

"I know exactly what reaction this causes in your body, and where," he whispered. "I'd like to touch you there. But this has already gone too far. I want you badly, Amanda."

She pulled his hand completely over the mounded flesh and pressed it to her, feeling the warmth of his palm cupping her. "I want you, too. Is that so terrible?"

"No. Between us, lovemaking would be beautiful," he replied, "a soft, sweet joining that would be very addictive." His fingers contracted tenderly. "And very wrong."

"You sound like a theologian," she whispered.

He smiled gently. "You're virginal," he whispered back. "In this, I'm hopelessly conservative. There are a few gentlemanly rules of conduct left that I still believe in."

She sighed. "Good girls wait until they're married," she murmured. "Why is it that only rakes feel that way?"

"Because we honor innocence, having deprived the world of so much of it," he teased. He moved his hand, enjoying the pleasure that came so readily to her eyes when he caressed her. Her sudden moan aroused him deeply. He breathed out and covered her with his big, warm hand. "I don't sleep," he said quietly. "I don't eat, I don't function. All I do is remember how you looked when I sent you away. That's why I came here today. I had to know that you were all right, that I hadn't hurt you too much."

"You didn't mean anything you said that day, really, did you?" she asked.

He laughed faintly, bitterly. "What do you think?" He watched the progress of his own hand from her breast to her collarbone and her soft throat. His eyes lingered with quiet awe on the beauty of her breasts. "I'll know what I need to know by the end of next week," he said enigmatically. His eyes lifted back to hers. "If I needed you, would you come?"

"What a silly question," she murmured lovingly.

"Yes, wasn't it?" He removed his hand. "You're the most beautiful woman I've ever seen, like this," he said matter-of-factly. His eyes caught hers. "I'm sorry there was ever a woman at all, do you know that?"

She did. His eyes told her so. "I don't know what's wrong in your life," she said. "But nothing would matter. Love doesn't make conditions."

He drew her blouse back together. "No. But sometimes it imposes them."

He was frightening her. It was as if he had some terrible suspicion that he couldn't, wouldn't, share. He was withdrawing from her emotionally all over again. She had to do something to lessen the tension in him.

"Is this all I get?" she asked suddenly.

He frowned. "What?"

"I'll bet you never stopped this soon in your life before," she accused.

He began to smile. "There's a first time for everything."

"Yes," she said, her lips tugging up and an impish look in her sparkling eyes.

His eyebrows arched. "Was that...?" He nodded toward the bodice she was lacing up.

"Wouldn't you like to know?" she teased. "I don't kiss and tell."

"You don't need to. You have a very expressive face. Well, well," he murmured, and he looked so smug that she glared at him.

"You puritan," she muttered when he put her back on her feet and sauntered into the kitchen to pour coffee into the cups.

He glanced at her with pure mischief as he put the coffeepot back in its holder. "Why? Because I won't let you seduce me?"

"I can't imagine why you make an exception of me," she said with a sigh.

He stood beside her for a moment, his face guarded. "Because I care too much to treat you that way," he said quietly. "I'm jealous of my own brother. Jealous of any man who looks at you." He sat down, his expression puzzling. "When I have no right to feel that way. None at all."

She was beginning to get the idea that it wasn't a dislike of marriage that was keeping him away from her.

"Joshua," she said, catching his big hand in hers, "we never used to have secrets."

He knelt beside her chair, his eyes almost on a level with hers. "We wouldn't have this one," he replied, "except that I can't make promises until I'm sure I can keep them. When I know exactly what I'm up against, I'll tell you."

Her stomach felt knotted as she considered the implications of what he wasn't saying. "You're not ill?!"

"No," he replied. "I'm not hiding a fatal illness."

She let out a long sigh. "You worry me."

"That works both ways."

He got up and sat down on his own chair, taking time to sip his coffee. "Not bad," he mused. "But I make it stronger."

"You can make it next time," she promised.

He checked his watch, swallowed the rest of the hot liquid, and got up again.

"You don't have to leave already?" she moaned.

"Yes. I'm due in Florence by midnight, our time." He pulled her up and held her in front of him. "I have to go."

She searched his eyes sadly. "You're always saying goodbye."

"Kismet," he murmured.

"Did you say 'Kiss me'?" she teased. "I'd be just delighted."

She reached up on tiptoe and put her mouth firmly over his. He tensed, but almost at once he lifted her closer and began to devour her soft, willing mouth. It only made her hungrier to feel the long, powerful line of his body completely against hers. She stepped closer, trembling. It was like alcohol, she thought dizzily, kissing him back. The more she had, the more she wanted. She lifted herself against him, shivering with pleasure.

He felt it and pulled back. But he was more than obviously aroused.

"Stop that," he muttered.

"Liar," she accused breathlessly. "You don't want to stop."

He gave her a rueful smile. "Shrewd guess. It must be the result of all that higher education."

She glanced down and up again. "Nope. Just keen observation," she whispered wickedly, and flushed in spite of her attempted sophistication.

He chuckled, unruffled. "I'll be in touch."

He walked to the front door. She went with him, subdued and sad, because it was always endings for them, never beginnings.

"I'm glad you don't want to marry my brother," he observed. "But don't turn your back on him, all the same. His reputation was honestly come by."

"Meaning yours wasn't?" she probed.

He turned and looked down at her, the open door beckoning. "Wouldn't you like to know," he teased, throwing the words she'd used earlier back at her.

"Brad won't come up on my blind side. Please try to get some rest," she added. Her long look was expressive. "You're exhausted already, and Florence is so far away..."

"Worry wart." He touched her face with his fingertips. His eyes adored it, adored her. He smiled wistfully. "It's dangerous to hope."

"It's cowardly not to," she returned, without really understanding why he looked so sad. "When hope is all we have."

He dropped his hand slowly. "So long, pixie."

She wanted to drag him back, hold him, prevent him. But he turned and walked back toward the black stretch limousine, where the driver sat with stoic patience until he approached. The liveried chauffeur got out to open the door for him. Josh got in. He didn't look back, even when the driver cranked the car and pulled out of the driveway.

Amanda watched, though, until he was out of sight. Even then she didn't close the door at once. It was only just occurring to her that he might love her.

CHAPTER TWELVE

Mirri was a nervous wreck by Saturday. She and Nelson Stuart had reached a sort of compromise in the office. She was plaguing him less and wearing clothes that were a shade more conservative than usual. He was somewhat less abrasive.

The odd thing was that he'd started giving her long, smoldering looks, the kind she'd read about in romantic novels but never seen for real. He had another look, too. Not a very pleasant one.

There was a new man in the office, Danny Tanner by name. Danny was a ladies' man, and he took to Mirri on sight. Unfortunately for him, he reminded her of one of the boys who'd hurt her so badly. She froze whenever he came near.

He'd been standing, talking to her past the lunch hour Friday. Through the glass window of his office, Nelson had seen him flirting with Mirri.

He'd gotten up, come into the outer office, and stood by Mirri's desk, just looking at Danny. That's all he'd done. He'd simply looked at him, with those deep-set black eyes in a face like honed leather.

Danny had stammered something and escaped.

"Don't encourage him during office hours," Nelson told her curtly.

"I wasn't," she said, defensive.

"He might as well move his pillow onto your desk, he hangs around it so much."

She glared at him. "I'm trying to do my job."

"I can't imagine what you think it is."

"Now, see here!"

They stopped and stared at each other, neither giving an inch. But during the long exchange of gazes, she began to melt inside and his body went taut.

"Are you still making Stroganoff for me tomorrow night?" he asked unexpectedly.

"Yes." Her voice sounded much softer than she wanted it to, and the smile she gave him unwittingly made promises.

"At six?"

She nodded.

He pursed his lips. "No arsenic in the sauce?"

She put her hand over her heart. "I swear."

"So do I, but mostly under my breath."

She couldn't believe he'd said that. He had a slow, deep drawl and, apparently, a dry wit to go with it. She started laughing. There was actually a twinkle in his eyes as he turned and went back into his office. *Mr. Stuart*, she was thinking, *there may be hope for you yet!*

Mirri worried about what to wear as she made supper Saturday night for her guest. In the end she decided to wear a simple pale yellow silk shell with a patterned rayon skirt. Her hair was loose around her shoulders, and she wore low-heeled shoes. She hoped she wasn't overdressed. If Nelson showed up in jeans, she was going to feel terrible. Then she laughed. She couldn't really picture the very dignified and citified Mr. Stuart in a pair of blue jeans. She pictured him very easily in the nice suits he wore to work, like the one he'd worn when they went to the cafe to talk that night. But not jeans.

When she opened the door there he was, wearing pale blue designer jeans pulled over hand-tooled brown leather boots. His Western-cut shirt looked just right under a denim jacket, and atop his dark hair was a tan Stetson that complemented his attire.

She was astonished, and it showed.

"Not dressy enough?" he drawled, his dark eyes slow and appreciative on her voluptuous figure. "You look smart in that rig."

"Thank you. You look like a cowboy."

"I was born on a ranch down near Victoria. My uncle got the ranch when my grandparents passed on," he added without mentioning his mother or her tragic end or his own bitter life. "He runs the ranch now. I go down there on holidays and help him out."

Her eyes watched the deft movement of his hand as he swept off the Stetson and sailed it onto her sofa. "Can I help in the kitchen?"

"Nice of you to offer," she said with a grin. "But it's already on the table." Thank goodness she sounded confident when inside she was shaking!

"Anticipating that I'd be here on the dot? I've heard you in the back room, making bets on my sense of timing," he mused.

She laughed. "Can I help it if some of your agents are stupid enough to bet against your sense of punctuality? I can't turn down good money!"

"It's a good thing for you that I'm on time," he said, following her to the elegant little table with its white linen cloth and fresh-cut flowers, place settings neat, and food arranged attractively on platters. "Cold Stroganoff is the very devil."

"I know. Do sit down."

He waited, though, seating her first with a gentlemanly elegance that made her feel feminine and vulnerable. It was the first time she'd ever been with a man alone in her adult life. She was frightened and nervous, so she was more animated than usual to cover it up.

But Nelson saw through her, and he was puzzled. Amazed, in fact. She wasn't putting on any act. She was really strung out by him. He let his eyes fall to his plate quickly before she could read the pleasure and triumph in them. She wanted him all right. This was going to be one hell of a sweet night. By morning he'd have worked her out of his system and, with luck, out of his life. He'd finally hit on the one best way to make her leave the agency. And the irony of it was that it had been at her own suggestion.

Mirri didn't taste anything, although she was aware that the homemade Stroganoff was one of her best efforts. Her dinner guest didn't seem to suffer from the same lack of appetite. He ate his way through two helpings of Stroganoff, vegetables, and a huge slice of apple pie to top it all off.

He leaned back in the chair, sipping his second cup of coffee. "Did you bake the pie?"

"Oh, yes," she said. "Killing the apples was the hard part. They scream so—"

He chuckled. "You're a very good cook."

"You seem surprised."

He shrugged. "I don't associate you with culinary skills."

Here it was, finally, out in the open. She moved away from the table and stood up. "You have some odd ideas about me. That's what I really wanted to talk to you about when we went to the cafe," she began.

But he was on his feet, too, towering over her, and the look in his eyes made her nervous.

"Talking wasn't what you had in mind when you invited me here, and we both know it, Mirri," he said with careless mockery. His long arm shot out and suddenly riveted her to the lean length of him. "So let's just skip the rationalizations altogether, shall we?"

She opened her mouth to ask what he meant, and his hard lips came down on it. She hadn't been expecting the kiss. She was totally unprepared for the fierce pressure of it, as well as the insolent assumption that she'd invited it.

Incensed by his conceit, she pushed at his hard chest and tried to tear her mouth away from the uncompromising demand of his. But he wouldn't let go. He laughed under his breath, and his lean arms tautened to bruising strength. She became aware all too soon that he had no intention of stopping and, furthermore, that his body was already capable of intimacy with hers.

That was when she knew her mistake. Fighting with him had only aroused him more. The harder she tried to get away, the closer he held her. He seemed to enjoy controlling her. And all the while his mouth was becoming more intimate, more demanding, on her lips.

She might have been able to respond to him if he'd been gentle. God knew she was attracted to him. But his headlong ardor left no room for response. It wasn't coaxing. It was demanding and harsh and lustful.

All of a sudden it was a dark night in a lonely street and he was a gang of drunken youths bent on conquest. Horrible memories filled her mind. She felt his hand at her hips, grinding her thighs against his aroused body, and she cried out with fear.

He hardly heard her, for he was totally at the mercy of his body for the first time in his life. The feel of her softness, the delicious taste of her open mouth, made his head spin. He couldn't think past her body under his in bed.

Aware only of a slackening in her flailing limbs, he picked

her up, keeping his mouth on hers, and walked down the hall until he found her neatly made bed.

He laid her down and settled alongside her, his mouth still covering hers. She'd gone very still; there was no fight in her. He lifted his head just momentarily to look at her. What he saw was an utter and total shock.

Her eyes were wide open, staring sightlessly. She was shaking all over, but not with passion or abandoned desire. Her face was quite white—so white that her freckles were blatant in it. Her bruised mouth was trembling, and tears were rolling down her cheeks in hot profusion.

He scowled. His heartbeat was shaking him, and his body was already aching with need. But the way she looked stopped him cold. He lifted himself a little away from her, fighting to get control of his scattered senses.

It was the opening she needed. She clawed her way off the bed, falling off it onto the floor in her frantic haste, bumping her arm on the railing.

He went toward her. She backed toward the wall, her hands crossed over her breasts. Unconsciously she began to sob with fear and shock, her voice so hoarse that the sound was barely even audible. She grappled her way back against the wall to a corner near her closet and huddled there, shaking, her hands toward him, palms out, when he kept coming.

"No!" she cried, reduced to begging by her fear, her voice breaking on an anguished sob. "No, God, please, not again. Not again!... I won't let you!" Her small fists clenched defensively. *"I won't!"* Her voice was shaking.

He stopped in his tracks and stared down at her with slowly dawning comprehension. During the years he'd spent in law enforcement, he'd seen enough rape cases to recognize her behavior. There was fear in her wide blue eyes, horror in the way she crouched like a whipped child waiting for the next blow to fall.

Something inside him curled up and died at the sight of Mirri's vulnerability. Everything fell into place in his mind with sickening certainty, and the enormity of what he'd almost done to her made him hate himself. He'd misread the situation entirely. She might dress and act wantonly, but it was all an act. And his limited experience with women had blinded him to it.

He moved back a step or two, still breathing heavily. He pushed back his disheveled hair and squatted down on one booted foot, his arm resting on his knee. After a minute, when she realized that he wasn't coming any closer, some of the terror went out of her eyes.

"It's all right, Mirri," he said softly, using the tone that he employed with hurt children. "I won't hurt you. I won't come near you. You're safe now."

She shivered convulsively, her wide eyes seeing through him to the past. "They…hurt me!" she whispered. "They hurt me…so badly!"

His face tautened. It was obvious that he'd brought back some deep-buried memory. He was ashamed. All his unwarranted assumptions about her fell away in a rage of helpless anger toward the person responsible for her torment.

But she'd said *they*!

Furious anger kindled in him, but he kept control of himself. He had to, for her sake. "Talk to me," he said softly. "Mirri, talk to me. What happened?"

Her eyes closed, and she began to cry and hug herself and sway back and forth as the tears fell. "I used to go out at night with my friends, when I was in my teens and living at home. It was dark, and I took a shortcut down an alley. Five of the boys I went to school with were passing around a cigarette in the alley, and they had a bottle of liquor with them. They saw me and started toward me, making the sort of catcalls men make to prostitutes."

She swallowed. "I ran. I ran very fast, but they caught me. They laughed and said I must want it, or why would I be out alone at night? And they raped me. All of them."

His breath caught. He damned the consequences and went toward her, scooping her up into his arms before she could be frightened, before she could protest. He carried her back into the living room and sat down on a big armchair, cradling her against his chest. She was stiff at first, but after a minute or so she began to soften in his arms.

"That's right. It's safe to let go with me now. I've got you. Nothing will hurt you, ever again," he said with gruff protectiveness. "I swear to God, nothing!" His arms contracted, and his face pressed through the thick, sweet-smelling curls of hair at her throat as he rocked her gently in his embrace. "You're fine, Mirri. I won't let anything happen to you."

His arms felt gentle and protective. She felt her muscles go lax, and she began to breathe normally. Her body shivered once, uncontrollably. His big, lean hand smoothed over her shoulders, gentling her, comforting her.

He smelled nice, she thought. He was wearing something spicy and sweet, and beyond that there was the faint odor of detergent in his shirt. She remembered that his flat nails were always immaculate at work. He had nice hands.

Her eyes opened and stared across the quick rise and fall of his chest to the window beyond. One small hand curled into his shirt trustingly while she laid her cheek on his broad chest and felt his heartbeat.

"My God," he breathed. "What have I done?"

The tone was unfamiliar. It was tender and full of self-reproach.

"I asked you out that time," she said wearily, "because I wanted to tell you that you were wrong about me. I know what you thought, but I'm not a tramp. Although I guess maybe I am, really, because those boys seemed to think I wanted what they did—" Her voice broke.

His arms contracted, and he groaned. "That's it, turn the knife," he said unsteadily. "Why didn't you tell me?"

She lifted her head and looked at him from tear-wet eyes. "But I haven't ever told anyone," she said, surprised. "Not anyone, except Amanda. My mother died, and my dad drank. He didn't care where I went. I was just turned loose on the streets, and I was stupid. I went to a movie with my friends and and took a shortcut home, all alone." She shook helplessly, closing her eyes. "I went to Amanda after it happened. She made me stay with her, got a doctor... I think I'd have killed myself afterward, but she wouldn't let me."

"Killed yourself! Good God, it wasn't your fault!"

"But it was," she said heavily. "I didn't have a brain in my head. I trusted everybody. I never thought, dreamed, anyone would do that to me."

"Did the police make an arrest?"

"I didn't...couldn't...go to the police," she said, her hand clenching into the fabric of his shirt. "They warned me, dared me to say anything. Their leader was the son of a local politician. He said the others would swear under oath that I suggested it. It would be their word against mine, and everybody would think I was just trying to get some money out of them. Everybody knew I was poor."

"Of all the...!" He cursed, roundly and profanely.

"Later," she continued after a minute, "the leader was killed in a wreck. I never saw any of the others. I never knew them." Her nails bit into his chest involuntarily. "I...there was a... I became pregnant."

His hand stilled on her back, waiting.

"My father made me...have an abortion." She took a slow, wounded breath, talking out her pain, her grief, her guilt. "I tried to run away, but he dragged me into the clinic. My God, nobody tells you what you'll feel like afterward!"

She burst into tears, crying as if her heart would break in two. His arms contracted and he held her closer, his cheek on hers, his eyes closed, in anguish for her.

"I'm sorry," he said gently. He rocked her against him. "I'm so damned sorry!"

"The suffering doesn't stop," she whispered. "It never stops. I don't sleep for thinking about it, for the guilt..."

"Perhaps for some women," he began quietly, "abortion is the best way after a rape. But it depends on the mental attitude a woman has toward it. Your father should have known you better than that. The decision should have been yours. Abortion is a deeply personal decision. It should rest with the mother of the child. With her alone."

"I'm too soft for it," she said, wiping at her eyes. "I haven't cried for years. I don't think I cried this much when it happened." She looked up at him through a mist. "You were right, weren't you? I'm a tramp."

He drew in a painful breath. His lean fingers touched her face gently. "Oh, no, you aren't. I wanted you," he said, his voice deep and slow in the stillness of the room. "Telling myself you were a tramp was the only way I could talk myself out of trying to do something about it. Maybe I was trying to make you resign as well. I don't like being out of control."

"You wanted me?" she asked slowly. "But you hate me!"

"No."

She forced a smile. "Sure."

She tried to get up, but he pushed her back down, gently but firmly. "Just stay where you are," he said. "I'm not going to do anything but hold you."

She subsided. "All right. Just don't make me feel that I couldn't get away if I wanted to," she said. "That scares me."

"So I saw." His face hardened. "I didn't know what I was

doing in there." He jerked his head toward the bedroom. "I just lost control. I'm sorry."

"I guess you've been without a woman for a while," she murmured, unconsciously defending him as she wiped her eyes again.

He felt that he owed her a secret or two. She'd been hurt badly enough that she'd probably understand. She might be the only woman on earth who would.

"Mirri, I've never had a woman," he said quietly, and with icy pride.

Her soft blue eyes searched his dark ones. He looked so defensive, as if he expected her to laugh or ridicule him. "By choice?" she asked.

He drew in a steadying breath. "Not really." He toyed with a strand of her hair. "I was shy when I was younger. Then I got tough. I had to, just to survive. I studied hard and worked hard. I went into law enforcement and never looked back. It became my whole life. I saw what happened to men who let themselves be addicted to women. I wanted no part of it. Until…" He hesitated, but she looked genuinely interested. He shrugged, the action lifting her closer to him. "Until a debutante staked me out for hot pursuit and tried to add me to her collection of men. To make a long story short, I didn't know what to do. She threw a fit and said some things I've never been able to forget. Finally she laughed me out of her room." His face went hard. His dark eyes were pained. "I never had the courage to try again after that. The older I got, the harder it was for me to think about being intimate with a woman, having her find out how naive I was and make fun of me for it. My pride wouldn't take it. After that, I guess work became my life."

She was watching him, her eyes quiet and curious. She reached up hesitantly and touched his thick dark hair. She smiled apologetically. "I never liked touching men, after what happened to me," she confessed. "I was never able to let a man hold me or kiss me without remembering…" Her eyes went cold, and her hand lifted away from his face. "I couldn't talk about it. Men made fun of me in places I worked. The ice virgin, they called me. I couldn't handle the teasing, so I changed my wardrobe and my image. When I did that, most men couldn't take the challenge I presented to their egos. You know, superwoman in bed. Maybe they were afraid they wouldn't measure up and I'd gossip about them. Whatever the reason, they were nice to me, but they left me strictly alone except to tease me. That was better than being ridiculed, at least. I suppose I've been hiding," she finished sadly.

"Maybe we both have." He sighed, studying her slight form in his arms. "I'm sorry for what I did to you. For what it's worth, it won't ever happen again."

"I know that. And you don't have to worry that I'll say anything about what you told me, either," she added, averting her eyes. "I'm a very private person, too. I don't gossip, ever."

"I'm amazed that I'm such a poor judge of character," he murmured dryly. "I suppose it's being inexperienced. One of the visiting agents, who really is a notorious womanizer, said you were the most innocent little creature he'd ever seen. I wish I'd listened. You'll have nightmares tonight, and it's my fault."

She smiled with a world-weary look. "I've had nightmares for years. Every night. Nothing will change that."

He scowled. "Have you ever had therapy?"

"No, and I won't. I'm not letting some stranger scour around in the back of my mind and charge me a hundred dollars an hour just to listen to me whine about it."

"Therapy would help," he said stubbornly.

"No."

He smiled and shook his head. "I'll bet you were a handful when you were a child."

"No, I wasn't," she replied, finding him surprisingly easy to talk to. "My father had a big stick."

"And beat you with it," he said as if he knew.

She nodded, looking down at the buttons on his shirt. "I don't like people very much."

"Neither do I. You're a better actress than I gave you credit for, did you know? You bubble, like champagne. My blood rushes through my veins every time you walk into a room. You're always smiling, cheerful, as if life is a constant joy."

"Parts of it are," she replied. "I have Amanda to talk to and a good job, and I like my own company."

"Will you like it for the rest of your life?" he asked gently.

"I don't know that I could be intimate with a man," she replied. "That would put a terrible strain on anyone I tried to have a relationship with. I'm aware of my limitations, so I keep to myself."

"But you were attracted to me, weren't you?" he asked thoughtfully.

"Since we're being so honest with each other, yes, I was," she agreed.

"But not after tonight."

Her eyebrows curled downward. "Why not?"

"I hurt you. Frightened you. Damned near forced you. That's why not."

"I know why you did it now, though," she said. "I'm not afraid of you."

"Did you hear what I told you?" he repeated. "I wasn't kidding. I've never made love to a woman completely in all my life."

"Yes, I heard you." She smiled at him shyly. "I feel sort of like that." The smile faded. "It hurt terribly," she said in a husky whisper. "They didn't even touch me, except for…" She averted her face. "I thought I was going to die for days afterwards."

"It's a miracle they didn't kill you."

"But they did try to," she returned. "One of them had his belt around my neck, and there was an ambulance siren. I guess they thought it was the police. They left me lying there and ran."

His face hardened. "You shouldn't have let them get away with it," he said coldly.

"I know that, now. I keep thinking what if they did it again, to some other poor girl. But I was very young, and very scared."

He brushed back her disheveled hair and looked at her. Finally he smiled. "You're very pretty, too," he mused. "Are you going to keep working for me?"

"Yes, I think so."

He nodded. He let go of her hair. "I'd better go home. Will you be all right?"

"I've lived with it for a long time," she said. "I can cope."

He got up, gently depositing her on her feet in front of him. His dark eyes searched her wan face. "I don't like leaving you, Mirri," he said. "If I give you my home number, will you use it if you need to? Sometimes a voice in the darkness is as good as a hand to hold."

"You'd do that for me?" she asked.

"Of course."

"For anyone who needed it," she guessed.

He didn't answer her right away. Finally he said, "I'm not a benevolent society. No one has the number except my uncle. It's unlisted."

She searched his eyes for a long moment. "Then, yes, I'll use it. But only if I have to."

He wrote it down on a slip of paper and laid it on the coffee table. He slipped the pen back into his pocket and retrieved his Stetson. "The Stroganoff was delicious. Thank you."

She walked with him to the door, her arms folded protectively over her breasts. "You're welcome. I like to make quiche, too."

"I don't think I've ever eaten that."

She didn't look up. "I make it on Saturday nights. I like the Saturday-night horror pictures on television, so I usually stay up late. Vampire movies and werewolves and such," she clarified. "But I don't like a lot of gore."

"Neither do I. I lived through Vietnam. I don't ever want to look at mangled human beings again."

"How old are you?" she asked.

"Thirty-seven." He touched her hair slowly. "I'm too old for you, anyway."

"I'm almost twenty-four." She studied her toes. "No, you're not."

"You don't look that old," he said with faint wonder.

"Neither do you."

He opened the door and stood looking out it, his hat still in his hand. "I've always wondered what quiche tastes like," he said without looking at her.

Her heart skipped. "You could come over next Saturday night and find out."

He didn't turn, but his hand contracted around the hat. "I'd like that, if I haven't made you afraid of me."

"You aren't the same man who came over earlier tonight," she reminded him. "I'm not afraid of you now. You know how it feels to be hurt."

He took a slow breath. "Yes."

She smiled. "I'll see you at work on Monday, then."

He looked down at her. "First thing."

Her body tingled when he looked at her. It was an odd reaction. She liked it. Her face began to heat at the way he smiled back. "Good night."

"Good night."

He left, reluctantly. Mirri watched him walk to his car and

get in it. She watched until he drove away, out of sight, before she closed and locked the door. For an evening that had begun as a disaster, it had ended surprisingly well. She went to clean up the kitchen and found herself humming.

The rest of the weekend was uneventful, but when Mirri was back at work, she noticed that Nelson's attitude toward her had changed drastically. He was gentle and polite, and he smiled at her. She warmed to him like a flower to sunlight, and her work suffered just a little because of her distraction.

On the other hand, Danny Tanner was becoming a real headache. He staked out Mirri like prey and began to flirt outrageously with her. The more she resisted, the more he persisted.

It was bound to come to a head, and it did. One day at lunch she was left alone in the office with him, and he made a crude remark about what he'd like to do to her.

Unfortunately for him, Nelson Stuart walked in the open office door and overheard him.

"What did you say?" he demanded, enraged at the thought of Mirri having to tolerate language like that in her own office.

"I was just talking to her," Danny blurted out. He was a whiz kid, a college dropout with a big ego and not much ability.

Mirri drew herself up to her full height. "Like fun you were," she said through her teeth.

Knowing what he did about Mirri, Nelson had to force himself not to take two steps forward and throw the other man through the wall. Tanner wasn't an agent, he was a clerk, a couple of steps higher on the pay scale than Mirri. He was also expendable.

"Do you want to file charges against him for sexual harassment?" Nelson asked her.

"Oh, good grief, it was just a joke." Danny laughed nervously.

"Yes, I want to file charges," she told Nelson. "I've had more than enough of Mr. Tanner's offensive language, and I've repeatedly asked him to stop it. He doesn't listen."

"Come into my office, please. Mr. Tanner, you are suspended without pay pending a formal hearing," he added, his very stance enough to make the young man step back. "Starting now."

"It was a friendly little discussion! She's a woman, I'm a man…"

"She's an employee of this agency, Mr. Tanner," Nelson said, his temper barely leashed. "You have no right to subject her to any action, even any language, which makes it uncomfortable for her to do her job."

"I'll file a countercharge," the young man threatened. "I'll say she encouraged me."

Mirri was sick inside. It was the past, all over again.

"If you do, make sure there are no skeletons rattling in your closet," Nelson said, and he smiled at him.

It was a calculated threat. But it worked. Danny paled. He glared at the two of them and went to his desk.

He left, and Nelson took Mirri into his office, closing the door behind him. He smiled at her with curious pride.

"You didn't back down this time. Good girl."

"Will he do what he threatened?"

He shook his head. "And if he does, it won't matter. I'll stand up for you."

She laughed nervously, pushing back her hair. "I couldn't make him stop. He's been driving me batty ever since he came here."

"Why didn't you come to me?"

"I didn't think you'd believe me, before," she confessed. Then she smiled at him. "He can say what he likes. He looks like a lizard. No sane woman would want to go out with him."

He chuckled. "Don't say that at the board hearing."

"It's the truth."

He searched her soft eyes. "I wanted to hit him. Imagine that."

"Because of me?"

His broad shoulders lifted and fell. "I feel protective toward you. Even a little possessive." His eyes narrowed. "Do you mind?"

Warmth kindled inside her. She began to smile. "No. I don't think I do."

A corner of his thin mouth pulled up. He studied her and suddenly scowled. She was wearing a simple gray suit with a pale pink blouse and black high heels. "My God, what's happened to you?"

"I beg your pardon?"

"Did someone die?"

"You said…!"

He moved forward and took her by the shoulders. "Put it back in the box, and don't wear it again," he said firmly. "Blind me with colors. Dangle bracelets while you take dictation. Just be yourself. I'll never make another discouraging remark about you as long as I live."

She chuckled softly. "Mr. Stuart, you're weakening."

"Don't I know it." He searched her eyes quizzically. "I have a first name, you know."

She formed it in her mouth. "Nelson," she said softly.

He stiffened. It was erotic, hearing his name on her lips.

She recognized the tautness of his face. "Amazing," she breathed.

"You don't know the half of it," he said through his teeth.

Her breath began to jerk out of her throat. She looked at his mouth, and all sorts of unsuitable behaviors occurred to her.

"You could kiss me," she said outrageously. "I promise not to say one word about sexual harassment."

"Not even if I bend you back over the desk?" he asked with graveyard humor. "Because that's what might happen."

She took a step closer, and then another. Doors were opening in her mind, in her heart. She went right up against him, feeling his sudden arousal and not frightened by it.

He put her away. "No," he managed.

"I won't tell if you won't," she whispered, lifting her face. She parted her lips and closed her eyes.

Nelson was only human. He groaned. His mouth hit hers with the same ferocity she remembered, except that this time she wanted it. She locked her soft arms around his neck.

He made sounds in the back of his throat that were erotic and arousing. She bit his lower lip and felt his mouth open, felt his tongue thrust into her mouth.

They strained to get closer to each other. Her breasts hurt from the pressure of his hard arms, and it was sweet and heady. She clung, feeding on his mouth, tasting him, while the world went on outside the office.

He put her down abruptly and stepped back until he could lean against the desk. He was blatantly aroused, with no way to hide it.

She didn't embarrass him by staring. But it was enlightening to know that he couldn't really resist her.

"This isn't the place," he said.

She nodded.

His hands tightened on the edge of the desk that was supporting him. "You don't want to run this time?"

She shook her head, very slowly. "I've kept men away since it happened," she replied. "I haven't wanted to know what real intimacy was. But I'll let you teach me, if you like."

If he liked. He drew in a breath that was audible. "I'm an old-fashioned man."

"That's all right. I have my principles, too."

"Quiche Saturday night."

She hesitated. "Tonight, if you like."

He had no willpower left. "Tonight."

"Okay." She left while she still could.

That night they shared a quiche and watched wrestling on cable-TV. Somewhere in the middle of it, she crawled onto his lap and coaxed him until he kissed her.

Neither of them had much practice at it. They spent the evening learning all the soft, sweet ways there were to make two mouths talk to each other without words.

But when she guided his hand on her breast, he pulled away and sat up. And despite all her pleas and coaxing, he wouldn't go any further.

"We'll make haste slowly, if you please," he told her, grinning through his desire. "We've got something good here. Don't let's spoil it by going too fast. All right?"

She couldn't argue with that. She moved nearer and closed her eyes, feeling his heart beat under her chest. "All right."

CHAPTER THIRTEEN

After a postponement of his appointment for several days that very nearly drove him mad, the examination was finally over, and Josh had been sweating out the results overnight. Today, it was time. He sat reluctantly and restlessly in his doctor's private office in Nassau.

He used the company doctor in San Antonio for routine examinations, required by the insurance company, but there was a good reason for his visit to this physician. He was having some very secret tests done, and he didn't want to run the risk of leaks in case his suspicions were confirmed. The Lawson name was well known enough that the tabloids would have loved a shot at him.

He wasn't a particularly religious man, but he'd done his share of praying. He wanted Amanda. The time he'd spent with her had convinced him that she'd be all he'd ever want. But until he was certain that he could go to her a whole man, could offer her the future she deserved, he didn't dare talk to her about his worries.

He put down the magazine he'd been trying to read and

stared around him irritably, with barely concealed impatience. He hated waiting, especially now. His brother had finally gotten up enough nerve to approach him for help, and he'd turned him down. Now he was worried. What if something happened to Brad and it was his fault?

He'd always had more than his measure of self-confidence, but now he began to question his own attitude toward weakness. He was afraid of vulnerability. Well, except when he was with Amanda, he amended, smiling softly at the memories. It didn't really bother him to let her see him with his mask off. But Brad didn't seem to know that he was wearing one. Had he been too inflexible, too impatient, with his brother's weakness?

The nurse motioned him into Dr. Edmonds's office, and he went in, frowning worriedly. Dr. Edmonds sat behind his desk and glanced up, motioning Josh to a seat. His eyes were on the test results.

"Well, how am I?" Josh asked impatiently. "I know my cholesterol is high, but I've given up cheese." He leaned forward intently. "Tell me the rest."

The Bahamian doctor, who was even younger than Josh, raised his dark head and grimaced. "I don't like giving prognoses like this," he said quietly, his very correct British accent crisp in the silence.

"I've got a week to live," Josh guessed cynically to cover up his sudden fear.

"No, nothing fatal." He tossed the file onto the desk and leaned back. "You're in perfect health except for one thing. That fertility test you had us conduct. I'm afraid it came out negative. You have a sperm count that is almost nonexistent. Did you have any childhood diseases late in your youth?"

Josh felt his blood run cold. All his adult life he'd suspected that he was sterile, because there had been occasional lapses with women and no one had ever brought a paternity suit or mentioned being made pregnant by him. He'd always suspected. Now he knew. His face went taut with disappointment. "I had mumps when I was in high school."

"You do realize that mumps can cause sterility?"

"Yes," he said dully. "I hoped it was an old wives' tale."

"I'm afraid it's documented. It can, and does, cause it. You won't be able to have children."

Josh felt the hope drain out of him. He couldn't father a child. He would die without issue. There would never be a son or a daughter with his blood. And because of that, he couldn't rob Amanda of a normal life. He had to let her go, forever.

"Sweet Jesus!" he whispered, and it sounded like a prayer for mercy.

"You can get a second opinion," Dr. Edmonds continued. "In fact, I've sent your tests to a colleague myself, just to make sure there's been no error."

Josh didn't answer. He stared into space, stricken.

The doctor looked worried. "Josh, it isn't the end of the world!"

To Josh, it was. He stood up on unsteady legs.

"Let me give you something," Dr. Edmonds said.

"I'm all right!" Josh's cold eyes glared at him. "You said so, didn't you? There's nothing wrong with me, after all. Only a nonexistent sperm count!"

"In time, you'll adjust to this," Dr. Edmonds told him. "You have to believe that you will, given time."

"Like hell I will." Josh turned on his heel and left the office, his mind in limbo. *Sterile.* He heard the word with each step he took. By the time he reached the cab he'd taken from the airport, he was hearing it with his heartbeat.

"Drive until I tell you to stop," he told the driver as he closed the door and leaned back against the seat.

Back in San Antonio, Brad and Amanda were having a meal together in an exclusive restaurant downtown on the

Paseo del Río. It was a nice night, very starry and warm, and Amanda felt comfortable with Brad. She always had. He was a sweet man.

He sipped his white wine and smiled at her. "Isn't this nicer than work?" he remarked.

"Yes. I've been busy almost every night this week."

"Too much work will dull your brain. Look at Josh."

Her heart skipped. She kept her eyes on her place setting. "How is he?"

"I haven't heard from him since I left Nassau," Brad said tersely. "And I don't care if I never do again. I'm sick to death of big brother reading me the riot act."

"You know you'd die for him," she teased.

"Not today I wouldn't."

"You look worried," she said.

"I am. I can't beg, borrow, or steal enough money to clear my slate in Las Vegas," he said. "I'm at a dead end right now."

"Did you talk to Josh again?"

"Finally," he said irritably. "And of course, he said no. He says I've got to get myself out of it. Fine thoughts, if they don't find me floating in the canal one night."

"They wouldn't kill you," she faltered.

"Wouldn't they?" He smiled cynically. "You're incredibly naive sometimes, Amanda."

She grimaced. "I suppose I am."

"That's why Josh fancies you, I imagine," he continued deliberately. "His women are always like the beautiful Terri, very svelte and sophisticated. You'd be a novelty in his bed."

She stiffened. "That'll be the day."

He turned away before she could see his face. He wanted to keep her from getting involved with his brother. The more time he spent with Amanda, the more she meant to him. Why, why had it taken so many years for him to realize that of all the women he knew, she was the only one he could ever really care about?

"Suppose we go dancing after we eat?" he asked quietly, smiling as he turned back to her. "You're divine in that dress. I can't wait to get my arms around you."

She laughed, but she didn't flush or stammer. Brad was a tease and a playboy.

The laughter hurt Brad. She wouldn't take him seriously, and it stung his pride. "You don't think I mean it?" he asked.

"I'm sure you always mean it, Brad," she replied. "You like women."

He stared at the tablecloth. "I like you especially, Amanda."

She touched his hand, smoothing over the back of it with affection. "I like you, too."

He held her clear green eyes for longer than he ever had before, and something stirred inside him. But she didn't tremble or flinch or retreat from the sudden hot glitter of his eyes. She simply pretended not to see it.

He didn't like his own reaction, and hers was insulting. He withdrew his hand with a forced laugh. "How long have we known each other?" he asked.

"Since I was in grammar school," she recalled. "Since we were both in the same grammar school, that is."

"You and your friend Mirri were inseparable," he mused. "But you were both a couple of years behind me, and I *never* associated with children."

She laughed delightedly. "You snob, you. Mirri had a crush on you."

"I know. But she was too shy to suit me." He shook his head. "I saw her a few weeks ago in a restaurant. What an amazing change. She's the most flamboyant little heartbreaker I ever saw. Incredible that she was sitting alone."

He didn't know about Mirri, and it wasn't Amanda's place to tell him. She only shrugged it off and changed the subject.

They went dancing at a popular nightclub. Brad was actually a much better dancer than Josh. But it was Josh's arms she remembered, and her heart ached.

"You're very quiet," he said at her temple. The feel of her slender body in his arms was doing strange things to him. He'd never felt desire for her before. How odd that it should happen now, when his life was fraught with complications.

"I'm dreaming," she murmured.

"About what?"

She couldn't admit that. She lifted her dancing green eyes to his face and laughed. Her black hair was loose tonight, falling softly down her back almost to her waist. Brad looked at it and pictured it haloed around her soft oval face on his pillow. The hunger it kindled in his body made him stiffen.

"I was thinking about my job," she remarked without noticing his momentary hesitation. "I think I'm making some headway."

"You watch out for Johnson," he cautioned. "He's a shark. He'll nibble you to death if you threaten his job."

"I know that."

"And don't ever think Josh would take your side against him," he continued coldly. "He may employ women executives, but only because his image requires it. Privately he has nothing but contempt for women in business."

She didn't agree with that, but she didn't argue. She smiled up at him dreamily. The liquor and the music were disarming her. "I don't want to talk about Josh," she murmured, and linked her arms around his neck. "Let's just dance the night away."

His heart was beating double time. She was the most beautiful creature he'd ever seen. Impulsively he bent and brushed his lips sensuously over hers.

"Hey, cut that out," she teased, lowering her cheek to his chest. "Honestly, Brad, you're impossible."

His face tautened until it was almost painful as he moved in time to the music. He didn't understand what was happening. He'd only recently considered Amanda in a romantic sense, yet he'd expected her to trip over his expertise and fall into his arms. She hadn't. She seemed immune to him. She was more than special; she was a challenge. He couldn't let it alone. He tried again, and again she parried his efforts.

Frustrated, he laughed and teased and pretended that it didn't matter. But it did. When he took her home and she offered him her hand instead of her mouth, it took all his willpower not to drag her into his arms and kiss the breath out of her.

He drove back to his house so fast, he got a speeding ticket. Nothing seemed to be going right for him!

Brad didn't sleep very well that night. When the phone rang in the early hours of the morning, he'd only just drifted into oblivion. He cursed and grimaced when he saw the time.

"Lawson," he said into the receiver, his voice slurred with sleep and alcohol.

"Brad? It's Ted Balmain."

He sat up. "Yes, what is it?"

"I think you'd better come down here to Opal Cay. Something's wrong with Josh."

"What?"

"He's drunk as sin and locked up in his den with a gun. None of us can get him to come out or talk to us. I've never seen him so out of control."

The speech didn't penetrate. He was too sleepy to understand what he was hearing. "Josh doesn't drink and you know it. He's just had a tiff with one of his women or something," he said irritably. "He'll be all right in the morning. Go to sleep, for God's sake."

He slammed down the receiver. Josh was a painful reminder that Amanda didn't want him, that she did want Josh. He couldn't have cared less at the moment if Josh drowned himself in a gin bottle. In fact, he thought angrily as he pulled the pillow over his head, he'd enjoy it! Damn Josh for being in the way!

Ted hesitated, staring at the telephone receiver in his hand. If Brad wouldn't listen, somebody else had to be made to realize how dangerous the situation was. In all the time he'd worked for Josh Lawson, he'd never seen the man so agitated.

That doctor must have said something terrible to him. Josh needed someone who cared about him. There was only one other person he could call. He searched on Josh's desk for the number and dialed it with controlled haste.

Several frantic hours later, Amanda got off the plane in Nassau and climbed aboard the helicopter Ted had sent to bring her to Opal Cay. She was still half-asleep, her face devoid of makeup and her hair long and loose because she hadn't had time to do more than run a brush through it. She'd had to drag Mirri out of bed to tell her she was on the way to Opal Cay, so her friend wouldn't worry. She'd already phoned Ward Johnson, who'd made a grumpy remark about being shorthanded and slammed the phone down on her. He'd pay for that one day, she promised herself.

Mirri had tried to tell her something about Nelson Stuart, but Amanda had cut her off. Time was precious. Josh was in bad shape, and she couldn't waste a second getting to him. She hoped she'd made that clear to a sleepy, puzzled Mirri, but it didn't matter right now. Nothing did, except getting to Josh.

Ted had mentioned that Josh had gotten some test results that afternoon. Amanda knew about his physical, and her blood ran cold. He'd been hinting about some condition. What if he had cancer? He'd said he didn't, but that was before the test results. He smoked those cigars. He kept threatening to quit, and presumably he'd gone to that smoking seminar. What if it was that or something worse than that? What if one of the women he'd slept with had given him some killer disease?

She'd never been one to bite her nails out of nervousness, but by the time she arrived at Opal Cay she'd gnawed them all off just barely above the quick.

"Ted? How is he?" she asked when the tall man joined her in the chauffeured limousine on the way up to the house from the airstrip.

"Still throwing things and cursing at the top of his lungs, thank God," Ted said heavily. "Thank you for coming. I couldn't get Brad to take me seriously."

"Brad took me out to dinner last night," she told him. "He was acting very strangely when he took me home."

"I noticed. He barely spoke to me. And we can certainly say that of Josh, I'm afraid. I've never seen him drunk." He grimaced. "I hope I never have to again. He's violent."

"The doctor must have told him something terrible," she said uneasily, her big green eyes expressive in a face like rice paper.

"That's what I thought," Ted replied. "I found him like this when I got back from Freeport on business. I couldn't get in there with him, and he wouldn't talk to me. He hasn't stopped cursing for the past two hours."

Amanda absorbed that all the way to the house. It seemed to take forever. What if he was badly sick? What could she do? More important, would he even let her near him?

"Good luck," Ted said when he left her at the door of Josh's study. He went on upstairs with her single suitcase.

"Thanks," she called, absently smoothing away the wrinkles in her simple green silk sheath.

She knocked on the door.

"Go away!" came a powerful, angry voice, and something smashed against the wood.

"Josh, it's me!" she called back. "It's Amanda!"

There was a sudden silence. Footsteps stumbled closer. A key turned in the lock, and the door opened.

Josh looked down at her from bloodshot dark eyes, his tall body taut and unkempt in a shirt and slacks that looked slept in. His blond hair was disheveled. He was flushed, and there were terrible lines in his face. He looked at her as if she were salvation itself. "Amanda!" he choked.

She went to him, sliding hungrily into his arms, holding him. He clasped her bruisingly close, and the face he pressed into her soft throat was hot. His big body shook with emotion.

"Oh, Josh," she whispered achingly. "Here...darling, let me close the door." She did, gently, and he wouldn't let go of her even that long, following her to it.

"I need you," he said raggedly, holding her closer. "Stay with me."

"Of course I will. Of course, Josh." She maneuvered him over to the sofa, but when he sat down he pulled her onto his lap and clasped her breasts to his face.

"Please, tell me what's happened," she said tenderly, smoothing back his damp hair from his broad forehead. "Talk to me."

His fingers stabbed into her back, and he drew in a shuddering breath. "Oh, God," he whispered.

"Tell me," she coaxed.

His face rubbed against her throat. "I don't want to. I wanted to hide my head in the sand, but I can't anymore."

Her hands tugged gently at his hair. "Talk to me. What did the doctor tell you?"

He took a deep breath, and another. He lifted his head, and his dark eyes met hers levelly. "I can't father a child, Amanda. I'm sterile."

"Oh, Josh!" She stared at him with dawning realization. "It was this," she said involuntarily. "This is what you've had on your mind for so long. You suspected it all along."

"Yes." He pushed back his damp hair. He looked older. His dark eyes searched her face with aching loss. "I didn't tell Ted to call you, did I?" he asked uncertainly.

The liquor was doing its evil work on him. It might be a blessing, considering how devastated he looked. "No," she said. "But I'd have come anyway. You silly man." She touched his lean cheek and looked at him with worshipping eyes. "I'd come from the moon if you needed me. I said so, remember?"

"So you did."

Her fingers pressed against his hard mouth. "I'm sorry. I'm so sorry."

"That makes two of us." His eyes narrowed on hers. "Are you crying?"

"I think I am, a little," she confessed, wiping away the faint traces with the backs of her fingers. "I'm sad," she told him. "You're so beautiful, Josh. Your children would have been beautiful, too." She saw the pain in his eyes and understood. "It hurts, doesn't it?"

"Yes." His jaw tautened, to keep emotion at bay. He struggled to master himself. He drew a knuckle under her eyes to take away the tears. "I'm drunk, Manda."

"I know." She smiled and smoothed back his hair. "I guess you need to be, don't you?"

"It numbed the ache."

She bent forward and kissed his eyes. He stiffened at the unexpected gesture and seemed to go boneless. A faint gasp escaped him. He sat back against the sofa, and she pressed her advantage. Her warm mouth brushed his eyelashes. They were thick and dark and soft. She smiled as she smoothed her lips over his eyebrows and his broad forehead, his high cheekbones, and arrogant straight nose. They brushed his square, jutting chin and then whispered onto his broad, sexy mouth.

He stilled, accepting the caresses with something like awe. His eyes closed and he sighed, giving her the freedom to touch him as she liked. She slid closer and put her mouth over his, kissing him with tenderness and wonder. But his lips remained firm and tightly closed.

"What a prude you are!" she whispered, teasing gently through the maelstrom of emotion she was putting behind her. She lifted her head and smiled into his dark eyes. "Won't you let me kiss you properly? You won't get pregnant from a deep kiss, Josh," she murmured dryly.

Almost at once she realized she'd said the wrong thing. His eyes blazed up like brown fires, glaring at her. His big hands went to her waist and started to push her away.

"Don't," she pleaded quietly. "I'm sorry. I'm not trying to make a joke of it. But you can't expect people to avoid the mention of the word *pregnancy* around you for the rest of your life."

His jaw tautened, but he stopped pushing. "I'm not a child," he said. "Stop treating me like one."

"I never have," she protested gently. "I never would. Josh, do you really think the ability to make a woman pregnant is what makes you a man?"

"It's a good part of it," he argued.

"But there are much more important things, like gentleness and compassion and intelligence and strength. You have all those."

He drew a long, harsh breath into his lungs. "I'm sterile."

"Yes. But not impotent."

He laughed. It was bitter and cold, but it was a laugh of sorts. "Should I thank God for that, do you suppose?"

"Most things that happen are for a reason, even if we don't know what the reason is," she told him. "I'm sorry that you can't father a child, Josh, but it certainly doesn't make you less of a man in my eyes."

"Aren't you prejudiced, though?" he mused, looking at her

almost hungrily. "You wouldn't mind if I lost a leg or an arm, or if I were crippled. You'd love me if I went ugly overnight."

She smiled, accepting the gibe. It was true, after all. Why pretend?

"I'd love you if you'd always been ugly and went lame, too," she murmured, and her eyes smiled at him. "Love doesn't ever change or wear out or go away. Not if it's the real thing."

"And is yours the real thing?"

She hesitated. But only for a few seconds. Her soft eyes searched his, and she gave him her heart along with the words he was asking for.

"I'm afraid so," she replied.

CHAPTER FOURTEEN

Through the fog of his pain and intoxication, the words softened him, comforted him.

He allowed her to draw him down again, to hold him. It had always seemed a weakness of sorts to be vulnerable in front of a woman. But Amanda wasn't just any woman.

He smiled against her cheek. "I never had tenderness, did I ever tell you? I can't remember ever being embraced by either of my parents."

"Not even when you were little and hurt?"

"Especially not then," he replied, then added sarcastically, "Big boys don't cry, Amanda, didn't you know? They pick themselves up and grit their teeth, but they don't show weakness. At least, that's what I was taught."

She smoothed her hands over his warm back, savoring the feel of the hard muscles. She smiled. "Sometimes," she whispered, "it's all right to let your guard down and ignore all the rules."

He chuckled. "Is it?" He lifted his head and searched her eyes. The effects of the liquor were still there, but it was only relaxation he felt now. That, and a dangerous lessening of control. "Suppose we both say to hell with the rules?"

"I thought I just suggested that," she whispered dryly.

Smiling, he found zippers and fastenings and slid the dress away from her breasts. He searched for the catch that held her bra and unsnapped it, smoothing the lacy wisp of it down to her waist so that he could see her. Even that wasn't enough. He wanted more. He eased the dress down. His big hand went to the lacy curve of the briefs that matched the discarded bra and removed them, too. She gasped with pleasure at the tender, intimate touch.

"No protests?" he asked, smiling.

"When I've been trying to seduce you for years?" she whispered back, laughter in her voice, love in her face.

"You're a miracle," he breathed. He bent his head, totally intoxicated by her welcoming smile and soft eyes. His mouth touched her breasts, and his big body relaxed on hers. "Don't be afraid," he whispered against her soft skin. "I won't hurt you, and I'm not drunk enough to force you."

"As if you'd ever have to." Her body moved slowly and began to go soft under his mouth. He smiled as he felt it, felt the pleasure kindle as he nuzzled her breasts and began to suckle at them.

She shivered. Her legs moved to accommodate his. He shifted so that he was between them, and when he pressed down she felt him in an intimacy they'd never shared.

He lifted his head briefly to make sure that she wasn't frightened or unwilling. He moved deliberately, letting her experience his full potency. She caught her breath, and her body flinched from the whip of hot pleasure the movement brought. And she laughed, softly, wickedly.

He smiled, too, delighting in her uninhibited response.

His big hands cradled her head as he shifted, nudging her leg so that he could get even closer. He moved again, a sensuous downward thrust of his lean hips that made her body aware of his capability and ache to respond to it.

"Maybe I can't make you pregnant," he said in a deep drawl. "But I can you make you moan like the damned with pleasure. Do you want all of me?"

He was offering her heaven. She wanted to throw her arms around him and give in without a protest. But he wasn't completely sober, and in the morning he might hate her if she gave in to him. She didn't want to put more on his conscience than he already had on it. It wasn't really honorable to take advantage of a man's weakness, she told herself.

"I want you very much, Josh," she whispered at last. But she stayed his hand when he moved it between her body and his. "But not now."

"Why not?"

"Because you aren't sober," she said softly. "I want my first time to be the most exciting thing that's ever happened to me. I want it to last all night and exhaust me. You're going to be impatient. You might even pass out, right in the middle of it, and where would I be then?" she added impishly.

He looked stunned for an instant, and then he realized what she'd said and began to laugh, softly at first and then uproariously. "Oh, my God!" He rolled off her, chuckling, then lay beside her on the wide couch with one arm thrown over his head and one knee drawn up. "Leave it to you to knock the desire right out of me."

She looked in spite of her resolve and discovered that he was no longer blatantly capable.

"Maintaining that takes a lot of concentration," he murmured dryly, glancing at her with such worldly knowledge that she actually blushed.

"Laugh, damn you," she muttered. "I'll get back at you one of these days."

She felt between them for her bra and started to put it on, but he stayed her hand.

"Not yet." He moved, holding her gently against the sofa while his dark eyes glittered down at her seminudity with raw possession. "Perfect," he pronounced finally. "Just perfect. I can't imagine how I've kept my hands off you."

"Willpower?" she suggested, tingling with pleasure from the contact with his eyes.

"Something like that." He bent and put his mouth on her soft belly, feeling it contract. "Do you like that? I can move my mouth down a few inches and make you crazy."

"I'm sure you could," she said.

He rolled over onto his back again, watching her as she got up and put back on the things that were still in one piece. "Shame about the dress," he mused. "Buy something that won't wrinkle so easily."

She chuckled involuntarily.

He stretched with a languorous sigh. "I suppose I really am too drunk to do you justice, anyway."

"I knew that."

"You know me better than anyone on earth," he agreed. He threw his legs off the sofa and got up. "I need a shower. Maybe that would sober me up."

He stripped off his shirt and draped it around a chair for Harriet to deal with. The housekeeper spoiled him, Amanda mused. So did everyone else, though. She stared hungrily at his broad, hair-roughened chest. He was so handsome that he made her head spin, and she loved being intimate with him. She ached for it.

Her hand went out involuntarily and pressed into the hard, warm muscle under the incredibly thick body hair. "I love the way you look under your shirt," she said. "I've always wanted to touch you this way, but you never would let me."

His heartbeat ran away, but he made himself catch her

hand, gently, and lift it away. "One day I will. But just now, as we've both already agreed, I'm intoxicated," he reminded her, smiling to soften the rejection. "If you want me, you'll have to wait until I'm back in my right mind."

Her pale green eyes sought his. "You won't go through with it when you're cold sober," she said with resigned insight. "You keep pushing me away when you're yourself."

"For your own good." He took her by the shoulders and studied her solemnly. "I want you badly. But an affair is all you can have now, and if I wasn't half out of my mind on liquor, I'd never have started what I did a few minutes ago. That isn't for you. Marriage without children would be a prison after a while. You've always wanted kids, Amanda. Well, I can't give you any."

Cold chills ran down her spine. "So you're going to save me from myself. How noble."

His fingers contracted angrily. "I'm sterile."

"You said that."

"I'm saying it again. And don't hand me that same old bull about your being nothing more than a career woman, because I won't believe it. You need...a whole man."

She could have hit him over the head. Her eyes blazed with anger. "You *are* a whole man," she said furiously.

"If you mean that I can have sex, yes," he said bluntly, smiling with cold determination. "Is that what you want, Amanda, to have *sex* with me?" He emphasized the word with cruel ferocity. "Lie down and spread your legs, then. I can give you that!"

The crudity made her sick. It wasn't a physical need she felt with him. He knew that. It was probably why he was taunting her, in his misguided efforts to spare her a life without children. She turned away.

Josh grimaced at his own lack of finesse. All he wanted was to make her see that he was no marriage prospect. Amanda deserved a full life, and he could no longer give it to her. Even with Brad she could have children. Pain hit him in the gut so hard that he almost went to his knees at the thought of Amanda in bed with Brad.

"I need to change my clothes," she said curtly. "As you said, I'm wrinkled."

"All right. Go ahead."

She did. But he wasn't fooling her. She was certain that he loved her. She'd seen it in his eyes, even in his determination to spare her a fruitless marriage. She could forgive him that crude remark he'd made because she understood, too well, why he'd said it. It wasn't that he didn't care. It was that he cared too much.

After she changed her clothes, she went into the kitchen and had Harriet make him some soup and strong coffee. She took them in herself.

He'd had a shower and cleaned up. He looked pale and worn, but he was clean and he smelled like spice.

She pushed him gently onto his desk chair and perched herself on its edge. She was wearing blue jeans and a tank top, her hair loose, and she made a pretty picture. He was trying to enjoy it when she stuck a bowl of soup under his nose and proceeded to ladle it into him.

"I don't like soup," he muttered, angry and dark-eyed.

"But you'll eat it, won't you, my darling?" she asked softly.

A dark flush shadowed his cheekbones. He opened his mouth and accepted the soup. "Daring, aren't we?" he challenged.

"Yes," she agreed. She smiled as he finished the soup. It was strange to be needed by someone as self-sufficient as Josh. She enjoyed the feeling it gave her. She dabbed at his strong mouth with a linen napkin, her eyes lingering involuntarily on it.

"What is it?" he asked.

"I was wondering," she murmured.

"Wondering what?"

"If I could have a kiss."

He smiled gently. "I suppose I could sacrifice myself, if you need it that badly."

She smiled back and leaned toward him. It was new and heady to be allowed to kiss him just because she felt like it, to savor the touch of his hard mouth so gentle and warm against her own. But he wouldn't allow her to deepen the kiss. He kept it chaste and tender, drawing back long before she wanted him to.

"No heavy stuff," he cautioned when her lips tried to follow his. "I refuse to let myself be seduced."

"Spoilsport." She sighed. "How am I ever going to learn anything if you don't teach me?"

"I'll decide when," he told her firmly. He averted his eyes. "While we're on the subject, I apologize for the crude remark I made earlier."

She didn't have to ask which one. It still rankled. "You'd been drinking," she said, rationalizing.

"And feeling sorry for myself," he added wryly. "I suppose I'll have to contend with that for a while. I'd only started to have dreams of dynasty building." He got up and moved away from her, sticking his hands deep into the pockets of his white slacks as he stared out at the ocean. "All my life, I've worked to make money, to build up a legacy for my descendants. What was it all for, Amanda?"

"Brad may father children…"

He whirled, furious. "Not yours!"

She was literally without words. She stared at him and couldn't even speak.

"If he touches you, I'll break his neck!"

"I'm sure Brad's never had those kinds of thoughts about me," she faltered, and then remembered the way he'd kissed her in the nightclub. She blushed.

Josh's face was livid. "He'll do anything to get the money he needs to pay back Marc Donner, even if it means marrying his childhood friend."

"He wouldn't," she began.

"He would," he said with certainty. "If I thought he had half a chance of seducing you, I'd have him kidnapped and flown to the Antarctic."

She flushed. "Does being my first man matter so much?"

"No," he said tersely. "But sleeping with a man would mean too much to you emotionally. To Brad, it would be just one more conquest. A man like that could destroy you."

Her lips parted on a quick breath. "But I don't want Brad, don't you understand?" she said. "I don't feel anything when he holds me, Josh. I feel nothing at all.

"You won't listen, will you?" she asked wearily. "Don't you want to believe me, is that it? You've discovered that you're sterile, so there's no possible future for us?"

It was too close to the truth for comfort. He pulled a cigar from the holder on his desk and lit it.

"I thought Dina signed you up for that smoking clinic."

"She did. It was great. I learned how to smoke a cigar while holding a smoking deterrent tablet in my mouth."

She laughed in spite of herself. "You're hopeless."

"I'll quit. Not yet," he added. "It's this or alcohol until I come to grips with myself."

"You look a little better. Ted was worried about you." She frowned, glancing toward the closed door. "Where is Ted?"

"Being discreet," he murmured dryly. "He probably thinks I'm making passionate love to you on the carpet."

She flushed and laughed at him. "Is that where you usually do it?"

"Sometimes. But I prefer the beach in the moonlight," he said deliberately, watching her reaction.

Her jaw clenched. "How *is* Terri? Wasn't she supposed to

come with her *husband*—" she emphasized the word "—for a visit?"

"Yes. Brad mentioned it, remember?" he asked mockingly.

"You make a lot of noise about his affairs, but you're as bad as he is," she muttered. "Women are just a commodity to you."

"They certainly have been," he agreed. He stared at the smoking cigar in his hand. "They'll probably figure that way in the future, now."

"Just because you're sterile," she said angrily.

She wondered what he'd do if she sat down on the floor and started screaming her head off with pure frustrated rage. "Suppose I'm barren?" she tossed back, trying to sound careless about it. "One woman in seven is, I believe."

"I'd bet money on your ability to have children, Amanda. But it's no longer any business of mine." He took a draw from the cigar and turned to her. "I think you've heard rumors about a throwaway paper moving into San Rio. Is that right?"

"Yes. Is it true?" she asked.

"I'm trying to find out. How will Johnson cope, do you think?"

"He'll drown himself in the bathroom sink," she muttered.

"Well, we'll see. Got any ideas?"

She had plenty, but she wasn't telling them to him. Not yet. "I'm just the bookkeeper, remember?"

"The *Gazette* will belong to you one day—partially, at least. If you don't go soft and let Brad get his hands on it by marrying him."

"Didn't you just tell me that you weren't ever going to marry me? Why shouldn't I marry Brad?"

He ground his teeth together. "That's your decision. But if you do it just to pull his irons out of the fire he got himself into, I'll block you somehow."

"He's your brother! Those gamblers play rough. Don't you care?"

He did. But her attitude infuriated him. "You seem to care enough for both of us," he said icily.

"Oh, you won't listen! You won't hear anything you don't like!"

He put out his cigar. "I may fly over to Nassau in the morning," he said, cutting off the discussion. "I have to talk to one of the ministers about my new project. Care to come along?"

"I'm a working girl," she reminded him. "I have to go back to San Antonio."

"To do what?" he asked. "Pull the newspaper out of Ward Johnson's hands or seduce my brother?"

Incensed, she picked up a holder of paper clips from the desk and hurled it at him with all her might. He ducked, laughing with surprise.

She leaned over the desk and fumbled at a box of diskettes, heavy enough to do a little damage if they connected. But he was quick. Before she could get up again, he was against her, his hand preventing hers from lifting the box.

"Mustn't throw things," he chided at her ear.

"You son of a…!"

He had her on her back in the middle of several piles of legal-looking papers, and his mouth was on hers before she could get the last word out.

She struggled, but only for the few seconds it took him to get his hips squarely over hers and press down. She felt the strength and heat of his arousal and began to tremble in helpless response.

His chest drew lazily against her breasts while he kissed her, making her nipples go hard. He laughed as he urged her mouth open and penetrated it deeply with his hard tongue.

His hand held her thick hair at her nape as he kissed her with an intimacy beyond anything she'd ever experienced.

His knee edged her legs apart, and he pressed between them with slow, deliberate insistence.

She gasped into his mouth, clinging to his broad shoulders as she tried to get enough breath to stay alive.

His hand was at the zipper of her jeans. He drew it down, and his hand went inside, under her briefs. He touched her as no man ever had, staying her instinctive withdrawal, his mouth hardening into passion as she moaned.

Pleasure caught her, and her nails curled into his shirt as she began to shiver rhythmically. Her mouth trembled under the sudden gentleness of his warm lips. His tongue traced and teased until she was mindless with abandon. And when she thought she couldn't bear the sweet tension another second, his mouth opened on her lips and his tongue thrust deeply into the sweet darkness of her mouth even as his hand did something incredible to her self-control.

She sobbed against his mouth as she flew into a thousand heated pieces of satisfaction. Her body throbbed, exploded. She couldn't live through it…

"Josh!" she cried, shivering. Her nails scored his shoulder as the pleasure built.

"It's good, isn't it?" he whispered as he kissed her wet face, his hand soothing now, calming her as she shivered in the aftermath. "All silvery explosions and heat. And now you belong to me. All of you, Amanda. You're my woman."

His hand intruded gently. He lifted his head and looked into her shocked, dilated eyes. "Lie still," he whispered. He pushed, and she gasped.

"Josh!"

"Shhhh." His hand in her hair contracted, holding her. "I want this. I need it. I won't hurt you any more than I have to."

She didn't understand until his hand intruded even farther. There was a hesitation, a flash of pain. She looked into his dark, intent eyes and realized only then what he was doing to her.

"Josh!"

The pleasure was back. She was helpless. She arched backward, unable to prevent her body's seduction or her abandon. She cried out harshly as he fulfilled her. There was more pain, but now it didn't matter, because she was touching the sky!

"There," he whispered, cradling her. He was carrying her into the bathroom. She didn't remember that he'd lifted her at all. She was close against him, her face in his throat as she shivered. "There, darling, it wasn't bad, was it?"

"You...you..." She tried to speak.

"Shhh." He brushed his mouth over her closed eyes. His lips were trembling. "You let me," he whispered, his voice raw, hoarse. "God in heaven, you knew what I was doing, and you let me!"

Her nails contracted and she burrowed her face closer into his throat. "It hurt."

"It won't again. When I have you, there won't be any pain, ever," he whispered. He clasped her close, his jaw clenching as he remembered the look on her face. He was violently aroused from it, but there was no way he could satisfy himself. He fought his devils until he conquered them, and by the time he put her down gently in the bathroom, he was pale but composed.

He ran water in the bathtub and slowly undressed her while it filled. She watched him, catlike, her eyes wide and soft and stunned. When she was nude, he touched the faint stain on her thighs and kissed her forehead.

"I'm sorry I hurt you," he whispered. He lifted her gently and put her down into the faintly scented water. "This will help."

She flinched, because the water stung, but after a minute it did seem to have a soothing effect. She lay there, letting him bathe her, his eyes slow and tender and possessive on her soft breasts. Their crowns grew hard and dusky as he touched them with the cloth, and her body responded to him involuntarily. And all the while she watched him, awed by what he'd given her.

"So that's what it feels like," she whispered when he was drying her with a big, warm towel.

"Yes, darling," he said quietly. "That's what it feels like."

She reached up and touched his face. "I want you," she whispered.

"I know."

Her fingers stilled on his mouth. "You won't?"

He shook his head. "Not just yet."

"But you—"

"I had the first and sweetest taste of you that any man could ever want," he whispered. "Without robbing you of your chastity. You haven't known me intimately. That gift is still yours to give some lucky man, to let him know the secret, warm tightness of your body enveloping him in passion."

"I don't want anyone except you," she whispered. "I never will."

"You think so." He smiled cynically. "That won't last. You still have illusions. I've lost all mine."

"I want to know how it feels to go all the way with you," she said gently. "You know that I won't get pregnant. Why...?"

"I told you. The first time belongs to your husband. I'll never be that," he said. He wrapped the bath sheet around her and tucked it between her breasts. "I'll bring your suitcase. You'll want a change of clothes."

She watched him leave the room, her eyes full of love and pain. He wanted her. She knew he wanted her. But this was all he was going to give her. He wouldn't marry her because he felt she couldn't be satisfied with what he could give her.

That meant he wouldn't sleep with her. To him, it was dis-honorable.

She smiled to herself. He didn't seem to realize that love allowed for any kind of sacrifice, even the certainty of never having a child that he'd fathered. She wanted Josh. Only Josh.

But he was inflexible, and he wouldn't argue. She knew certainly that if she tried to go to him in the night, he'd put her out of his bed and his life with finality. He said no, and it wasn't an arguable position. But he'd said "Not yet." That could mean a lot of things. And he did care for her very deeply, she knew it. A blind woman could have seen it. There was hope. She had that, if nothing else, and she was going to hold on to it until he put her bodily on a plane home.

His delight in her was evident. All she had to do was find a way to convince him that where love existed, nothing else mattered.

She moved to the window and looked out, trying to lift her spirits by thinking about the changes she was going to make at the *Gazette*, her secret project to save the job press. But she couldn't get her mind to stay on it. It would stray back to the feel of Josh's touch bringing her to ecstasy.

Minutes later he deposited the suitcase in the bedroom with her and looked at her for one long, anguished instant. She smiled and started toward him, but he went out and closed the door without saying a word. The gesture was as audible as if he'd spoken. And as final.

She didn't see him again. When she got up the next morn-ing, he'd already left the island.

CHAPTER FIFTEEN

Amanda didn't bother to ask where Josh had gone when she was ready to leave the next morning. She knew that Ted wouldn't tell her. He'd been instructed to take her across to Nassau in the launch to hitch a ride on the Learjet. Josh had taken the helicopter himself.

She had to give him time, she decided. When he worked it out in his own mind, perhaps he'd come to her. In the meanwhile, pushing him wouldn't accomplish anything. And she had some needs of her own to attend to: saving her family business.

She hadn't been home long when Mirri, her radiant face full of excitement, came in through the front door of the cottage without knocking, an old habit from school days.

"I didn't even remember you were out of the country until I phoned your office to invite you to lunch! How is Josh?"

"He was sick," she said, refusing to divulge more. "He's much better now. What in the world has happened to you?"

"Can't you guess?" Mirri grinned. "The very starchy Mr. Stuart turned out not to be starchy after all. I asked him out, and we've been more or less inseparable ever since."

"You told him."

Mirri grimaced. "Well, sort of. We got off to a pretty rough start, but everything just fell into place. I love him!" She sounded, and looked, awed. "What's more, I think he's on the road to feeling something similar for me. We went to a rodeo the other night, and then to a concert in the park... He won't kiss me anymore, but he does seem to like being with me."

"Why won't he kiss you?"

"Because we're too explosive, and he's old-fashioned." She chuckled. "He doesn't think unmarried single people should make love. Isn't he priceless?"

Amanda lifted her brows and smiled. "Are things progressing?"

"I'm not really sure. He's hard to talk to lately," she replied. "He's gone broody. All silent and tense..."

Amanda leaned forward. "I'll bet he's bad-tempered, too, and snaps at you for no reason."

Mirri laughed. "Yes, he does."

"He's in love," Amanda said. "You should read more novels and you'd know things like that," she added, teasing.

"I guess I should. So that's it!" she exclaimed, radiant.

"And I thought I was stupid about men. Look at you!"

"Well, I'm in the learning stages of love." She chuckled. "He's very repressed, you see." She didn't add that the sexy Mr. Stuart was as virginal as Amanda. That was her own special secret.

"Then why don't you ask him to marry you?" Amanda suggested. "You might buy him a ring."

Mirri clapped her hands at the outrageous suggestion. "Candlelight, soft lights, soft music, all the trimmings? It's great! I'll do it!"

"I was only joking!"

"Yes, but isn't it a great idea?" She was beaming now. "I can't wait!"

"Mirri—"

"You won't be able to talk me out of it, so shut up," Mirri said impishly. She noticed for the first time how tired Amanda looked. "Say, you don't look very well."

"It was a hard two days," she said, averting her eyes. She couldn't tell Mirri what had happened. Josh's rejection had taken its toll on her, even if she didn't really believe he was saying goodbye forever. Hope was all she had left.

"Can I do anything to help?" Mirri asked.

"What? Oh. No, thanks, I'm fine."

"You don't look it," came the perceptive reply.

"Josh won't have an affair with me, and he won't marry me," she said finally.

"And you gave up that easily?" Mirri teased.

"He needs time. I'm giving it to him. He'll either come around or he'll find someone who doesn't want or need a commitment or children."

The wording made Mirri curious, but she didn't pry. Amanda was like her: a clam. Especially when she was hurting. Diplomatically she changed the subject. "How about lunch?"

"You aren't having it with Mr. Stuart?"

Mirri grinned. "Well, yes, but you could come along."

"Thanks, but no thanks. I have to go and see if I'm still working for the newspaper."

"As if Mr. Johnson could fire one of his employers."

"I'll only have forty-nine percent ownership," Amanda said wearily. "Josh keeps control. He's afraid I might want to help Brad pay off his gambling debts."

"What gambling debts?"

Amanda told her. "They've threatened him. Josh is jealous

of Brad. He doesn't want me, but he doesn't want Brad to get me, if you see what I mean," she said bitterly.

"Curiouser and curiouser," Mirri murmured.

"Isn't it, though?" Amanda's eyes flashed.

"Are you going to help Brad?"

"I can't, unless I want to marry him," she replied. "And I don't. The poor old soul will have to do what he can for himself. I don't know if Josh is right or wrong about making Brad stand on his own two feet. But I can't bail him out, and Josh won't. He's on his own."

"Poor old Brad."

"Yes." Amanda nodded.

She reported in at the office, but Mr. Johnson was staring at Dora as if she were the beginning of life, and she wasn't sure that he'd even missed her.

After going over the books just briefly, to make sure she hadn't missed anything damaging in her absence, like making out payroll checks or leaving deposits undeposited, she eased into the printing office and discussed another few quick changes with Tim while Ward Johnson was occupied.

Several lonely days later, she went into San Antonio on her lunch hour to see Brad. She was still fuming because he hadn't phoned in all the time she'd been back to ask how his brother was.

He ushered her into his office and seated her, smiling personably. "I phoned Ted yesterday," he confessed, irritated by her impatience with his behavior. "But I knew Josh would be all right," he said when she confirmed it. "He's indestructible."

"It's nice to know that you're so devoted to the only brother you have," she replied with quiet sarcasm.

He lifted a careless eyebrow as he dropped onto the big leather chair behind the desk. He was smarting over Amanda's studied rejection of him. Big brother always got the choicest tidbits. He even had Amanda in his pocket. The old competition that had always simmered between him and Josh boiled over.

"Brother Josh has been taking care of himself for years. He doesn't like people to see his weaknesses. Or didn't you find that out when you went rushing down to the cay?" he added bitterly.

"If you mean did he throw me off the island once he was sober again, of course he did," she replied. "I know he doesn't like people seeing him when he's vulnerable. But better that than finding him dead."

"He wouldn't commit suicide," Brad said, but he didn't sound quite sure.

"Ted and I weren't quite that positive," she replied without giving away anything about Josh's reasons for being drunk. She knew that Ted wouldn't have, either. It was up to Josh to tell Brad what he wanted him to know.

She half expected Brad to ask her what was wrong with Josh, but he didn't. He smiled at her, and his brown eyes twinkled warmly. "Did you miss me?" he asked with a sensual chuckle. "Are you dying of unrequited love yet?"

"You know better than that," she replied, laughing.

He swung his chair back to face her. His eyes were full of unholy glee at his own predicament. "Marc's going to kill me because I haven't paid my gambling debts, and Josh has thrown me to the wolves. You won't give me the time of day." He shook his head. "I think I'll go dive off the roof."

Amanda wondered about his remark that she wouldn't give him the time of day. "You might at least call Josh and talk to him."

He got up from his chair with cold anger. "He takes it all," he said without choosing his words. "He gets everything. It's always been that way!"

"If he does, it's because he works at his life," Amanda said defensively. "You're good at your job, but you don't take your work seriously—it, or life. You go from woman to woman, playing at love, and squander your money as fast as you earn it. Then you get mad because Josh won't bail you out. You want it all, Brad, but you want it handed to you. Life doesn't work that way."

"You sound very knowledgeable."

"I'm learning that the way you get things is to fight for them. If they're important to you." She got to her feet elegantly. "I've been walked on most of my life until just recently. I got tired of being on the receiving end and settling for handouts. What I want I'll get for myself from now on."

"You won't get Josh," he said mockingly. "He won't marry you."

She forced a smile, to show him that he hadn't hit the target he was aiming for. "I know that."

"He won't love you, either! You're just another woman in a line of women who've slept with him!"

"I have not slept with your brother!" she raged. "But for your information, he was the reluctant one, not me!"

He glared at her, furious at her admission that she wanted Josh even while he was oddly relieved that she hadn't slept with him.

"He's got Terri," he rasped. "Why would he want you?"

She lifted her head proudly. "Terri is married, and she hasn't been to the cay."

"Is that what he told you?" he asked with a harsh laugh. "Amanda, how can you be so gullible?"

She was sure he was lying. He had to be! But then he'd seen Terri in Jamaica and he hadn't told her. She'd found out from Brad. Couldn't he be keeping other secrets about her as well? "Why do you keep trying to turn me against Josh?" she asked impatiently.

"Don't you know?"

He moved forward, catching her in his arms. He bent and

kissed her, holding her roughly when she would have drawn back. With all his expertise he tried to win a response from her, but she only stood quietly in his arms, neither responding nor protesting. He groaned and forced himself to be gentle, to woo instead of demand.

Amanda adored him, but not like this. She didn't want to hurt his feelings any more than she'd already done. There was no one but Josh for her. All the same, thoughts of Terri and Josh's refusal to enter into any kind of a relationship with her claimed her mind. Perhaps Brad wouldn't be such a bad choice. Once he cured his gambling fever…and he had admirable traits. He was kind and generous, and no one underestimated his ability to stand his ground in a fight.

She hesitated, not fighting him, while those thoughts chased each other around her mind. She put her hands on his shoulders, and for an instant her lips softened.

The door opened silently, and the man standing outside it, who had started to speak, closed his mouth at the sight that met his dark eyes. Brad, with Amanda. He felt sick to his soul. With a black scowl, unseen, he closed the door as gently as he'd opened it, turned on his heel, and walked past the openmouthed secretary without saying a single word.

Back in the office, Brad stood, breathing roughly, his emotions in turmoil. Amanda had gently pushed away from him and moved back.

"I'm sorry, but no," she said, lifting her hands protectively when he started toward her again. She felt miserable that he wanted something she couldn't give him.

Her expression told him everything. He almost hated her at that instant for the weakness she'd kindled in him. She felt nothing when he kissed her. Nothing!

"I even look like him," he said tersely. "But it isn't enough, is it?"

"I love him, Brad," she said, more gently than she'd meant

to. She'd tried not to notice how much he cared about her. Too much, and in the wrong way. "I've always loved Josh. I'm sorry."

He winced and turned away, as if he couldn't bear the sight of her a second longer. "What now, Amanda?"

She stared at him, stunned. It was incredible, that vulnerability in a man who used women like toys. He'd kissed her with real feeling, not with base passion. But she couldn't give what she couldn't feel.

"I'm so sorry," she said helplessly.

His back stiffened. "Yes. So am I," he told her. He didn't look at her. He rammed his hands into his pockets and stared at his desk. His eyes closed. "I love you, Amanda."

She didn't know what to say. She'd never felt so helpless or guilty, and she'd really done nothing deliberately to hurt him. He was upset and confused, and when he came to his senses he'd more than likely realize that he was emotionally scattered. But that wouldn't help him right now. They'd been friends for a long time. She hated hurting him, even when he was doing his best to hurt her.

"Brad…"

"Leave it. You can't help what you feel for Josh." He turned, smiling mockingly. "We're both trapped."

She managed a faint smile in response. "I suppose." She searched his eyes. "What are you going to do?"

"I had my attorney check those stocks I told you about, that I inherited. It seems that they aren't worthless. They won't bring in much money, but they're worth enough to make a down payment on what I owe Donner. So I'm going to fly out to Vegas and work out a payment schedule," he said with a shrug. "Afterward, I suppose I'll have to learn to work harder for a living, because I'm out of allowance and Josh won't let me borrow. When I get back," he said heavily, "I'll get help. He was right about that, too." He smiled. "What do you think?"

"I think I'm proud of you."

He looked embarrassed, but he smiled lazily, back in character.

"If you'd ever given your brother the chance, he'd have been just as caring about you," she told him. "You've threatened and begged and hounded him, but you've never really put out a hand and asked him to help."

"I shouldn't have to. Damn it, he's my brother!"

"But not your keeper," she added. "You don't help people stand alone by giving them crutches."

He shifted, leaning back against his desk. He felt older. He looked at Amanda and felt deprived. Alone. He managed a smile. "You look pretty frazzled."

Her slim shoulders lifted and fell. "I'm lusting after your big brother, and he won't let me within ten feet of him," she said with a self-mocking smile. "How's that for irony?"

"You could always seduce him," he said.

She shook her head. "He's set traps all around the bed. It's just as well. There wouldn't be enough room for Terri and me both in it."

He hesitated. He almost told her that he'd lied, that Terri was deliriously happy with her Greek husband and she was even pregnant. But hope died hard, and he couldn't help thinking that Amanda might one day turn to him if his brother kept her at bay.

"If you ever need a shoulder, here it is," he said softly, patting it.

She smiled for him. "Thanks, Brad. I do care about you, you know," she added.

"I know."

She picked up her purse and started toward the door. As

she turned, she was surprised to see a pained, bleak look on his handsome features. "Ain't life terrible?" she drawled.

"It is that. Don't walk under any taxicabs."

"Don't jump off any roofs."

He smiled and opened the door for her. "Not today, at least," he agreed. "I've got a few things to do."

She nodded. Impulsively she reached up and kissed his darkly tanned cheek, feeling him stiffen at the contact. "You'll make it," she whispered. "I have confidence in you."

He flushed. "Thanks. That means a lot."

She smiled and left him standing there, nodding at the receptionist.

"Mr. Lawson?" the receptionist said hesitantly.

Brad had been in thought. He turned, his eyebrows lifted. "Yes?"

"I, uh, didn't like to tell you in front of Miss Todd, but your brother was here about five minutes ago."

He felt pale. "Josh was?"

"Yes, sir. He opened the door and looked in and closed it. He left in a rather angry rush."

"Check and see if he's in his office," he said quickly, knowing all too well what Josh had seen.

The receptionist buzzed his office and asked, but Josh's secretary said that he'd gone to the airport. He'd moved up his flight for his business trip to Europe.

"I see," Brad murmured. He went back into his office, deep in thought. Josh had gone off without a fight. Leaving him a clear field with Amanda? He smiled to himself. Well, here was an opportunity he wasn't about to waste! He'd take care of his gambling debt, then he'd take care of Amanda.

Josh was onboard a jet headed for New York, where he was to catch the Concorde for Paris. He hadn't planned to leave this early or without saying goodbye to anyone, but when he'd seen Brad kissing Amanda, he knew he didn't dare stay in the building a minute longer. In all his life he'd never known such murderous rage.

What made it worse was that Amanda hadn't been resisting. She'd been standing docilely in Brad's embrace, without a single protest.

He'd wanted to knock the door down and rage at them both, at the top of his lungs. But that would accomplish nothing. If Amanda wanted Brad, how could he say anything? Despite his threats, he had no right to decide Amanda's future for her.

Brad did care for her, and he could give her children. The thought made him sick. He stared blindly out the window, knowing that a child would give Amanda a kind of fulfillment he could never offer her. He'd just done the only decent thing he could do: he'd left, giving Brad a free hand, an open field. If Amanda wanted his brother, she had every right to decide that for herself, without any pressure from him.

He remembered so well how her body had felt in his arms that last time, how sweet it had been to have those soft cries of passion from her, to be the first to touch her innocent body. He'd have that, and the memory of her compassion and tenderness, until he died. Perhaps he could live on it, if he tried.

CHAPTER SIXTEEN

It was late, and Nelson Stuart was just bringing Mirri home from the theater. He'd dressed for the occasion, as had she. But this time her simple black dress had been very conservative. She dressed to please the man in her life, without guile or flair. She wore a conventional amount of makeup and perfume as well. The way Nelson responded to her was all the reward she needed. He looked at her as if she were his whole world. Day by day his barriers fell, his closeness to her grew. She wondered sometimes if he'd ever have said a word to her if she hadn't blatantly invited him over for supper that night. Now she wished she'd thought of it sooner.

"You're grinning," he teased as he walked her to her door. "Why?"

"I was wishing I'd made supper for you two years ago," she confessed.

He took her hand in his and held it gently. "So do I. I feel bad about the way things happened with us," he said, his dark eyes apologetic. "I'd do it differently, if I could start over."

"We're doing very well as we are," she replied. She reached up on tiptoe and touched her lips to his.

He drew back at once, softening the rejection with a smile. "Not too much of that, if you please," he murmured dryly. "I have my reputation to consider."

"Bosh! You and your reputation are maddening," she muttered. "You never kiss me."

He cleared his throat and looked uncomfortable. "There'll be plenty of time for that later on. Right now, it's important that we get to know each other as people."

"Maybe so, but you could still kiss me," she reminded him. "I'm not untouchable."

His big, lean hand brushed her hair gently. "Mirri, you had a hard time of it. I don't want to rush you. The way we're going, it looks like we'll have years and years together to learn each other in bed. I want you to be certain before you take that last step with me."

She started to argue, but, as usual, he stopped her with a light, brushing kiss.

"Good night," he said, and smiled. "See you at work day after tomorrow."

"Aren't you going to church with me in the morning?"

"I wish I could," he said, and meant it. "But I've got to fly out to New Orleans first thing in the morning to meet with one of our special agents. It's an unusual situation. I can't talk about it."

"I understand," she said sadly. "I'll see you Monday, then."

"Work isn't more important than you are to me," he said unexpectedly, his stare level. "This is the last time I'll do any work after hours, for anyone. You'll come first, with me."

She actually blushed. "I didn't ask you..." she whispered.

"Should you have to?" he replied. "I..." He cleared his throat. "I care about you," he said quickly, and averted his eyes.

She cared about him, too. She loved him half to death. She

wanted to tell him, but he was looking at his watch and muttering, as he did sometimes.

"I have to go. Lock up after I leave, and don't go out at night by yourself," he said firmly.

"You, too," she returned just as firmly. "Men can get knocked over the head, too."

He chuckled. "I know that. I work for the FBI."

"Do you, really?" she asked, grinning up at him. "What a coincidence."

He tweaked her nose and winked before he left her standing there. She went in and closed the door, but she watched him out the curtains until he drove out of sight.

He loved her. She was certain of it. But as time passed, he was just as distant from her physically, even as they shared meals and television programs, movies and theaters and concerts. He wouldn't let her within arm's length. Finally she decided that any progress was going to be up to her. She debated her next move carefully, weighing all the consequences. It would be a big step for her, with her memories. But she felt whole and reborn and ready for a full life. So she began to plot Nelson Stuart's downfall.

She invited him to supper the next Saturday night. All that week she was demure and standoffish. She gave him the same physical coolness that he'd been giving her, which made him hesitant and uncertain as the days passed. By the time Friday rolled around, he was smoking like a furnace and visibly off balance around her. That worked right into her plans.

Two could play at his game, she thought merrily, and proceeded to cook the most exquisite dinner she'd ever made. Then she dressed and made up her face carefully and waited for her victim to show up. This, she promised herself, was a night Nelson would never forget!

CHAPTER SEVENTEEN

When the door to Mirri's apartment opened, Nelson Stuart stood in the doorway and stared. Mirri was wearing a low-cut electric blue cocktail dress, her gorgeous hair curling down her back. The lights were low, candles graced the table. Soft music was playing. If he'd planned her seduction himself, he couldn't have done better. But it looked as if the tables had been turned.

"Is anything wrong, Nelson?" she asked with a vacant little smile.

"No. It looks nice. So do you. Here." From behind his back he produced a bouquet of fresh-cut flowers wrapped in green paper, smiling at her delight.

"Thank you!"

He chuckled as he bent his head. "Can't you do better than that?" he drawled.

"Sure. But you were the one who didn't want me to," she reminded him.

He sighed ruefully. "It's been a long, dry week," he replied. "Maybe I've gone overboard a little with restraint."

Her sly tactics had worked! She'd actually made him approachable. She smiled wickedly as she reached up and put her mouth gently to his, kissing him with tenderness and warmth. The time they'd spent together recently had been magic, for both of them. They grew closer as they learned more about each other. If Mirri hadn't already been in love with him, she certainly would have been now. He was her whole world.

"Very nice," he murmured against her mouth. "Have you been taking lessons?"

"I have this sexy Texas tutor," she whispered. "He's very good at kissing."

"Don't tell him, but I expect he's a beginner, just like you." He laughed, thinking how easy it was to tell her all his secrets. She was already part of him.

"Think so?" She smiled. "I hope you're hungry. I cooked Stroganoff, specially."

"Am I being bribed?" he asked as he closed the door and tossed his Stetson onto a chair.

"In a way," she said demurely, her eyes lingering on his nice white shirt and tie and the sports coat and dress slacks he was wearing with them. "I thought if I filled you full of good food and excellent white wine, you might let me make love to you."

He lifted both eyebrows. "Why, Mirri, I'm shocked! I never dreamed you were setting me up for seduction."

"And you're an FBI agent?" she chided.

He grinned at her with evident delight. "I want to see you carry me to bed. That ought to be one for the record books."

She grimaced, eyeing his tall figure. "Does it count if I have to drag you in feet first?"

"You might consider the sofa. It's closer."

"It's lumpy," she remarked. "And things live under the cushions. Old knives and forks, paper towels, paper clips, stuff like that."

"We wouldn't want you to bruise your back," he agreed.

"*Your* back," she returned. "If I seduce you, I get to be on top."

She realized what she was saying and blushed. So did he, before they both laughed. The thought of sex was no longer frightening to Mirri, who found her Texas boss so desirable that she wanted him all the time. Rarely did she think about the rape unless she was with her therapist. Nelson had gently coaxed her into therapy, and now she was glad he had.

Their romance had made working together difficult; they both beamed and flushed when they got near each other, and everyone in the office noticed. Even the most hard-boiled agents were smiling behind their backs.

"I think we'd better eat before we decide who gets seduced," he murmured dryly.

"All right. But I must tell you that playing hard to get won't deter me," she assured him as she led him to the table. "It only makes me more determined."

"You wicked girl!"

She laughed. Her eyes wandered lovingly over his broad shoulders and down to his chest, dark under the white shirt.

"Are you hairy-chested?" she asked, lifting a spoonful of fruit to her mouth and taking her time about putting it in.

He was feeling less rational by the minute. "Yes," he said. "Could you…eat that, and not play with it?" he asked, his eyes on her mouth.

"Why?" she asked, and slowly sucked a grape past her teeth.

"Mirri!" he groaned.

She swallowed and smiled with pure delight at his discomfort. She'd waited a long time to feel like a whole woman again. His innocence was a potent aphrodisiac, as if she needed one! She was on fire for him.

The nightmares were forgotten as she got out of her chair

and went to him. Her eyes were a soft blue, hungry, as they met his.

He watched the way she moved toward him, and his heart threatened to beat him to death. "This is seduction," he accused.

"I notice that you're not fighting very hard," she whispered. She bent and put her mouth gently against his. At the same time she eased onto his lap, feeling the rigidity of his thighs under her with delight.

His lean hands held her waist while his mouth answered the tender play of hers.

"It's always been dangerous. That's why I've tried to keep you at arm's length," he breathed into her mouth. "But tonight it's explosive. I'm losing control."

"I know."

He could barely breathe. He lifted his mouth and looked down at her. "Mirri, I don't want this," he said roughly. "I don't want a quick little roll in the hay."

She smiled against his throat. "Neither do I. Does this shirt button or snap? Ah!"

She unfastened the buttons while he tried to stay her fingers, but she soon had the shirt open to his belt buckle, and her caressing hands made him groan.

"I never knew you were this hairy," she said, smiling with delight. Her fingers pushed insistently into the thicket of dark, curling hair, and she tugged at it sensuously. "I love it, Nelson."

"Listen, you little fool, I may not be very experienced, but I sure as hell am capable!"

"I noticed." She reached between them and slowly unlaced the bodice of her dress before shrugging out of it. She wasn't wearing anything underneath. Her bare, pink breasts pressed into his hairy chest, and he cried out, his hands contracting on her back.

"God in heaven!" he groaned, shuddering.

She lifted herself enough to find his mouth. But she was in control no longer. His mouth opened, pushing her lips apart. His tongue darted into her mouth and made her gasp with the onrush of passion.

He was whispering something, his voice desperate, his mouth trembling. He got up, cradling Mirri in his arms, and carried her into the bedroom.

"I warned you!" he groaned as he slid alongside her, his hands feverishly undressing her. "Mirri, forgive me, I must!"

"It's all right," she whispered, her hands smoothing his thick hair. She lay completely vulnerable to him, her body pink and soft, waiting. She watched him as he shucked off his clothing, cursing as he sat down to pull off his boots.

She eased close and pressed her bare breasts to his broad, cool back. Her eyes closed as she felt him move and heard the sound of fabric rustling.

"I don't want to frighten you," he bit off as he turned and eased her down onto the coverlet.

She stretched out accommodatingly, her eyes soft and trusting. They dropped to his aroused body and lingered there for an instant before she blushed and jerked them back to his eyes.

"I'm not afraid of you," she said. "How can I be? I love you, Nelson. I've never loved anyone so much."

His chest stilled. He looked into her eyes with stark wonder and monstrous desire. His body trembled. "I'm like a boy," he whispered. "I don't even know what to do!"

"Neither do I, really," she said, her voice as hushed as his. "I didn't get to choose before. Now I can." Her hands reached up to touch his broad chest. "I want you. However it happens, it will be all right."

He groaned. His head fell to her breasts and moved against them. He remembered reading about women who enjoyed the feel of a man's mouth on them, so he turned his cheek and his

lips began to explore one firm, hard-tipped breast. He heard
her breath catch. He did it again, harder, and worked his way
slowly to the nipple. It felt hard and warm in his mouth. He
tasted it and she gasped. He sucked at it and she shivered and
began to moan.

It wasn't as difficult as he'd imagined. By listening to the
sounds she made and following her reactions, he discovered
what pleased her best. He eased her back against the pillows
and discovered her body with more pleasure than he'd ever
experienced in his life. There was a sweet, warm smell to
her skin, her own perfume. She tasted of woman. He drew
his face against her stomach and caught his breath when she
began to plead with him.

He knew what she wanted. He wanted it, too. His body
was taut with anguished hunger, but he didn't really know
what to do beyond the obvious.

He slid between her legs and kissed her eyelids, so that the
thick lashes came down over her wild eyes. His lips eased over
her mouth, and one lean hand slid under her thigh, gently
lifting her hips. He moved, settling on her, and began slowly
to penetrate her body.

She stiffened and made a sound. She shuddered. Her breathing stopped. He lifted his head quickly and looked into her
dilated eyes. He felt her nails stabbing into his arm and was
afraid that she was remembering what had been done to her
long ago.

"Are you frightened? I can stop, even now, if you want me
to," he whispered unsteadily. Although his body hurt from
having to hold back, he would have borne the pain for her
sake. "The choice is yours. It always will be."

"Oh, I don't…want you to stop, Nelson," she gasped. "You
don't understand. I…" She flushed and bit her lip. "It wasn't
fear…" She couldn't find the words. Instead she lifted her hips

and pushed upward in a soft, tender rhythm. She gasped and her teeth clenched. "It's…that!" She cried out and shivered.

"My God, is it hurting? Is that it?" he asked in anguish.

"No!" She caught his mouth and dragged it down onto hers while her hips writhed under his. "Nelson…don't you know…what's happening to me?" she groaned.

She whispered to him, finally, embarrassment giving way to exasperation. She arched and shivered, and he looked as if he'd just been given the crown jewels.

"For the love of heaven!" he exclaimed, astonished.

Through her violent satisfaction she began to laugh. "I never dreamed…!" She cried out again.

Neither had he ever dreamed of such pleasure. But he couldn't get the words out. He drove for his own fulfillment, finally convinced that whatever he was doing to her, it wasn't painful. He pushed down, hard, and convulsed. His body flew into the sun, splintered into rays of exquisite pleasure, in the first complete fulfillment he'd ever known.

When he collapsed on her, Mirri was still riding the clouds. She shivered one last time and gave up the greedy search for even more satisfaction than he'd already given her. She clung to him, her mouth touching his shoulders, his throat, his chin. She shivered with him in the glorious aftermath.

"I thought you didn't know what to do," she whispered when they were lying together quietly.

"I didn't. I must have gotten by on instinct." He chuckled, delighted with himself. He stared at her with such arrogant pleasure that she hit him. "Damn it, I'm good," he murmured, trying not to sound too conceited. "And here I thought I was killing you."

"So did I for a few seconds." She laughed and kissed him softly. "It felt like death, but it was sweet and heady, and I want it again and again and again."

"So do I." He lifted himself above her and joined his body

to hers in one smooth motion, smiling at her look of surprise. "I think we're going to discover that I'm one of those rare fellows who can go all night," he murmured. "I always thought I might be, with the right woman."

She smiled through her building excitement, gasping when he began to move. "I'm glad that I'm the right woman, Nelson!"

"No nightmares?" he whispered.

"No. Not ever...again. Not with you."

"Good."

"You have to marry me now," she whispered as she lifted to him.

His heart felt as if it might burst from happiness. "As soon as it's daylight," he promised, smiling as the pleasure built. "Did you buy me a ring?"

"Of course I did." She laughed, panting now from the exertion and the joy of belonging to him. "Do you want me to get up and look for it?" she asked innocently.

"Not right away." He drew his body against hers from side to side and watched her groan and shudder. "I'm glad you like that, because I like it, too." He brushed his open mouth over hers. "I love this with you. I love every...second of it!" he groaned as he began to lose control.

"So...do I!"

"Oh, God, Mirri...!"

His voice broke, and as his lean body arched down in a fierce rhythm, she began to cry. The poignancy of it was beyond bearing. She felt as if she were shooting among the clouds, a firefly being tossed against the sun and wind. She felt herself become one with the universe, one with the blazing sun and sky and sea. She was an empty vessel, being filled with the sweetest substance in the world.

"Nelson!" She hadn't dreamed anything could be so awesome. She did, in fact, lose consciousness.

An eternity later, a worried Nelson bathed her face with a cool cloth held in trembling hands.

"Oh, my God, I thought I'd killed you," he whispered when her huge, wet eyes opened. "Really killed you!"

"I'm not dead," she murmured drowsily, and reached up to kiss him. "But I'll bet you just made me pregnant."

The cloth stilled in his hand, and he looked incredibly radiant. "Do you think so?" he whispered.

She did, although she had no idea how or why. She smiled up at him with awe. "You don't mind? Would you like a baby, so soon?"

"I'd like a baby anytime, with you," he murmured adoringly. He wrapped her up against him, unembarrassed by his nudity or his vulnerability. "I love you, Mirri," he whispered. "All the way to the grave."

Her eyes closed. She knew that already, but it was nice to hear it. "I love you, too. I'm hungry."

"We missed dinner," he pointed out.

"Yes. And that was hours ago."

He looked at the clock, and his eyebrows levered up. "My God! It *was* hours ago!"

"Didn't you realize how long we'd been in here?" she murmured. "Why, Mr. Stuart!"

He managed to look indignant through his grin. "I was seduced," he accused. "Seduced and compromised."

"You don't have a thing to complain about," she reminded him. "I've bought the ring and I proposed to you. And if you get pregnant, I'll stand by you," she added, placing a firm hand over his heart.

He grinned. "If I get pregnant, you sure as hell will."

She nuzzled her nose against his. "You aren't planning on going home?"

"No," he mused. He turned her into his arms with a long

sigh and tucked her close to him. "Because I am home, right here."

"So am I." She closed her eyes and smiled against his chest. When she slept, there were no nightmares. This time she dreamed of babies.

Ward Johnson was just getting home. He'd been at the office with Dora. It was sweet, being with a woman who wanted just him and not what he couldn't give her.

"So there you are. It's about time," Gladys said sourly, swaying a little as she came into the room. She was wearing a see-through blue gown, but there was nothing under it that would interest her husband.

"I've been working," he began.

"Sure you have," she agreed, her pale blue eyes flashing at him. "Working on some woman. Who is it this time?"

"I don't have other women," he lied wearily.

"I wouldn't care if you did," she muttered. "You're a loser, Ward. That's all you'll ever be. A no-account little pencil pusher with no ambition. Someday they'll tip you right out into the street."

"Go to bed," he said.

"Want to come with me?" she teased, striking a seductive pose. "Even if you did, I wouldn't let you. You're a real bust in bed, honey. A nothing."

He could have told her that Dora found him exciting and satisfying, but that would only make things worse. His life had become bearable since he'd been seeing Dora. But the minute he walked in his own front door, it all fell apart. He was sick to his stomach of what passed for his marriage.

"Why don't you get help?" he asked curtly. "See a doctor. Join Alcoholics Anonymous…"

"I don't have a problem," she murmured, and smiled at him. "You have the problem. And I'm it. Why don't you kill me?"

He hated the thought that flashed through his mind. He turned away. "Where's Scotty?"

"I don't know. He went off with some people."

"He's on drugs," Ward said harshly. "Don't you care?"

"It makes life with you bearable, why shouldn't he use it?" she asked with laughing sarcasm. "If you cared, you'd stay home at night. You don't give a damn about Scotty. You never even wanted him!"

"I never thought he was mine," he corrected. "You've had half a dozen men since we married…"

"To get the taste of you out of my mouth!" she threw back. "I hated you. I still do!"

"Then why don't you get out?"

She swayed a little more and began to laugh. "You ruined my life. Why should I do anything to please you? I like the way we live. I like watching you suffer. You're too damned honorable to leave me. You'd feel guilty if you threw me out. No, you're stuck, honey. Stuck, stuck, stuck. Like a fly in flypaper."

She laughed even louder. He pushed past her and went to the guest bedroom where he'd stayed since Scotty's birth sixteen years before. When he closed the door, she was still laughing.

The next morning at work, Ward managed to maneuver around Amanda long enough to get a word with Dora.

"Can you stay tonight?" he asked her.

She gnawed her lower lip worriedly. "I don't know. Edgar doesn't like my staying out past dark. Oh, he doesn't suspect anything," she whispered. "But he's worried that something might happen to me."

"Something might all right," he murmured dryly, and reached out to caress her full breast.

"Stop that!" She slapped his hand away playfully. "I'll stay, but the boys have to be picked up from baseball practice at seven."

"Okay."

He slipped back out. Amanda looked worn out, he noticed in passing, and wondered if she was seeing someone. But that was none of his business. As long as she didn't interfere in the way he ran the paper, or get between him and Dora, he wouldn't disturb her.

Amanda went back to her desk, glancing disinterestedly at a flushed Dora. She sat down at her desk and began combing through the classifieds for ads to mark and charge out. She had raised the advertising and printing prices without consulting Ward. She'd simply made up new rate cards and had Lisa set them and slide them in. None of the advertisers or old print-ing clients had complained so far, and Ward hadn't noticed.

She wondered if he'd noticed anything. He seemed to spend most of his time watching Dora and working late, although Amanda would bet he wasn't working. His distraction had made lots of minor changes possible. By working behind his back—the only course open to her, although she hated having to do it—she was slowly raising the efficiency of the business. He'd remarked that making up the paper certainly seemed easier. She hadn't told him about the changes in procedure she'd initiated. She'd only smiled slyly and remarked that she didn't notice anything different at all. She'd noticed that Lisa quickly left the room, hiding a smile.

Amanda met Brad for coffee later in the day. He'd already been to Las Vegas to make his peace with Donner.

"Well, I'm off the hook," he said wearily, smiling at her in his old irrepressible way. "Donner agreed to accept thirty-five hundred a month as a 'friendly gesture to Lawson, Inc.' Jake, our controller, is arranging it so that the payments are made straight out of my salary."

"Good for you!" Amanda exclaimed. "I knew you'd find a way."

"I'm glad you did. I wasn't sure." He hesitated. "Amanda, I've done a lot of thinking about addiction lately. You were right. I'm not going to solve this problem by denying I have it. I talked to Jake about a clinic. He told me that Josh had already okayed the funds for it, anytime I got my head together and asked. So I asked."

She knew what courage it must have taken for him to admit he had a problem and get help for it. Her eyes glistened with pride and delight. "I'm so proud of you I could just burst," she told him.

He flushed, embarrassed. "At least you were in my corner. Josh never was," he added with bitterness.

"Wasn't he? All he ever wanted was for you to admit you needed help and get it. By forcing you to stand on your own two feet, he made you strong, don't you see? You'll never have to depend on anyone again." She frowned. "Well, maybe on the power company for electricity," she amended.

He laughed. It had been a long time since he'd felt like it. "Maybe on them. I'll have to make my peace with Josh."

"That wouldn't hurt." She'd heard nothing from Josh, and she missed him terribly. "I suppose Josh is all right?" It was the closest she could come to asking outright.

From the tone of her voice it was obvious she wasn't even trying to get over Josh. Brad knew she couldn't help how she felt. Yet he also knew she was making herself miserable.

"Of course Josh is all right. He's self-sufficient to the bitter end," he replied tersely. "Ted said he's in Europe at a conference." He eyed her cagily. If Amanda could get angry at Josh, maybe she'd be able to forget him. "I hear Terri's getting a divorce," he lied glibly.

Amanda wanted to die. The knowledge that Josh might

even now be with Terri made her sick. Had she gone with him to Europe?

She forced her chin up and even smiled. "Is she? How nice for her. Tell me more about this clinic, Brad."

He did, hating himself for lying to her, even by default, but he'd begun to believe he was doing her a favor. After he returned from the clinic and Amanda got over Josh, anything could happen. If she wanted control of the damned newspaper, he'd help her get it. All he wanted in the world now was Amanda.

CHAPTER EIGHTEEN

The chamber of Commerce held its luncheon on the third Tuesday of the month. Ward Johnson never attended, even though the newspaper was a member, but Amanda went.

She wore a nice pale green silk suit with a matching scarf around her neck, and she looked every inch the professional. She introduced herself to the other members as they arrived, making sure she knew their names and places of business.

By the time lunch was served, she was on a first-name basis with two of them and competing openly for their printing business. She went back to the office afterward feeling quite pleased with herself. It might not be a bad idea, she thought, to join some other civic organizations and get to know their members.

She mentioned to Ward, very casually, that a couple of the chamber's members had asked her about their printing prices. She'd given them a rate card, she added.

He scowled, pausing as he cut up a column of copy to paste it onto the makeup sheet with hot wax. "We don't have a rate card," he said.

"Yes, we do. Don't you remember?" she murmured, hiding her eyes as she lied through her teeth. Again. "I asked you a few weeks ago if I could have Tim print one and you said yes."

He scowled harder. He didn't really remember that at all.

"It was about the same time you agreed that we could change our paper supplier and sell off those old flats of paper."

"I did that?"

"Oh, yes. And you said Lisa could do some soliciting for the print shop when she wasn't setting type… Don't you remember the three new customers we got last week for brochures and flyers?"

"I remember the new customers," he said slowly.

"You were going out to lunch when I talked to you about those things," she persisted.

Out to lunch. With Dora. He smiled dreamily and glanced across the room to where Dora was running out headlines in the developing tank. "Oh. Sure. I remember."

Amanda was delighted. She was taking over his operation right under his nose, and he was too smitten with their new employee to even notice.

She went back to her bookkeeping. So far, so good. She was already noticing a difference in revenue, just from the few changes she'd managed to slide by him. Now she wanted to up the quality of their work in the job press, to go into real competition with the other print shops in the metro area of San Antonio. Some of them were cut-rate, some were sloppy. If she could keep their prices competitive and their work above average in quality, they could get even more business.

Tim, when he listened to the modifications, whistled softly. "We're doing good business with the copier, now that you have it working right. But for the kind of printing you're talking about—four-color jobs—you need a quality typesetter. You can't afford mistakes on that sort of job. Lisa's good, but she averages several errors per page. And some of them," he added, showing her a copy of a recent newsletter they'd printed, "don't get caught before they're processed. I'm too busy, and she can't catch her own typos."

There were red lines through the errors and a note from the client saying that he expected correction lines he'd marked to be put in before jobs were printed. Amanda had already discussed this with Lisa, and she said so. They needed someone to do nothing but job-work typesetting, while Lisa sold ads. The girl was a whiz; she'd already brought in two new advertising accounts for the paper in addition to the three printing job customers.

"How about Addie Wright?" he asked suddenly. "She works for old man Tellman's ad agency. She used to set type here about ten years ago. She's the best. We might coax her into some Saturday work. You know, correcting Lisa's copy and even setting more."

"Ward would never go for that." Amanda sighed. "He'd go through the roof if he even realized what I've already done."

"It's going to be partially your business one day, isn't it?" he asked belligerently.

"Yes, it is, when I can sneak control of it under the table," she replied. She glanced at him. "I could pay Addie out of my own pocket."

"No need for that. You do the checks, don't you?" He grinned at her. "Tell Ward we need extra help on Saturdays."

"I've made too many changes already. He's getting suspicious. He'll never agree to it."

"He will if you wait until just before we go home and hang around for a few minutes," he said, his eyes narrowing.

Amanda glanced up at him. "Playing with fire."

"So?"

She shrugged. "It's worth a try, I guess."

"That's my boss. You've got grit. More than old Johnson ever had."

"I hope I can keep enough to stay here," she said.

She stayed late that afternoon, noticing that the longer she hung around, the more impatient Ward got.

When he was to the point of chewing his thumbnail, she told him what she wanted. "Just on Saturdays," she persisted. "A little extra typesetting will put us over the edge, and there are these two new clients—"

"All right," he said finally, his eyes on Dora. "All right, go ahead, hire the girl. But only on Saturdays! And I'll want to see a sample of her work."

"Yes, sir!" So far, so good. "And Lisa brought us two new ad accounts, did you see? She's a whiz of a salesperson. She even took college courses in marketing. We could let her spend two or three days a week just canvassing for new customers, for the newspaper and the job press."

He scowled, trying to balance business with Dora and failing miserably. His body ached. "She has to set up copy for the paper," he reminded her.

"Our revenues are picking up. That throwaway they're threatening to start up won't put us out of business if we can increase our printing business. Having Lisa out there showing samples of our printing even one day a week would be nice," she relented. "She could sell refrigerators in Antarctica."

Somewhere in the back of his mind, Ward remembered the threat of the shopper. He hadn't checked the books lately, but he was aware that business had picked up. "All right," he said after a minute's deliberation.

"And we need more toner for the copier. We only have one bottle and it's going down fast. You wouldn't let Tim order more than one bottle because it's expensive, but the quality of copies depends on it."

He stared at her. "It does?"

"Yes. Didn't the man who installed it explain it to you?"

"I was out. He explained it to Lisa... Oh, all right, I'll authorize the purchase. Is that all?" he asked impatiently.

"Yes, it is." She grinned at him. "Thanks! Good night!"

Tim was a genius! she thought. In seconds she was out the door, noticing that Ward locked it behind her with undue haste. She should have been ashamed, even allowing that situation to develop. It was worse to take advantage of it, despite the fact that the business wasn't going to survive without some intervention.

She thought about that as she started toward her small compact car. She should do something about Ward and Dora. But what? She had no proof that anything was going on. Just suspicions.

She had to wait until there was concrete evidence, and then she might have to approach Josh for help. Meanwhile she hoped Dora's husband was thicker than he looked, and that Ward's wife didn't care that he was never home. Those two were heading for tragedy. She could feel it.

As she got into her car, she noticed an old, loud-motored car pull up at the curb. A young man climbed out of it and walked toward the door of the office. Almost as an afterthought, he moved toward the window and stood there for a minute.

Amanda jumped out of her car and all but ran toward him. "We've just closed!" she said, loudly enough for Ward to hear her. "Can I help you?"

The young man paused and glowered at her. His eyes were very bright. "Who are you?"

"I'm Amanda Todd," she said. "Who are you?"

"Scotty Johnson," he mumbled, avoiding her eyes.

"Oh, you're Mr. Johnson's son!" she exclaimed with just the right mix of curiosity and pleasure. "He's finishing up some bills in the office. If you need to see him..."

The front office door opened and Ward came out. "Hello,

son," he said pleasantly. "Nice of you to drop by and see the old man. Come on in!"

"No," Scotty said quickly. "No, I, uh, just thought I'd say hello. I'm on my way to a party. Got twenty I can borrow? There's a girl…"

"Sure." Ward peeled off a twenty and handed it to the boy.

"Thanks, Dad. Nice to meet you, Miss Todd," he added to Amanda. He went back to his car and got in. His tires screeched as he tore away.

Ward glanced at Amanda with eyes she couldn't quite read.

She stared at him until he flushed and went back inside. He didn't dare say anything to her, even admit that his son had a reason to suspect anything was going on. He had the upper hand right now, but it was going to be touch and go to keep it. Amanda was like Josh Lawson in her old-fashioned attitudes. She had a weapon to use against him now, and he knew it. He had to keep his head.

Amanda went back to her car, feeling as if she'd finally gained a little ground. Ward Johnson knew that she had a pretty good idea what was going on with him and Dora. He'd be careful about pushing her too far, for fear that she'd go to Joshua. He couldn't intimidate her anymore, and she could make sure that he didn't put the *Gazette* in the red.

Ward went slowly back into his office. Amanda had saved him, for reasons he couldn't quite grasp. Scotty suspected that something was going on. Maybe his mother had sent him to spy on his father. He was in danger of having this sordid little affair blow up in his face, and if it did, his job was the last thing he might have to worry about. Josh Lawson might have women, but he had conservative views concerning adultery.

"What was that about?" Dora asked worriedly, wringing her hands. "Who was it?"

"My son," he said. He caught her hand in his and held it. "Don't worry, he's gone now."

"I heard Amanda."

"It's all right. She doesn't suspect anything."

Tears stung her eyes. "I'm scared."

"So am I," he muttered. He pulled her into his arms and held her tight. "Dora, you're all I've got now."

She put her arms around him and clung. But inside she was already regretting her indiscretion. Things were getting out of hand. If his son was suspicious, his wife had to be. If Mrs. Johnson started making wild, drunken accusations, people might listen. This was a small community, even though it was a suburb of sprawling San Antonio. Edgar would be devastated if there was any scandal, and so would her children.

She could never do that to Edgar, to her children. She'd missed her chance at happiness by marrying out of desperation, but now her actions would affect other people. Edgar had never hurt anyone. He shouldn't have to suffer because he couldn't satisfy her. And God knew her children had done nothing to deserve that kind of contempt.

"We've been living in a dream world, Ward," Dora said sadly. "We're going to have to stop seeing each other."

"No, we aren't," he said. He bent and kissed her. She struggled at first, but she gave in, as she always did, after a few seconds. "You want me and I want you," he whispered. "God knows we're entitled to a little happiness in this lousy world!"

Perhaps they were, but at what cost? she asked herself. Then his hands slid under her neat blouse and she stopped asking questions.

Edgar was sitting on his easy chair when Dora got home later that night. He glowered at her as she put down her purse.

"I don't like cold suppers," he told her. "And having to put the kids to bed myself."

"I'm sorry, dear, but we're getting a lot of new business at the office, and I have to help out."

He put down his newspaper and stared at her. Dora felt dirty under the level look and had to work hard at not letting her shame become visible.

"Well, try to get home on time, can't you?" he muttered after a minute, and went back to the paper. "I couldn't find a clean shirt, either. And will you please make some effort to let me know when you won't be in time to pick the boys up from ball practice? They had to call me from the field. Everyone else had gone home. They were out there by themselves."

The boys! In her passion for Ward, she'd actually forgotten her own children. Her hand went to her throat. "They were all right?"

"Yes, fortunately." He sighed and shook his head. "Honestly, Dora, this job has changed you. You were always so efficient. Now you're just scattered. Honey, I wish you'd come home," he added, his face faintly pleading. "You were a brick to get the job to help me afford those courses. I think you're wonderful. But I'm getting a substantial raise next month, and we did agree when the boys were born that one of us needed to be here when they came home from school; that both of us should share their upbringing. Lately," he added gently, "I've been doing it for both of us."

That's right, she thought, feeling even more guilty by the minute, even though it had been Edgar's idea for her to get a part-time job. Her lower lip trembled with mingled dislike and fury. "I like my job. I don't want to quit. I'm entitled to do something I want to do," she said.

He laughed. "You sound like a mutinous teenager who's just been told that she can't go out with a college senior."

Her face burned. "You aren't my father."

"No. I'm your husband." His eyes narrowed. "Dora, this isn't like you."

She realized that just in time. Soon she would lose sight of any possible future for her family. What was she doing? She was having an adulterous affair, and she was furious at her husband for asking her to care about him and her children. Perhaps the guilt of her clandestine life was beginning to warp her thought processes.

"Maybe it isn't," she faltered.

"You don't even go to church with us these days."

She'd found excuses for weeks now. Headaches. Lack of sleep. She knew it was because she felt too tainted to walk into a church. A woman who was having a love affair was betraying everything the church stood for. But she loved Ward! She did!

"I'll...go this Sunday," she promised, knowing she wouldn't. "I'll look in on the boys before I go to bed."

"I'll see a doctor," he said wearily as she paused at the doorway.

"What?"

"I know that I have a problem with intimacy," he replied without looking at her. "You've been patient, and I've been a fool. I'll see a doctor, Dora."

"No! It's not your fault! I...maybe it's my age, but I don't... I don't care about that anymore," she said in a heated rush. "I must go to bed, Edgar, I'm very tired!"

She almost ran out of the room. She'd never felt so guilty or so ashamed in all her life. She had a wonderful, caring husband and two little boys who loved her. She'd tossed all that away for a sleazy affair with a man hanging on the edge of disaster. Now she had to wonder whether a little attention and mediocre sex was worth the devastation of her whole life.

Brad's rehabilitation would be in an out-of-state clinic, so that the tabloids didn't get wind of his problem or the impending solution. Amanda saw him off at the airport.

He looked down at her with quiet regret while he waited
to board the plane. She looked worn and sad. "Still mourning Josh, aren't you?"

She shrugged. "Like you, I'll get better."

"I wonder." He tilted her face up to his, and deep feeling
burned in his dark eyes. But when he bent to kiss her, she
turned her face so that his lips landed on her cheek. He drew
back, a pained expression momentarily hardening his features.

"I'm sorry," she told him, her green eyes compassionate. "I
really am. But it will always be Josh, no matter what happens."

Brad could have cursed until his face turned blue. Nothing
had hurt so much in all his life. Maybe it was only his pride,
but he was used to women falling into his arms, and Amanda
wouldn't. His ego was shattered.

"I'm sorry," she repeated helplessly.

"I wanted you to bail me out," he choked. "That's how
it all started. I was going to use you to bankroll me so that
I could get out of trouble with the casino." He laughed bitterly. "It all came back to haunt me, though. In the end, I
couldn't do it. I cared too much. But like everything else, big
brother has you, too."

"Not the way you mean, Brad," she said proudly.

"Give him time." He sounded almost violent. "But I won't
make it easy for him," he added. "No, I won't."

"What are you talking about?"

His handsome face hardened. "He saw us."

She blinked. "I beg your pardon?"

"In the office, when I kissed you. He came in the door and
saw us, and went right back out again." He watched Amanda's face go pale. "Try telling him you weren't kissing me
back. Try telling him we aren't involved. He'll believe me,
Amanda, because it will save him from having to admit that
he's human enough to love. You don't deserve someone that
hard. Can't you see that?"

She leaned against a pillar for support, her eyes wide and tragic in her oval face.

"I love you. My God, I do. If I can't have you, he certainly shouldn't! He's not capable of loving anyone more than his work."

She could barely find words. A voice came over the intercom, the last call for boarding the plane. "How could you, Brad?" she asked with building anger. "You say you love me, and you could hurt me like this, knowing how I feel about Josh? *You* don't know what love is! You're too selfish and vain to learn!"

In a fever of pain, she reached out and struck him across the face as hard as she could. "That's for me, and for Josh, and for all the other people you've used for your own gain!"

He touched his cheek. "You could love me, if it weren't for Josh," he said, his voice hoarse.

"Pigs could fly," she said levelly. "You're the most self-centered, shallow man I've ever known. I thought you were my friend!"

"Friendship is less than I wanted."

"Now it's more than you have."

He smoothed his cheek and looked down at her with blatant hunger. "Maybe you'll change your mind. After all, Terri has Josh," he added with a cold smile.

"It doesn't matter. You won't have me," she returned with contempt.

He flushed. After a minute he picked up his suitcase and turned, walking quickly down the boarding ramp. Amanda shivered with pure rage. She'd trusted Brad, and he'd sold her down the river. She could imagine what Josh had thought when he saw her in Brad's arms. She could, of course, call him and explain. But if he had Terri, it would accomplish nothing to open her heart to him. No. Brad had helped her dig her own grave there.

When Mirri and Nelson Stuart stopped by the office later, she was deep in her own misery.

"My, what a gloom-and-doom look that is," Mirri said, glowering at her. "I came by to cheer you up. Look!"

She held out her hand. A small but respectable diamond ring graced it.

"Congratulations," Amanda said, rising to hug her best friend. Obviously she was meant to pretend that Mirri hadn't already told her about the engagement, so she did. "I wondered where you'd been the past few days."

"In heaven, I think," Mirri murmured, looking up at Nelson with pure adoration. "We were going to just go ahead and get married and not tell anyone, but Nelson said we should do the thing right."

"I'm very happy for you both," Amanda said warmly. She smiled at Nelson, who looked like a different man altogether in jeans and a casual knit shirt. "When did you propose to her?"

"It was the other way around." Nelson chuckled and looked down at Mirri in a way that made her blush. "I got the works. Soft music, soft lights, a candlelight dinner, and a proposal of marriage. How could I turn her down? She's got a good job, so she can keep me in style, and anyone can see she worships the ground I walk on...oof!"

Mirri had clipped him in the ribs. "Don't get conceited," she told him.

He laughed with pure delight, pulling her close. "Anyway, we're going to have a small wedding. A quick small wedding," he added ruefully, "next Monday. You're invited."

"I'll be very happy to come and be a witness. Where and when?"

They told her. Nelson went outside to smoke a cigarette, and Amanda hugged Mirri warmly.

"I'm so happy for you," she told her friend.

"Me, too." Mirri laughed. "Can you believe it? He's nothing like I used to think. We get along so well together. He'd die for me, Amanda," she added, almost choking on emotion.

"I think that's mutual. Be happy."

"I don't see how we couldn't. He's my world."

Long after Mirri and Nelson had left, Amanda sat at her desk and wondered how it would feel to have that kind of happiness. Love, it seemed, didn't come with guarantees of happiness.

The telephone rang. She answered it, since everyone else was in the makeup room.

"Is this Amanda?" asked a faintly slurred male voice.

"Yes. Who—"

"Listen. That old tart had better stop making a play for my dad, or she's going to wind up in a cemetery somewhere. My mom just tried to kill herself!"

She caught her breath. "Scotty?"

"Yeah. Scotty. If my dad can drag his ass away from his latest conquest, tell him Mom's in the hospital. He might like to pretend to care, for the sake of...of appearances, you know."

He hung up. She got to her feet. The boy was obviously under the influence, and he sounded dangerous. The situation here was getting complicated. Too complicated.

"May I speak with you for a minute, Mr. Johnson?" she asked from the doorway.

"Sure."

He came out into the hall. But Amanda opened the front door and gestured him outside. It was warm and sunny. Birds sang nearby, their songs mingled with the incessant sound of traffic and car horns.

"Well?" he asked impatiently.

"Your son just called," she said. "Your wife tried to commit suicide. They've taken her to the hospital."

He paled. "Which hospital?"

"He didn't say. He was intoxicated."

"I think I know which one," he said shortly. "God knows it's not the first time."

"Your son made a threat, Mr. Johnson," Amanda said, and met his wary eyes levelly. "I'll say this one time. If anything happens to involve my mother's newspaper in a scandal, I will do everything in my power to have your job."

"You'd like that, wouldn't you?" he asked coldly. "Well, better employees than you have tried!"

"I'm not exactly an employee," she reminded him. "This newspaper has been in my family for over a hundred years, and I stand to inherit forty-nine percent of it."

"But Josh Lawson owns the other fifty-one," he countered. "I've been here fifteen years. He'll never agree to fire me."

"You're bluffing," she said with certainty, and watched his eyelids flicker just slightly. "If Josh finds out that you're having an affair with a married employee, you won't have a leg to stand on. He's extraordinarily conservative."

He took a sharp breath and just barely kept his head. "First you'd have to prove that I'm having one. And you'd better be able to," he added. "Because I could fire you for defamation of character."

"Don't make the mistake of underestimating me," she replied quietly. "I'm not the only employee here who isn't blind."

He didn't want to back down, but he had no other recourse. He walked back inside. Amanda glared after him in cold fury. He was threatening her business, threatening her job. She was sick of conspiring to save the business. She wasn't going to let him get away with endangering lives to continue his pitiful love affair. That had to stop, and now!

Late Friday afternoon she got on a plane for Nassau without

telling anyone where she was going. She'd learned from Josh's secretary, Dina, that Josh was at Opal Cay. He was going to get an earful, and not only about the newspaper.

CHAPTER NINETEEN

Amanda phoned the house when she arrived in Nassau. Joshua was due in that night, Ted told her. He brought the launch over to fetch her, and she boarded it with patent relief. It would have been a shame to spend the money to come down, only to find Josh gone. Thank God for Visa cards, she mused. Until money was released from her trust fund, she depended totally on her job at the newspaper.

"Did you tell Josh you were coming?" Ted asked her after she had changed into slacks, a white knit shirt, and sneakers, and was back downstairs.

"I didn't dare," she replied. "He wouldn't have been here. But I have to talk to him. We've got a major problem at the office, and I can't discuss it over the phone."

"Business brought you here?" Ted looked disappointed. "I see."

"You don't think I came rushing down here in a fit of passion, surely?" She laughed. "Josh would have kittens!"

He frowned. "Why do you say that?"

"I know about Terri, Ted," she said with forced carelessness. She stiffened. "She isn't here, on the island?"

"Of course not. Why should she be here? And what do you know?"

"That Josh is having an affair with her," she said.

"It's news to me," he replied. "Terri and her husband are in Greece, in fact. They're very happily married." He lifted his eyebrows at her disbelieving expression. "Terri's been sticking very close to home. And there was a rumor that she poured a bowl of conch chowder over a woman who made a pass at her husband just recently." He laughed. "Besides all that, she's pregnant. Hardly the best time for a woman to have an affair."

"Brad said..."

"Ah. Brad."

The two words were enough. She searched Ted's eyes and understood exactly what he was saying.

"I'm glad you came, Amanda," he added quietly. "Josh has been...different since you left."

That was all he said. But the expression in his voice said much more.

Amanda wandered around the house listlessly all day, waiting for Josh to show up. Ted's revelations had exhilarated her. She felt like a child on Christmas morning, waiting for permission to tear open the bright wrappings. When she finally heard the whine of the jet engines it was almost dark, and she was a bundle of nerves.

Josh didn't know she was in residence. She didn't know what kind of mood he'd be in. He'd made some violent threats about Brad even before he'd seen Amanda in Brad's arms. She dreaded the confrontation, even as she anticipated the joy of being with him again. If they could just clear up the misunderstandings once and for all, there might yet be hope for them.

Josh walked into the house yelling orders. He tossed his

case down and shed his jacket in the living room. On his way to the bar, he noticed Amanda for the first time and froze in place. For one long instant his dark eyes met hers.

She was seated on his big armchair by the window overlooking the bay. Her hair was long and loose, as he liked it, and her jeans clung lovingly to her body, like the partially unbuttoned white knit shirt that emphasized the small thrust of her breasts. He felt as if he'd come home, much as he tried to deny the hunger she roused in him.

But he remembered his last sight of her, in his brother's arms, and his face went hard. "What are you doing here?" he asked coldly. "I don't remember inviting you."

"Don't be sarcastic," she said quietly, pretending a serenity that contrasted violently with the turmoil inside her.

He poured himself a drink. Whiskey, she noticed, and no water. He threw it into the back of his throat and bent forward as he swallowed it.

"We have a problem," she began conversationally.

"Do we?" He turned and set down the shot glass. "Has Brad made you pregnant already?" he asked with a mocking smile.

So it was to be that kind of conversation. She might have expected it.

"If he had, we'd both be on national television doing the talk show circuit," she informed him. "That was sarcasm," she added, in case he'd missed the insinuation.

"Forgive my ignorance," he replied pleasantly, although something in him unclenched. "I had a vivid impression that you and Brad were at least on the way to a love affair when I stopped by his office recently."

She sat up and folded her cold hands in her lap. "I didn't come here to talk about Brad," she said, although she wanted to. This wasn't the time, when he was so unreceptive. "There's a problem at the newspaper that I need to discuss with you."

"Johnson's trying to seduce you," he guessed.

"Will you stop? Nobody's trying to seduce me," she said bitterly.

"Pity. Stick around a day or so and I might see what I can do for you."

"You love to think the worst of me, don't you?" she demanded. "Even knowing how I felt about you, all it took was one glance at me in your brother's arms to make you certain I was having a wild affair with him! And believe me, I was there against my will."

He shifted his eyes and looked uncomfortable. He ran a hand over his thick blond hair. It lingered at his taut nape. He poured himself another drink. But he didn't throw it down his throat this time. His dark eyes stared into it. "Brad can have children," he said.

"And you can't." The bluntness of her remark brought his eyes up.

"That's right," he agreed with a cold glare.

"So, that being the case, you very nobly sacrificed yourself so that I could sleep with Brad and have babies."

His jaw clenched. He moved away from the bar, one hand idly unfastening his tie and the top buttons of his shirt. He stared out at the ocean. "What do you want?"

"To talk to you."

"Talk," he invited. He sipped his whiskey.

She hesitated, her eyes on the long, elegant line of his back. "I don't know where to begin. So much has happened."

"Why isn't Brad with you?"

"He's in Atlanta," she said.

He turned, scowling. "Explain that."

"Brad's voluntarily checked himself into an exclusive clinic to kick his gambling habit."

"I wasn't told," he said, and she knew that someone in his office was going to catch hell for that.

"Your office okayed the visit to the clinic," she told him.

"You wanted Brad to realize that he had a problem and ask for help. All right. He's done both. Have you really got it in you to turn away from him now?"

He hesitated. "No," he said after a minute. "Was he...all right?"

"If you mean did he have bruises all over him, no. He went to Las Vegas to see Marc Donner personally, and he said he's had the company set up a garnishment of his wages so that his debt will be paid off in the shortest time possible." She glanced down at her clasped hands. "I thought you knew. Brad talked as if you did."

"I knew about the garnishment—not about the clinic!" Josh's eyes narrowed. "Ted!"

The man came as quickly as Josh called, looking sheepish and guilty.

"Did you know that Brad was going to a rehabilitation clinic in Atlanta and that his salary was being garnished?"

Ted grinned. "I believe Jake was going to be the one to tell you when you got back to San Antonio."

The taller man gave him a furious scowl, but Ted didn't back down an inch. When he left the room, Josh shook his head. "Dina had to be in on it with them," he muttered.

"You have good people on your staff," Amanda remarked, smiling. "Brad will recover this time. He'll work hard at it."

"I hope so."

"There's one other little tidbit of news," she said, diverting him. "Mirri is marrying Nelson Stuart on Monday."

His eyebrows arched. "I don't believe it."

"Neither did I, but after seeing them together, it's not so hard to imagine."

"After years of bad-mouthing each other, too." He chuckled faintly. "Amazing."

"But none of that is why I came down here." She moved to the window to stand beside him. "Josh, I'm almost certain that Ward Johnson is having an affair with a very married part-time employee. His wife has just tried to commit suicide because of it, and his son is either an alcoholic or a drug addict. The son telephoned today and threatened to kill Ward's paramour. Unless something is done, it could be dangerous for anyone connected with Dora."

He scowled. "Can you prove any of that?"

Her face tightened. "I shouldn't have to prove it," she told him. "My word should be enough for you, even after all that's happened."

His broad shoulders rose and fell. "You're right, of course. And it is. I'm sorry."

"Proof is the problem, though," she confessed. "Ward said that he'd deny it, and so would Dora if I went to you. He seems to think that he owns the newspaper."

"He does run it," he reminded her.

"But my family owned it!" she raged. "Part of it is still mine!"

His eyebrows flew straight up. He could hardly balance this new Amanda against the old image he had of her. He began to smile at the leap she'd made from reticent bookkeeper to independent businesswoman. "Amanda?" he asked.

"Who do I look like, the tooth fairy?" she demanded. "I tell you, I won't stand for it! I've had to go behind his back to print rate sheets, to solicit business. I've had to conspire with Tim to upgrade the quality of our printing and hire a typesetter who can spell two words running! I've worked nights and holidays and weekends on sample books so that I could go door to door looking for new business. And all the while Ward Johnson is locking up the office at dusk every day so that he can have Dora on his desk!"

He laughed. He couldn't help it. She wasn't at all the woman he'd known. Business had honed her, polished her.

"What's so funny?" she asked belligerently.

"You're beautiful," he mused, watching her. "Don't you really know how much you've changed, Amanda?"

"I haven't changed!"

"Oh, but you have. You've taken over the reins of a flagging business and pulled it out of the red, and you've done it in record time. Do you really think I don't know what you've done? I've certainly had access to the more recent accounts," he asked with keen scrutiny.

She hesitated. "You mean you knew Ward had altered my figures?"

He nodded. "He isn't very good at embezzlement. Not that he was trying to steal from me. He didn't want you to make him look worse than he already did."

"He's been destroying the business," she pointed out.

"I know that, now. I didn't until you went in there and started pointing out fallacies. Your father must have been blind, deaf, and dumb to hire such a poor manager in the first place."

"My father didn't care if the business failed," she said quietly. "I think you know that already."

"It's fairly obvious." He put down the whiskey and lit a cigar.

"You're still smoking."

"Looks like it," he agreed, and repocketed his lighter. He opened a window with great care.

She laughed. "You'll never change."

"It isn't a perfect world. Since you can't please everyone, it's sensible to only please yourself. Within limits," he added, his dark eyes sweeping over her body.

"How's Terri?" she asked deliberately.

"That look is a dead giveaway," he remarked, studying it. "Ted obviously told you that she's crazy for her own husband and pregnant."

"You lied," she returned.

He nodded. "At the time, it seemed the best way."

"And now?"

He laughed curtly and turned his attention to a passenger ship far off on the horizon.

"About Ward," she persisted. "What are we going to do?"

"Kick him out," Josh said.

"Oh, that's not fair," she said gently.

"You're the one who's been jockeying for his job," he reminded her.

"Yes, but I don't want to cheat him out of it."

"You yourself said that the possibility for tragedy is growing by the day."

"And I meant it," she agreed. "But there must be something less drastic. He does have a family to support."

"Name it."

"Well…" She was thinking on her feet. "He's a good journalist, you know. He runs the newspaper itself very well."

"But not the job press."

She smiled. "Not that. And the job press helps support the newspaper. I'm sure you know by now that there probably is going to be a shopper publishing in competition with us. Close down the print shop and the newspaper will fold. I promise you it will."

"I can see the direction your mind is taking. Make them into two separate businesses with two separate managers."

"Exactly." She told him what else she'd done, too, outlining the changes one by one.

He listened, smiling at her enterprise. "You are smart, Amanda," he commented. "And I agree that the job press, properly run, can become a paying enterprise. I won't say anything else about closing it down. However," he added, "that doesn't solve the personnel problem."

"I hate to suggest it, but firing Dora makes good sense. It

does at least get the problem off our property." She hesitated. "We could fire Ward as well..."

He nodded. "And kiss the newspaper goodbye. You don't just walk out the door and hire someone off the street to run a newspaper."

She grimaced. "Point taken."

"We'll make personnel decisions when we have to. Meanwhile, you'll be in charge of the print shop, even if you don't have control of the stock in both operations until your twenty-fifth birthday," he continued. "But Ward will run the newspaper on a trial basis. We'll see how that works."

Josh saw the disappointment in Amanda's expression. "You have a good business head, but you're one person, Amanda. Even if I eventually sign over two percent to you and give you controlling interest in the business—and I haven't said I will—you'll still have to have a manager for the newspaper. You know nothing about journalism. Running a newspaper properly requires a reporter."

"I guess you're right."

"I'll bet it hurt to admit that."

"Not really." She smiled at him. "You're a good businessman."

"You're going to make one," he replied. "You have a flair for it. Harrison underestimated you, right down the line."

"Thanks."

He stretched wearily. "I'm tired. I've done ten countries in ten days."

"Idiot."

He chuckled at the face she made. "Nobody dives in to protect me from myself when you aren't here."

"They're all afraid of you," she mused.

"And you're not."

"Not in any way that matters, I guess." Her eyes softened on his lean, handsome face.

He met that searching look, and his body began to ache. She was so lovely. Independent, fiery, saucy. His own pixie. But she was a person in her own right now, an independent businesswoman with class and style. He wanted her, needed her, ached for her; she wanted him, too. Would it be so wrong to love her for just one night? He tormented himself with the exquisite thought. No. He couldn't. He would have to get out of the house...

His hands clenched in his pockets, and it was an effort to stand there and not pull her into his arms. "I won't be in for dinner," he said in a forcibly calm tone. "But I'll see you off in the morning."

"Okay," she said huskily, managing to smile. She turned and left the room. When she closed the door, he still hadn't looked at her. She knew how badly he wanted her. If only she had the nerve to go to him.

She ate a lonely supper and wondered why she'd been so impulsive in coming down to Opal Cay. It had been for nothing. She'd accomplished little more than affecting a change in management at the office. She had cleared the slate about herself and Brad, but it hadn't made any difference. Josh wouldn't give in now. She knew how stubborn he could be. She would have to resign herself to it. He was simply going to ignore the feeling between them. He'd made that clear without even discussing it.

When she went to bed the room was uncommonly hot, and the air conditioner seemed to have stopped working. Smothering, she opened a window and let the sound of the sea and the ocean breeze into the room. They calmed her, but only a little.

The touch of even the thin gown on her hot skin made her uncomfortable. Being in Josh's house, remembering how it had been that day in his study, made her blood run like fire through her body.

She threw off the gown, pulled the lightweight sheet over her, and stretched. With her eyes on the ceiling and the sound of the tide in her ears, she began to drift.

It was the feel of the sheet being lifted from her heated body that awakened her from a faint doze. She opened her eyes, and in the moonlight she saw Josh standing over her.

He was holding up the sheet, his eyes blazing in the dim light as he stared down at her nudity. He himself was nude, his body taut and firm and blatantly aroused.

The breath sighed out of her as she looked up at him. Her breasts began to peak, giving away the fact that she was not only awake, but aware.

His dark eyes levered up to hers. He searched them in a tense, heated silence. His chest rose and fell jerkily, in time with his breathing. His body shivered noticeably with the urgency of his desire for her. He'd fought it all day. And lost. He was giving in to it because he loved her, even if he couldn't quite admit it.

"I have no right to be here," he said harshly.

"Yes, you have," she said, her voice soft and loving. "You're the only man in the world who does, or ever will. I love you so much, Josh. More than my own life."

His eyes closed and he shuddered. "It's wrong. It's all wrong, Amanda. But, oh, God, I want you so! I can't sleep, I can't eat. I can't work. All I do is ache for you."

She opened her arms. "Come here, darling," she whispered. "It's all right."

With a groan of utter anguish, he tossed aside the sheet and threw himself down against her.

The contact with his nudity made her gasp. It was like touching a live wire. His skin was hot, his body hard and rough and totally unfamiliar to her. She stiffened a little in reaction.

"You feel good against me," he whispered, smoothing her against the length of him. "You feel like satin."

"Your chest is very hairy," she murmured, awed by the feel of him in her arms like this.

"Hairy, and shocking, too, I imagine. The reality of this is very different from those novels you read, isn't it, little one?" he asked gently. He shivered as he drew his mouth against hers and down her throat. "I'm terrified of you, Amanda. I've never wanted anyone so badly before, and you're a virgin. If I lose control, despite what I did to you in my study that day, it's going to hurt. I'm better endowed than most men, and you're going to be very tight inside."

The intimacy of the conversation made her blush. She clung to him while his mouth worked its way down her collarbone to her soft breast.

"Josh, I never…never thought it would be like this," she breathed.

"Are you afraid?"

"A little. But that wasn't what I meant. It's so intimate."

He chuckled, despite the tension that was stringing him out. The feel of her soft body was making his mind spin. "You don't know the half of it, just yet."

Her leg drew slowly, sensuously, against his, and she moved into sudden, stark intimacy with the heated masculinity of him. She stopped breathing.

"Ah," he whispered. "Yes, that's the idea." He caught her hip and moved suddenly, pushing forward with a deft, expert lunge.

She cried out in mingled fear and pleasure. It all became clear at once, the role of male and female, the domination of a man's body, the submission of a woman's.

"Lie still," he said, his hand smoothing down her hip and thigh, calming her. He had to stay in control. It was getting more difficult by the second. She was warm and moist, and

the touch of her made him crazy to complete his possession.
"Yes, darling, that's it. That's it, pixie. Now ease close to me.
Don't be afraid, Amanda," he whispered into her soft mouth
as he probed it gently. "Your body is like a flower in the rain.
No matter how tight the bud, a raindrop can slip inside and
touch it. Yes." He smiled against her mouth as he began to
invade the sweetness of her. She was making soft noises as his
fingers tightened on her thigh and pulled gently, steadily. He
moved closer, and closer, until she stiffened.

"No, it isn't possible… I can't," she whispered frantically.

"I know." He stilled and began to kiss her with exquisite
tenderness. His hands smoothed down her spine and over the
bowl of her hips, tugging rhythmically, pulling her to him
in a rocking motion that did incredible things to her senses.

Her nails bit into him and she began to moan. "Josh…what
are you…doing?!" she gasped.

"Possessing you," he breathed into her mouth. "Taking
your virginity. Making you my woman. Softly. Softly. Softly!"

He repeated the word like a litany, all the while pulling
her into him, over him. She felt her body suddenly expand
and contract in sensations she'd never experienced in all her
life. She began to tremble and then to shudder. She pushed
against him, trying to get closer, and all at once he was over
her, above her, his hips grinding into hers as he drove against
her and into her.

She clutched at his hips and began to wail, her voice dis-
torted, like her face, his face, the room, as the pleasure built
and suddenly exploded into a oneness and a heat like the end
of the world.

She sobbed rhythmically, her body throbbing with unbearable pleasure as he fulfilled her. He barely managed to
look at her abandoned face before the tide caught him, too,
and he cried out her name as he let go of his control at last.

He was heavy. His skin was cool now, and damp, and she

held him as if she never wanted to let him go. She was shivering, as he was, despite the heat of the room.

She could feel his heart beating down into hers. She could feel his blood flowing through his veins. She could feel his breathing, the very pulse of his life, because they were joined so intimately.

He groaned as he lifted away from her, despite her attempt to cling, and threw himself onto his back. "Damn it!" he whispered.

She sighed and moved close to him, sliding a languorous arm over his broad, hair-roughened chest. "That's it," she murmured. "Turn the air blue."

His fingers slid affectionately over her smooth arm. "I tried to stay away," he said. "God knows I did. Tonight, all I could think about was the way you looked at me when you walked out of the living room. When I got home, your eyes haunted me. I meant to wake you up, to talk." He laughed ruefully. "Well, I did wake you up."

She moved her hand against him, smiling at the delicious feel of his body against her. "In more ways than one," she murmured.

"Did it hurt?" he asked quietly.

"Oh, no. I think it frightened me, at first," she confessed. "I wasn't sure that we were going to, well, to fit."

He chuckled at the way she put it. "A woman's body is designed to accommodate a man's, unless there's a great disparity in their sizes."

"I read about that once, though," she said. "The couple couldn't get married because of it."

"A very rare instance," he replied drowsily. "And one that certainly didn't apply to us. We should have had a long, and intimate, talk before I initiated you."

She hit him. "It wasn't initiation."

"What was it?" he asked, levering up on his elbow.

She touched his face with fingers that worshiped it. "We made love."

He nodded slowly. "We did indeed, Amanda."

Her fingertip touched his broad mouth, lingered on his full lower lip. "You never said that you love me," she whispered.

"And you think that in order to make love to a woman, a man has to be in love with her?"

"No. But in my case, you would," she said. "You'd never have touched me at all if you didn't love me."

He breathed deeply, his eyes full of need and pain. "You're too perceptive. I never meant for this to happen."

"I want nothing that you can't give me, Josh," she said, her voice still and gentle in the big room.

"Not now, perhaps, in the aftermath of your first loving. But later…"

"My first loving." She pressed against him and slid her arms around him. "It was so beautiful."

His arms enfolded her. He settled back on the bed, drawing her close. His eyes closed as he cradled her, feeling a surge of love and possession that knocked the breath out of him. "I won't marry you."

"I know."

"Amanda, for God's sake!" he groaned when he felt the tears on his chest. "Amanda, listen to me. It's for your own good. Honey…!"

But the tears kept coming. He turned, kissing them away, staying them with lips that were tender and loving and then, suddenly, urgent.

"Don't cry," he whispered feverishly. "Don't cry, I can't take it. Amanda…!"

His mouth found hers. His body tautened with an uprush of desire too strong to stem. While he tried helplessly to fight it, she turned and slid against him, urging his body to hers, in a slow, sweet joining that was more profound even than the last. She whispered to him, coaxed, urged, until he was hers. The tenderness was unbearable. Contractions of exquisite violence bonded them together in a heated climax that left Amanda exhausted.

"No one else can give you that," she whispered with her last sleepy breath. "And you'd throw it all away because you can't make me pregnant."

He cradled her in his trembling arms and cursed himself and fate for the trick life had played on him. When he finally let himself sleep, he was no closer to a solution than he had been. But his body, for the first time in years, was at peace.

CHAPTER TWENTY

Amanda was alone in the bed when she woke up. She remembered the security she'd felt in Josh's arms and mourned for its loss. He wasn't going to change his mind. She'd felt it at the last, just before they slept. He loved her, even if he hadn't said it, and he wanted her. But he felt that she couldn't accept him as he was. Silly man, she thought sadly. She'd have taken him limping and blind, but he had too much pride to give in to his own need.

She slid into a pretty, multipatterned shirtwaist dress and tied her hair back with a matching ribbon, then went down to breakfast.

Josh was sitting at the table with Ted, going over paperwork.

"No wonder you never gain weight," Amanda mused, smiling shyly at Josh. "You eat paper for breakfast."

He smiled at her. "Just checking a few figures. Go get your own breakfast, Ted. We'll discuss this later."

"Sure thing, boss." He winked at Amanda as he strode off

toward the front door, obviously bent on breakfast at a restaurant in Nassau.

"Am I leaving today?" she asked Josh.

He leaned back in his chair and let his dark, possessive gaze wash over her. "Yes."

"What if I refuse to get on the plane?"

"I'll carry you on it."

"I'd start kissing you. You'd never get out the door."

"Don't bet on it," he said implacably. "I want you, but I'm not at the mercy of my loins."

"You were last night," she said daringly.

He nodded. "Very much so. I wanted you to the point of madness, and took something I had no right to take. This morning I'm bristling with regrets and shame. As you should be," he added.

"I can't be ashamed of it," she replied, sitting down beside him. "I love you. It was the most beautiful experience of my whole life."

"It belonged to your husband, when you marry," he said.

"And I gave it to you," she replied, her eyes loving on his hard face. "Because I'll never marry anyone else. Never love anyone else. I'll grow old and die, all alone."

His hand clenched as she traced the back of it where it lay on the table. "You could have children..."

"I would only have wanted yours, Josh," she replied sadly, and removed her hand. She helped herself to bacon and eggs. "Maybe you haven't realized it yet, but carrying a child is part of loving someone, for a woman. I could no more allow myself to become pregnant by a man I didn't love than I could fly over a mountain in a car. I've loved you since I was in my teens and my cat scratched you. In all that time between, I haven't... I haven't been able to want anyone else, much less love them." She lifted her eyes to his. "Only you."

The words were haunting. The way she said them made

him ache inside. He averted his eyes to his coffee cup and abruptly picked it up and drained it.

"I have to fly down to Rio today on business. I won't be here to see you off."

"All right, you don't have to rush away without your breakfast to get rid of me. I won't make a scene or any more confessions of love. I know how you are when you've made up your mind."

"I'll let you know what I find out about Ward Johnson and his love interest."

"What will we do?"

"First we'll get facts instead of suspicions," he said with forced humor. "I don't want to spend the next ten years in court with him."

"Neither do I." She searched his face with quiet longing. "You're sure, aren't you? About us?"

He got to his feet and looked down at her, his eyes dark with sadness and irritation. "Try to see the other side of it, can't you? Reverse the situation and think how you'd feel."

"I'd feel sad, just as you do," she told him honestly. "But I'd love you enough to marry you anyway. Josh, what happened to you was quite obviously an act of God. You don't go to church, but I used to, with Mirri. Don't you know that God never closes a window unless He opens a door? You won't believe that life works if you're not always in control of every facet of your life. But even at my age, I've learned how to let life happen instead of trying to master every minute of it."

"I've gone through all those arguments, too, Amanda."

"I love you," she said fiercely. "Argue with that!"

"Damn you," he said through his teeth. "Damn you!"

He jerked her out of the chair and into his arms. His mouth hit hers like a weapon, twisting and hurting, his arms slamming her into his body. She didn't struggle at all. She met his ardor headfirst, with sweet grace, her arms around him, her mouth soft and sacrificing, giving him everything he asked for.

She opened her mouth, and he groaned as he accepted the invitation. His tongue shot into the soft darkness, probing, possessing. He lifted her, and the kiss took on new dimensions, broke new ground. He forgot his anger, forgot everything except the glory and wonder of Amanda in his arms, loving him. It was the night before, all over again, and he shivered with delight.

"You love me," she whispered into his devouring lips. "Say it. I dare you. Tell me, Josh…"

"Shut up," he ground out against her mouth.

She kissed him back until they were too breathless to keep it up. He let her slide down his aroused body until her feet touched the ground. She was trembling. His hands were none too steady, supporting her.

"You don't even have to marry me," she managed unsteadily. "I'll live with you. Whatever you want. Anything."

"No." His fingers bit into her arms, and he looked as if he were being tom apart. "Go home."

"Josh!" she moaned.

His eyes closed as he fought to resist the unbearable temptation. "You're overwrought," he said after a minute, and put her gently away from him, letting go reluctantly. "You'll get over this. Time will cure it."

She could barely breathe. Frustrated tears blinded her. She fought for control, for pride. Her hands clenched at her side, and she leaned against the table for support as her legs threatened to collapse. "Just tell me one thing. If you were fertile…?"

His chin lifted, but he wouldn't look at her. He forced a laugh. "Haven't I told you, time and again, that I don't believe in marriage, Amanda? My parents were certainly no advertisement for it. My mother is already working on prospective husband number five when she's still legally tied to number four! Happily ever after exists only in books."

"You said it was because you were sterile."

His shoulders straightened. "It is, but only partially." He turned. His eyes were strange, his face white. "Last night was wonderful. I loved it." He lit a cigar. He chose his words carefully. She'd been innocent. She had no idea how it was between lovers, and he could sound convincing. "Haven't you ever heard that a man hungers for something until he's had it? I've had you. Now the ache is gone, and there are new conquests waiting." He gave her pale face a cynical appraisal. "Sex is sex, Amanda. What I had with Terri was just as good as last night."

Pride, she thought, could save her every time. She drew herself to her full height and ignored the red-hot pain in her heart. She managed a tight smile. "I see. Then it would be the same with another man as it was with you?"

He didn't like that. His whole face changed. His eyes went very nearly black with shock and contained rage.

"Yes," he said firmly. "It probably would."

"That's that, then." She turned away. "All right, Josh. Business again, as usual." She moved away from him. "I won't come here again," she added, her pride rearing up to spit at him. "Not even if you damn well beg me!"

"Do the words *fat chance* strike a familiar note?"

The contained humor was the last damned straw. She'd been certain that he loved her. Now she wasn't. His behavior was as maddening as it was final. She sat back down at the table and deliberately poured herself a cup of coffee with hands that were unnaturally steady. "I assume you have a plane to catch," she said stiffly.

"So do you. If you see Brad," he added reluctantly, "tell him that I asked about him."

"He'll appreciate your concern, I'm sure."

He hesitated in the doorway, allowing himself one last look at her. She was so beautiful, sitting there almost strangling on her pride. He hadn't wanted to hurt her. But one day she'd thank him for not putting his own selfish wishes ahead of her happiness. He'd become her first lover. She was letting her emotions blind her to reality right now. When she'd had time away from him, time to realize that her body had wanted him much more than her heart, she'd come to grips with it. Self-sacrifice had a warped nobility about it, but, God, it hurt!

"Goodbye, Amanda," he said softly.

"Goodbye, Joshua," she returned. She didn't look at him. He walked away. The silence in the room became suddenly stifling. She looked into her coffee cup. It took a minute for her to realize that she could no longer see clearly what it contained.

Gladys Johnson was in a private room at the general hospital, after having had her stomach pumped out. A handful of barbiturates, mixed with the amount of alcohol she usually consumed, had overloaded her system almost fatally.

Sitting beside her bed, Ward Johnson was surprised at how old and worn she looked. He scowled as he discovered her frailty.

"If she dies, I'll cut your girlfriend's throat," Scotty muttered, looking at him with hate-filled eyes. He jerked at the voice, because he hadn't heard his son come in.

"I don't have a girlfriend," he lied.

"I saw you," Scotty said coldly. "The Todd woman wasn't quite quick enough. I looked in the window and saw you kissing that fat slut. You had your hand up her dress."

Ward put his head in his hands and took a deep breath. "You don't understand."

"I'm not that dim, Daddy," he said sarcastically. "You're running around on my mother, while she sits at home up to her eyeballs in booze. If you gave a damn, you'd make her get help."

He looked at his son irritably. "Sure. Like you got help."

Scotty shrugged. "I tried," he muttered. "I went away and dried out. But when I came back and I had to watch the way she lives, I couldn't take it. You treat her like dirt. You never even look at her."

"I can't stand to look at her," Ward exploded, white-faced. "Damn you, she's an alcoholic! She drinks all the time! When she isn't drinking, she's telling me what a simple-minded failure I am, a loser she hates having to tolerate. She hasn't slept with me in sixteen years! How the hell am I supposed to treat her?"

"She's your wife!"

"Big deal," he spat.

"What does that fat slut give you? Love?" Scotty laughed coldly. "She gives you hot sex. That's all she gives you. Maybe she tells you you're handsome, huh? You're a middle-aged man with a big pot gut and the compassion of a squirrel in heat!"

Ward jumped to his feet and caught the boy by the collar, shaking him. "Don't you talk to me like that, you piece of scum! You're nothing but a juvenile delinquent! A filthy little thieving drunk, just like your mother!"

Scotty pushed him away and tore loose. His glassy eyes glared at Ward. He pointed a shaking finger at him. "I'm going to fix you," he said. "I'm going to kill that fat slut you're sleeping with! And everybody is going to know what you really are!"

"You're out of your mind," Ward began.

"I'll kill her!"

Scotty slammed out the door. Ward felt chills run down his spine. He'd never felt so tangled in all his life. He stood over his wife's unconscious body and looked down at her with utter disgust.

"You miserable excuse for a human being," he said furiously. "It's all your fault!"

But Gladys was beyond answering him. Five hours later she slipped into a coma and died.

Ward was shaken out of his mind. He'd never dreamed that Gladys would do something so stupid. But he should have realized that her drinking was leading her that way. Scotty was right; he hadn't paid her any notice lately, hadn't cared that she might be on the edge looking for a way over.

Scotty blamed him, and why shouldn't he? He hadn't listened to Gladys in years. Perhaps part of her wild behavior was due to his very indifference. He'd turned his back on her, and she'd killed herself. He had to live with that. That, and the guilt of knowing that while she lay dying, he was lusting after Dora.

He telephoned the office to tell them about his wife. Amanda had taken time off to go to her best friend's wedding that morning, but he told Lisa that he wouldn't be in for a few days. Then he asked for Dora and cautiously told her what had happened.

"Don't go out alone at night," he told her worriedly. "Scotty made some wild threats. You be careful."

"Your son? He knows about us?" Dora asked frantically, hushing her voice so that nobody in the office would overhear her.

"Yes. I'm sorry, but he does. He blames both of us for what happened to his mother. He's wild drunk, and he doesn't care how much damage he does," he said. "Dora, I'm sorry I got you into this. I'm so sorry."

"It's all right." She said it automatically, but she felt sick. If Edgar found out, she could lose her children. And that wasn't the worst of it. What if Scotty decided to take his vengeance out on her sons instead of on her? She was suddenly stricken with the enormity of what she'd done. She'd put her secure, happy life at risk by engaging in a sordid love affair. And now her chickens were about to come home to roost.

Mirri and Nelson Stuart beamed as they came out of the courthouse, marriage license in hand. Amanda, walking with them, was delighted for her friend. Mirri didn't look anything like the frightened young girl she remembered from their childhood. In her off-white suit and orchid corsage she was beautiful and radiant, all the things a bride should be. Beside her, Nelson Stuart looked like a man who'd captured a fairy. He clung to his wife's hand, while around them FBI agents congratulated them and went away trying to decide how the impossible event had come about.

"They're puzzled," Mirri said, chuckling softly.

"They can't imagine how a stick-in-the-mud like me wound up with a pretty butterfly like you," he teased, bending to kiss her forehead tenderly.

"I think the women are wondering how I landed such a hunk," Mirri replied.

"And I know how a fifth wheel feels." Amanda laughed, shaking Nelson's firm hand. "You people go away and act like newlyweds. I've got a job press to run."

"Don't let the boss get the upper hand," Mirri cautioned.

"Never in a million years. I'd wish you happiness, but you already have that. So I wish you half a dozen children and years and years together," she added with a sadness that was lost on her friend.

"You'll marry one day," Mirri told her, hugging her warmly.

"No," Amanda said. She returned the hug. "I'll talk to you when you get back from your honeymoon. Love you." She smiled at Nelson and walked back toward her car.

Nelson clasped Mirri's hand warmly, frowning after Amanda. "Something's wrong there," he murmured.

"It's Josh. Again. She'll never get over him, and he'll never want marriage," she told him. "I feel sorry for both of them."

"I feel sorry for me," he murmured dryly to lighten her mood. "I haven't slept with you since the night you proposed. I ache all over."

Her eyebrows lifted gleefully. "That was your idea, you prude! You felt guilty that we'd jumped the gun and kept me at arm's length for weeks!" She leaned into him, amazed at the ease and comfort of being intimate with him. "I've got half a mind to push you down in the grass and ravish you right here."

"Go ahead," he challenged, grinning.

"Oh, Nelson," she said adoringly. "I do love you so!"

"Same here, kitten. Let's go back to my apartment and legalize the ceremony."

She chuckled as she slipped her hand into his. "Lucky, lucky me," she murmured.

"Double that on my account."

Amanda took her time getting back to the office. It was almost lunchtime, so she stopped for a sandwich and coffee on her way. When she got there she learned that Ward's wife had died and he wasn't expected back for several days.

"Did anyone send flowers?" she asked when Lisa and Tim and Dora were gathered around.

"Well, no," Lisa asked.

"I'll call them in. How about assignments for the rest of the day?" she asked Vic and Jenny, the part-time reporters.

"He didn't give us any," Vic murmured. "Sometimes he forgets."

"Advertising? Do we have the ad copy in hand?"

"We're missing four," Lisa said. "They usually come in at the last minute, though."

"They won't this week," she replied. "Write down the names of the sales managers and their telephone numbers for me. Vic," she added, "isn't there a rally today at the civic center for one of the returning Desert Storm officers?"

"Why, yes," he replied. "But we usually pick up that kind of story from the dailies."

"Take a camera and go cover it," she told him.

He beamed. "Actually report a story?"

"Get out of here," she muttered.

He laughed and ran for it before she could change her mind.

"How about me?" Jenny asked.

"Don't you people listen to the news? An archaeologist is digging up a site over at Taggart Lane. They found some prehistoric bones in a construction area. See what you can find out. When you're through, there's always something going on at City Hall. Make friends. Ask questions."

"I thought you weren't a reporter," Tim mused when the others had gone about their business.

"I associated with a lot of journalism majors in college." She grinned. "I kept my ears open, too. While Mr. Johnson is away, we're going to implement a few more quick changes," she added shrewdly. "Game?"

"You bet!"

Like a whirlwind, she tore into the job at hand. She taught Dora how to paste up ads and use ready copy from the news services to fill holes around them. She called the tardy advertisers and diplomatically manipulated them into getting their ads to the paper a day earlier than usual. She noticed the date, figured a seasonal campaign for advertising, and began calling local businesses, while Lisa, for once, had a structured series of tasks at the word processor. By the time Amanda went home, she had enough copy for the front page and more than enough ads to put up two new pages.

She fell into bed that night, and it was a good thing. She didn't have time to worry about Josh or grieve over having been thrown out of his life. She was too tired to think.

Dora had been restless around the office that day. When she went home she began checking windows and looking out them. Edgar puzzled over her behavior.

"Is something wrong?" he asked her after supper.

She gnawed her lower lip. Beside her, Tommy and Sid stared at her with the curiosity of preadolescent boys.

"Yeah, Mom," Tommy agreed. "You sure are dizzy lately. You even forgot us at ball practice last week."

"Yeah," Sid muttered. "You forgot us."

She had to still her trembling hands. "Things have been very busy at the office," she said to excuse her behavior. "But they'll be better now that I'm learning my job."

"I heard that Ward Johnson's wife died," Edgar said. "Tragic woman. She drank, they say."

"Yes."

"Well, he has a son. That should be some comfort to him. Dora, this coffee is much too weak. Can't you make it stronger? And you forgot to salt the peas."

"Yes. I'll take care of it."

She went into the kitchen, listening halfheartedly to Edgar's patient voice explaining homework math problems to the boys. She glanced back at him. He was a kind man, a good man. He wasn't exciting, and she wasn't passionately in love with him. But he'd provided for her and given her a good life and two wonderful sons. Now she stood to lose it all, because she'd been selfish and greedy.

A sudden thump at the back door made her jump. Slowly she went toward it, her hand at her throat. Was it Ward's drunken son, come to kill her? She peeked out the curtain.

"Hi, Mrs. Jackson!" A redheaded boy grinned at her through it. "Can I come in? I'm going to do my homework with Tommy and Sid."

"Of course, Billy," she said. She opened the door and let him in.

"Gosh, you look funny, Mrs. Jackson." He frowned. "You okay?"

"I wish people would stop asking me that!" She laughed nervously. "Of course I am. Go right in, Billy."

He shrugged and went on into the dining room with his books, greeting the boys loudly. Dora leaned against the cabinet and took deep breaths. She had to get herself together!

But the next day she was all thumbs at work. Amanda took her to one side.

"This won't do," she said quietly. "What's wrong, Dora?"

The older woman started to prevaricate.

"I know about you and Ward," Amanda said, cutting her off. "Your private life is your own concern, but when you put my business at risk, you make it mine. I want to know what's going on."

Dora didn't question the self-command in Amanda's voice. The younger woman was strong and efficient, and it seemed so easy to lay her burden on those slender shoulders.

"Scotty is threatening to kill me," she confessed shakily. She pulled at her fingernails. "He says it's my fault his mother killed herself, because Ward and I...well, he drinks, like his mother did, and he's crazy mean when he does it. He takes dope, too, Ward says." She looked at Amanda with desperate eyes. "I wanted a little attention. Ward said I was pretty." Tears rolled from her puffy eyelids. "Edgar never noticed me at all. Now I'm going to die, or maybe my boys are, and I brought it on all of us. Gladys Johnson would be alive except for me!"

"Stop that," Amanda said, refusing to let the other woman give way to hysterics. "Stop it immediately. You're a grown woman. Certainly you're old enough to know that you can't play with fire and not get burned. Have you sworn out a peace warrant against Scotty, so that he can be arrested if he comes near you?"

Dora gasped. "I can't do that! My husband would have a fit. He'd want to know why!"

"You don't think he'll find out?" Amanda asked quietly. "You can't be that naive. One way or the other, your affair is no longer secret. Everyone on the staff knew weeks ago, Dora. If you don't realize that, you're fooling yourself."

"Oh, my goodness!" Dora put her head into her hands and cried brokenly. "No!"

"Listen to me," Amanda said, tugging the woman's hands from her contorted features. "You have to tell your husband the truth. I know it won't be easy. But if he loves you, it won't matter."

"He'll take my children away," she whispered.

Amanda didn't remind Dora that she could have taken time to think about her children before she leaped into Ward Johnson's arms. The woman was distraught enough already.

"Maybe not," Amanda replied. "But your life may be in danger. And not only yours," she added. "Everyone who works here and everyone who lives with you could find themselves right in the line of fire. First you have to tell your husband. Then you have to go to the police."

"He might be bluffing," she cried, grasping at straws, "he might just be saying it!"

"You can't afford to take that chance," Amanda said. "Neither can I."

At last Dora relented. "All right," she said weakly, drained. "I'll tell him tonight. And first thing in the morning I'll go to the police."

"I'm sorry," Amanda said, her green eyes sympathetic. "I know what it is to love without hope. But you've run out of options."

"I suppose I knew that already," Dora replied. She went back to work without another word.

CHAPTER TWENTY-ONE

Amanda had the office running smoothly by the end of the week. She'd doubled the advertising revenue and the content of the newspaper in one edition. Leaving Dora to post bills, she'd sent Lisa out to take the rate cards and printing samples door to door down just one city block of San Rio. The response from the community at large, and advertisers, was exciting. In fact, she decided, it would pay to replace Lisa on typesetting altogether and turn her into a full-time advertising person. Now all she had to do was convince Ward Johnson that it was a good idea—a thought that rankled.

She'd put Ward and his son to the back of her mind. The staff had sent flowers, but she hadn't gone to the funeral. She'd sent Tim instead, so that she could get the paper out with the help of the other employees. Wednesday was the day it was mailed. Papers had to be stamped and single-wrapped and taken to the post office. It had to be done quickly and efficiently, or all the advertising revenue would be wasted. Ward would know all that already, she rationalized, and understand her absence at the funeral. Despite her dislike for the man, she could still feel sympathy for his situation.

Dora had promised to tell her husband about her affair and swear out the peace warrant against Ward's son. But while she'd managed to make Amanda believe that she'd done both, she'd done neither. Her nerve had failed when she'd tried to explain her betrayal to Edgar. She couldn't make herself hurt him. So the trip to the police was out, too. She just prayed that nothing would happen and that she wouldn't be found out.

Meanwhile it was business as usual. Ward came back to work early Friday morning, looking older and in need of comfort. Dora ached to pull him into her arms and give him solace, but there was no opportunity.

"What the hell have you done to my newspaper?" Ward exploded. He'd called Amanda into his office after he'd thumbed through the paper he hadn't yet had the time or presence of mind to read. "We're a weekly, not a daily, we aren't supposed to be competing! And I told Bob Vinson he could have the page two spot that he's always had! You've moved him to the obit page!" He looked at the sheets, horrified. "My God, you've taken out Tartoni's Pizza Parlor ad!"

"Indeed I have," Amanda said, leaning back against the desk with her arms folded. In a neat gray pantsuit, and her hair in a chignon, she looked every inch the executive. The contrast between her and Ward Johnson in baggy slacks and a frayed knit shirt was blatant. "Tartoni hadn't paid for his ad in six months."

"He was having financial problems!" Ward exclaimed.

His proprietorial attitude, and the vicious anger he was showing toward her, put an end to her sympathy for him. It was her newspaper, and he was trying to tell her she had no right to run it!

"You might not have noticed," she began, "but we've been having financial problems ourselves. And no wonder. Did they

teach you in journalism school that you can give free advertising and keep the doors open?"

He flushed. "I didn't go to journalism school. I got my
education in the school of hard knocks!"

"Then you weren't knocked hard enough," she said angrily.
"You run this office like a weekend hobby! You wouldn't raise
prices, even when every other newspaper in the state did. You
very nearly let the job press die because you wouldn't update
your printing prices. You wouldn't make clients proofread
and okay printing jobs before they were put on the press. We
lost money hand over fist because of that. Worse, you kept
old paper for printing that was worthless in spots where new
paper should have gone, and you practically gave away photocopies. You probably had to, because nobody knew how to
get the machine to put out decent copies. Even if they had,
you were too cheap to buy toner to keep it running properly.
It does now, and you're going to notice that we're attracting
a lot of new customers. You wouldn't add new people, you
wouldn't give raises to the old ones...my economics profes-
sor in college would have loved you as an example of every
'don't' in business!"

"This is my business," he began hotly.

"This is *my* business!" she flashed back. "It's been in my
family for a hundred years, and I'm going to own forty-nine
percent of it year after next! On paper you work for me, mis-
ter, and don't you ever forget it! I have enough legal control
even now to kick you right out the door if you don't show a
profit. And I will. Josh and I agreed that we need two managers. When we get the details sorted out, you'll manage the
newspaper, and I'll manage the job press. But believe me, if
you don't hold up your end, I'll get someone who will!"

"Who do you think you are?!" he raged, red-faced.

"Harrison Todd's daughter," she said with cool insolence.
"Your boss."

"I'll go to Josh Lawson," he threatened.

"I already have," she replied, and watched him melt. "Josh and I are of one mind on your recent behavior," she said meaningfully. "You are now here on sufferance. I suggest you get into your assigned slot and do the job you were hired to do. Run the newspaper to show a profit, not as a charity."

His fists clenched by his side. "You'll regret this," he said, his voice rasping.

"No, I won't. But you might, if you don't straighten out your life. Just one more thing. There will be no more late working hours here, Mr. Johnson. The doors close at five. For everyone," she added.

He swallowed. His eyes darted through the open doorway to Dora, who stood there, hesitating to interfere. She turned away and avoided looking at him. He'd had a hell of a week. Scotty hadn't stopped drinking and popping pills since his mother's death. He'd made threats but, fortunately, had been too drunk to carry them out. Still, there had been something ugly in the way he'd looked at Ward that morning, and he'd made a very odd remark about how he would "get Daddy where it hurts."

Now he had Amanda Todd on his neck. He still could hardly believe the change in her, from frightened bookkeeper to manager. She was more than a match for him now. She was like her father, and he'd only just found it out.

"All right," he said stiffly, swallowing his pride. He couldn't afford to lose his job, and she'd all but ousted him. "All right. I'll make a few changes."

"I have every confidence in you, Mr. Johnson," she said politely. Pushing away from the desk, she returned to her office.

She sat down behind her desk and breathed rhythmically for five minutes, trying to slow her heartbeat. She'd never been so scared in her life, but apparently you could bluff anyone if you worked at it. At last she grinned, pleased with herself as she'd never been before.

Later there were a few heated glances from Ward and nervous looks from Dora. But by and large it was business as usual for the rest of the morning.

Ward had an unexpected visit from a Georgia newspaper editor he'd met at a conference earlier in the year. The man, along with his wife and two teenaged sons, toured the operation, remarking that it looked well run and prosperous.

Amanda was hard-pressed not to thank him for the compliment that Ward accepted.

"We have a weekly newspaper up in the Georgia mountains," the visiting editor murmured, smiling through his mustache. "My mother-in-law owns it, but it's sort of a family operation. One of these days, though, I'm going to get out of the newspaper business and write books."

"I think anyone who can run a weekly newspaper can do anything," Amanda said, grinning.

"They tell me it has something to do with full moons," the visiting editor said, and he and his wife exchanged loving smiles.

Amanda excused herself, touched by the obviously happy relationship the visitors had. She would never know those secret smiles that loving couples exchanged or the joy of a marriage that lasted for years and years. She would grow old alone. And all because Josh couldn't settle for less than perfection.

She was still brooding about Josh as it neared lunchtime. Ward had shown his visitors out and gone to the back to check on some negatives with Tim. Amanda was standing up at her desk, looking out into the reception room, when the opening of the front door caught her attention. She glanced toward it curiously just in time to see the same disheveled young man she'd met several nights back waving a gun around the office.

She started to move. He jerked around and pointed the gun right at her, leveling it shakily with both hands.

"C-come out of there!" he ordered. "Quick!"

She edged around her desk and out the door past him on unsteady legs. His pupils were dilated. He was shaking. He was on something, and his eyes told her that he meant business. This was no bluff. She thought almost hysterically that Josh could forget the arguments now, because the whole staff was about to be murdered here.

"Scotty!" Ward burst out when he saw the boy. "You fool, give me that gun!"

Scotty pointed the gun at him and then, suddenly, shifted it to Dora, who walked out to see what the fuss was about.

"You slut!" he shouted at Dora. "You filthy slut! You killed my mother! She died because of you!"

Dora went white and caught the door facing.

"And you, you horny old fool, you were never home, and she's why!" He laughed sarcastically at Dora. "She's fat and old and ugly. Is that the best you could do?"

"Scotty, you need help," Ward said, trying to be calm. He moved forward.

"Don't," Amanda cautioned him. "Don't dare."

Ward stopped. Scotty looked at her and blinked. He even smiled. "Smart lady. You're Miss Todd." He nodded. "He complains about you all the time. He says you're trying to get his job. Good for you. He never does anything except watch television. When he isn't humping the fat lady, that is."

Dora went white and red alternately. "You don't understand," she said, her voice squeaking.

"You had a husband and two little kids," he muttered. "Didn't you think about them? Poor little kids, some mother they got!"

Dora bit her lip. "If you want to shoot me, go ahead," she said hoarsely. "But you won't…you won't hurt my boys?"

He lifted his eyebrows. "Lady, you're the one I came here to kill," he said. He lifted the gun and pointed it at her. "Only you. This is for my poor mother, you stupid slut!"

Amanda knew that he was going to fire the gun. It was make a jump for it or watch Dora die.

She never knew where she got the strength to push forward and knock his arm just as he fired. The pistol, an automatic, discharged three times in the struggle, and the shots brought screams from two subscribers who'd just pulled up in the parking lot.

Scotty went wild. He swung the pistol barrel, catching Amanda's shoulder, and knocked her down. He fired at the ceiling and the glass in the front window, shattering it.

Amanda stayed on the floor, cursing silently as she held her bruised shoulder and flinching at the shots. She couldn't let him shoot Dora, but her action had caused something in his brain to snap. They were all going to die. She'd never see Josh again. She whispered his name and closed her eyes.

"Damn, damn, damn!" wailed Scotty. He backed up and grabbed Lisa around the neck, the pistol to her jaw. "Don't come near me," he said hysterically. "If you come near me, I'll kill her!"

Everyone froze. Scotty backed away with Lisa until he reached the steps that led down through a hall into the print shop. He locked the door and then pushed Lisa away from him. He had them cornered, Amanda and Ward and Dora and Lisa, all at gunpoint, in the one office.

"Sit down," he said, gesturing toward the floor as sirens approached. "Hurry!"

He was nervous and wild, and they knew better than to make him more nervous. The automatic held several shots, and he'd used only five. He had at least enough left, Amanda reasoned, to account for every one of his hostages.

A police car screeched to a halt in front of the building and a door opened. A voice called out to them through a bull-horn. "This is the police. Throw down your gun and come out with your hands in the air."

"Fat chance!" Scotty yelled, and laughed. He was enjoying himself now. For the first time he had his old man in a tangle. "I've got hostages!" he called.

Amanda looked at Ward and could have cursed him blindly. It was going to be a long day.

Josh flew in from Nassau just after lunch, his head throbbing from too much business, to confront Ward Johnson about Dora. First he tried to find Amanda, without success. Next he tried Mirri, who had apparently gone off on her honeymoon; no one answered the telephone at her office.

Now, tired and irritable, he buzzed Dina. "Still no answer at Johnson's office?" he asked.

"No, sir," she replied. "I called the telephone company. They're going to send someone out."

He frowned. "Doesn't it strike you as rather odd that the phone at a newspaper office would be out this long without it having been reported?"

"I wondered about that. There's... Just a moment, sir." After a pause she came back on the line, sounding not at all like her usual efficient self. "Mr. Lawson, it's Ted. He wanted to know if you'd heard that some madman is holding the staff of the *Gazette* hostage."

He was on his feet and in her office before she could repeat herself.

"I won't be in this afternoon," he said.

She watched him go out and turned back to the phone. "Ted, he's on his way over there. Are they all right?"

"So far. The guy's on dope and high as a kite. I'm sorry Amanda's in there with him. It looks bad, Dina."

"Poor Mr. Lawson," she said softly.

★ ★ ★

Scotty was enjoying his play for power. He waved the gun around and watched with pure pleasure as his father chewed on a thumbnail. His mother had suffered because of this man. He wanted his father to know how it felt to be helpless and alone.

"This won't accomplish anything," Amanda said, holding the arm he'd injured as she sat against the wall with her colleagues. "You'll only make things worse for yourself."

"You talk too much," he said.

"Someone hasn't talked to you enough," Amanda continued quietly. "Would your mother want you to do this?"

"Of course she would!" he exclaimed, astonished. "She hated him! He gave her nothing but heartache. This…woman of his was the last straw. She cried." He seemed to puff up with outrage as he looked at his pale-faced father. "She cried, damn you!"

He pointed the pistol at Ward, who went paper white.

"Don't shoot him," Dora pleaded, sliding close to Ward. "Kill me, but don't hurt your father!"

Ward looked at her, stunned that she cared that much. He didn't know what to say, but his eyes were eloquent. "Dora, don't, honey," he said gently. "Don't."

"Why couldn't you love my mother?" Scotty cried at him. The gun in his hand shook. "Why!"

Ward looked up at him. "Your mother never wanted me in the first place," he said coldly. "She wanted money and position. I just wanted to run a country newspaper. I could never do anything right in her eyes."

"She was a saint!"

"She was a selfish, whining drunk!" Ward raged. "And you know it! You're heading down the same road she took, can't you see?"

"I ought to blow a hole in you," Scotty said with cold

determination. He aimed the gun right at Ward's chest. "It would be so easy. All I have to do is pull the trigger…"

"Scott Johnson!" called a voice through the bullhorn.

Scotty jerked around, wild-eyed. "What?!" he yelled.

"I'm the police negotiator," came the reply. "I want to talk to you."

"Yeah? What about?"

As he spoke, the power went off. The telephone had long since been shut down. Now the office went dark.

"Turn that back on!" Scotty yelled.

"Come out and talk to me," the negotiator returned.

"Like hell!"

A big black limousine pulled up just past the roadblock, and Josh got out of it. He found the officer in charge and drew him to one side.

"I own this place," he told the officer without pausing to elaborate. "There's a back door through the print shop and a hallway that leads to the newspaper office where he's holed up. If you've got a man who can pick a lock, you can get in behind him."

"I've got one," the watch commander said tersely.

"Are they all right in there?" Josh asked.

"So far, so good. We don't know what he wants. He's done some shooting, but we don't think he's shot anyone yet."

Josh's face hardened. "Oh, God," he said as thoughts of a wounded Amanda filled his head.

"Is there a gun in that office besides the one he's got?" the watch commander asked.

"Not that I know of. The manager won't have one in the building. I can sketch the layout for you, if it would help," he offered, trying not to think about Amanda in that building with a madman. All around the streets, shopkeepers and pedestrians were trying to get a look across at the action. Motorists slowed as they passed the police and sheriff's cars.

"It's a sideshow," the police officer muttered while Josh penciled in a notebook the man had produced.

"Just consider that he's holed up in a newspaper office," Josh replied with black humor. "What a story they'll have when it's over."

"I hope they all get to write it."

"My God, so do I," Josh seconded.

He stood and smoked a cigar while the negotiator tried to talk Scotty out of the building. But Scotty was enjoying himself and wouldn't budge. As the day wore on, though, he began to show signs of withdrawal, and he got more nervous by the minute.

"I need a drink," he said uneasily at last. "Is there a bottle in here anywhere?"

"No. You know I hate liquor," Ward said coldly.

He went to the door and yelled, "I want some liquor. Get me a bottle of whiskey. Now!"

"Finally," the negotiator said on a sigh. "An opening!"

They sent for a bottle of whiskey. It was doctored first, of course. A new seal was put on so that it would look as if it hadn't been tampered with. And if the boy was as desperate as he sounded, he wouldn't be looking at it very closely.

"Are they crazy?" Lisa gasped when they put the bottle of whiskey next to the door and left. "They're crazy!"

"No, they aren't." Scotty chuckled. "They're smart. They know what I'll do to you people if they don't give me what I want. God, I need a drink!"

He eased to the door, looked out, and swept up the bottle. He checked the top. They couldn't inject anything into a metal cap without it showing, and if they'd opened it, the tax seal would be broken. It wasn't.

"Good boys," he mused. He moved back inside and ripped off the seal. "Nice brand, too. High quality. I couldn't afford this," he added, glaring at his father.

Ward, who'd been a newspaperman for a long time, knew almost certainly what the police had done. He didn't blink an eye.

"Don't drink it," he told his son. "You've had enough."

It was a calculated risk, and it worked. Scotty glared at him and deliberately upended the bottle, swallowing two large mouthfuls.

Ward averted his eyes so that his son wouldn't see his triumph.

"That's pretty good." Scotty nodded. "Pretty good." He swallowed some more.

Ward checked his watch without being obvious. The stuff would take several minutes to work. He hoped everyone outside realized that and wouldn't take any foolish chances.

Amanda's arm was throbbing. She leaned back against the wall and closed her eyes. It all seemed unreal somehow, except for the throbbing of her shoulder. Only days before she'd been in Josh's arms for one long night, touching heaven. Now she was faced with death. She remembered too well what Josh had said to her at the last. If it was true, and all he felt for her was desire, he probably didn't miss her at all. She'd die, and his life would go on without interruption. That hurt most of all.

"I'm very sorry," Dora managed through tears as she looked at the others. "It's my fault."

"No, it isn't," Ward said. He clasped her hand in his. "We were looking for something we'd never had, and we had the misfortune to find it in each other. I'm sorry, too, but nothing's really changed except that Gladys is dead."

"And you're glad, aren't you?" Scotty demanded, red-faced.

"I'm glad for her, Scotty," he said simply. "She was unhappy, and she made everyone around her unhappy as well. Maybe now she's at peace."

"You wouldn't care if she was. You never loved her!"

"Actually, I loved her very much when we married," he

replied. "But I wanted a child, and she didn't. I took away her choices," he added quietly. "She tried to have an abortion, but I found out and stopped her. She never forgave me. She got even in ways you can't imagine. Once, she told me that you weren't even my child. She had other men, Scotty," he said, hating to admit it in front of his coworkers. "She had plenty of them."

"You're lying!" Scotty burst out. He raised the gun again. "You take that back! She wasn't like that! She was my mother and she loved me!"

"She loved using you against me," he corrected. "And she did a good job of it. Look at you. You're her image, right down to the drunken stagger!"

Scotty lost his grip on the gun, and it fired accidentally. The bullet ripped into the wall just an inch above his father's head.

Outside, Josh froze at the sound. His heart shook him, and he seemed to stop breathing. "Amanda..." he choked, terrified.

The hostage negotiator and the police officer in charge exchanged glances. "Bill, see if you can get a glimpse inside the office!"

An officer with binoculars homed in on the glass window. He didn't see blood. "It's all right," he said. "And the bottle's open. He's drinking from it."

"That's one break," muttered the officer in charge. "But it's going to take another few minutes for that drug to work, and he's got ants in his pants. If we wait much longer, he may decide to shoot somebody."

He considered for a minute while Josh clenched his teeth in impotent anguish.

"We go in," the policeman said quietly. "Carefully, but we go in."

"Couldn't you call in the SWAT team?" Josh muttered.

The policeman smiled at him. "What do you think we

are, daisies?" he mused. "I started out with the SWAT team. Hawkins, with me," he said, motioning to another officer.

They put on flak jackets and armed themselves with shotguns. Josh felt sick to the soles of his shoes as he considered the consequences. All his arguments against marrying Amanda vanished as he wrestled with the nightmare of her predicament. He loved her. That was all that mattered anymore. If she loved him enough to marry him, he was ready. Past ready. If she died now, how would he bear it? The law enforcement people started to move. He stopped them, worried.

"The drug should work, shouldn't it?" he asked.

"Listen," the officer said sympathetically, "this kid is used to drugs. It will probably be less effective on him than it would be on a nonuser. You don't want us to bet those people's lives that it's going to work in time?"

He sighed wearily. "No. I don't."

The officer clapped him on the shoulder. "Trust me. I've done this since I was in my early twenties." He had to be forty now, Josh observed, and found he was less worried than he had been.

The police squad moved in. Incredibly, the entire operation took less than three minutes from beginning to end. They entered through the print shop and stealthily picked the lock that led into the *Gazette* office. Outside, as arranged, a squad car siren went off at a designated time to camouflage the soft noise picking the lock made. Then, simultaneously, the men armed with shotguns stormed in behind a shattered Scotty.

There were shots.

Josh cursed roundly and made a break toward the door, but two of the officers caught and held him, cursing and white-faced.

"Just stand still," one policeman told him. "You won't help by walking into a bullet."

A minute, a very long minute, later, the front door of the

Gazette opened. "All clear!" the police officer called from the doorway. "No fatalities!"

Josh slumped. "Oh, God," he breathed, and as the officers let him go, he ran for the front door. They weren't going to stop him this time, not if he had to tackle someone!

He got past the uniformed men and found Amanda on the floor, holding her arm. He knelt in front of her and touched her with shaking hands.

"Oh, baby," he whispered. "I've been out of my mind!"

"Josh? Josh!" She reached up with her good arm and felt him hold her so close that her ribs ached. She clung, whispering to him, her voice breaking as she gave in to the strain of the past few hours and began to weep.

The others were led outside and turned over to the paramedics. Scotty had a flesh wound in one arm, and there was a rather large hole in the wall where he'd been standing. The sedative in the whiskey had finally taken effect. He was being led away. He didn't look at his father, who was standing with his arms around Dora, almost in shock.

"Was it bad?" Josh asked her.

"It could have been much worse," Amanda said.

Josh looked at Ward Johnson and then at Dora. "He's your son, I gather," he said, his eyes blazing with fury as he held Amanda.

"Yes," Ward replied. That look made his knees go weak. He pulled Dora closer. "My wife died and he blamed me. And Dora."

"I blame you and Dora myself," Josh said icily. "If you have one shred of sense left, you'll get out of my sight while you still can. If anything had happened to Amanda, hell itself wouldn't have been far enough away to save you."

Ward had never seen that look in another man's eyes. He pulled a shocked, sick Dora out the door and never looked back.

Lisa was being comforted by Tim and Vic and Jenny, who'd

been at lunch when Scotty invaded the office. Lisa was giving them an abbreviated version of the standoff.

Josh got Amanda to her feet and lifted her in his big arms. "Let's get you taken care of, sprite," he said softly. His face was still pale, but he was smiling.

"Wow," Jenny was whispering to Lisa as she spotted Josh. "Who's the hunk?"

"Your boss," Josh said with a teasing glance in her direction. "But I'm already spoken for. And flattery will not keep you at your desk. Get a camera, for God's sake, and start asking questions! Where's your sense of exclusivity?"

"Yes, sir!" Jenny said, giving him a mock salute. "You can count on me, sir!"

He turned to Tim. "Can you take over the job press temporarily?"

"Yes, sir!" Tim grinned.

"It's my newspaper," Amanda grumbled as he turned and carried her to the paramedics. "My job press, too!"

"I'm only making suggestions, as your partner," he said soothingly. "Any decisions you don't like, you can countermand later. We have to keep the doors open, darling," he whispered, and bent to brush his mouth over her pert nose, "until I decide what to do about a replacement for Johnson."

"How about me?" she teased.

She tingled at the tone and the touch. But when she moved to put her arms around his neck, she winced.

"How did this happen?" he asked as he turned toward the paramedics.

"He hit me with the gun," she said reluctantly.

He didn't look at her. But his tall body shuddered with feeling, and the paramedic he was looking at came running.

"Yes, sir, can I help?" the man asked.

"She's hurt," he said, putting Amanda down gently. "Her arm might be broken."

"I'll check. Not to worry, I've had hours of extra training." He frowned as he felt her arm. "Badly bruised, but I don't feel any breaks. We'd better get an X-ray, though. Never know about hairline cracks that might come back to haunt you."

"I'll run her down to the hospital," Josh said. "Come on, little one."

He picked her up again, despite her protests, and carried her to the limousine.

"You either have to let me be protective or watch me follow that boy to jail and beat him half to death," he said through his teeth. "Take your pick."

She relented. She laid her head back on his shoulder and looked up at him with soft wonder. "In that case, it's all right if you want to be protective. I'll lie here and try to look properly helpless."

His eyes slid down to meet hers, dark with feeling. "There's only one place I want you totally helpless. I think you already know where it is."

"That isn't enough anymore, Josh," she said sadly. She averted her eyes to his hard mouth. "I'm sorry."

His arms contracted. "I'm sorry, too. Sorry that I hurt you before you left Opal Cay, and sorry that I've been so damned pigheaded and stupid. I should have kept my mouth shut."

"The truth is always best."

"You don't know the truth, yet," he said, his dark eyes sweeping her face hungrily. "But once I have you properly looked after, I'm going to give it to you. All of it. Then," he added, easing her into the limousine while the driver held the door open, "we'll make decisions."

CHAPTER TWENTY-TWO

Dora stayed beside Ward while he fielded journalists and policemen and paramedics. But when they were finally in his car, she went to pieces.

"It will be all over town," she whispered. "Edgar will hear it on the news before he hears it from me."

"I'm sorry," he said, miserable. "Dora, honey, I'm so sorry."

"He'll take my boys away from me."

"Maybe not." He pressed her hand. "Listen, suppose you get a divorce and marry me. Then we'll ask a judge for visitation rights. You won't lose your sons, I promise you."

"You've lost yours," she said sadly. "All because of me."

"It's been building for years, Dora. You only helped me precipitate matters. It will work out. If Lawson fires me, I'll find another job. I can always go back to reporting if I have to. Trust me. I feel like a new man. I can do anything, if I've got you. How about it?" he asked, glancing warmly at her. "Will you take a chance on me?"

It was only then that Dora fully realized all she'd given up. Ward was nice to her in bed. He was a kind man. But she'd sacrificed respectability, a secure future, and her children. There was no way she could ever get them back again. She had Ward. But now that she had him, she wasn't going to be allowed to give him back. His wife was dead. His son was probably going to prison. And she was the catalyst. She would have to live with his failures all her life and know that she'd caused them.

"Of course I'll take a chance on you, Ward," she said dully. She forced a smile for him. "But you'd better drive me home now. I owe Edgar an explanation when he and the boys get home."

He was reluctant, but in the end he let her go alone. When she walked in the door, she noticed an unusual stillness. There was no one in the house at all. A note was propped on the immaculate dining room table. It had her name on it. She picked it up, hating the clean feel of it, and ripped open the envelope.

Dora, I'm sorry you didn't feel you could be honest with me about your affair. I've taken the boys to stay with my mother, where, hopefully, the press won't harass them. They're very upset. I thought you were happy with us. I wish you could have said something before it was too late.
Edgar.

She sat down on the sofa and clutched the paper in her hand. After a minute she began to cry. When at last Ward called her she had a bag packed, and she asked him to come and pick her up. It was all she could do. She'd given up everything she had. So had Ward. They might not be ecstatically happy together, but there was no going back. She'd wanted Ward, and an ironic fate had given him to her. Now she had to make the best of what she'd salvaged of her life. It would be all right, she told herself. All the same, her last look at her old home was a bitter one when she drove away in the car next to Ward.

Amanda's arm was only bruised, but the doctor told her to take Tylenol for the discomfort and get a good night's rest. He gave her a couple of tablets to take that would make her sleep.

"You won't need that," Josh murmured as he stuck the sedative in his pocket. His dark eyes slid over her face with warm possession. "I've got a much better way to make you sleep."

"Have you?" she asked with building excitement.

"Oh, yes." He pulled her close as the limousine wound its way to his house through the night traffic of San Antonio. "Have you heard from Brad?"

"I had a letter yesterday. He says he's doing well." She looked up at him. "He thought he was in love with me, but he's decided that it was mostly a case of a wounded ego. He's very sorry for all the trouble he caused."

"I'll forgive him if you will."

"We have to. He's not a bad man, really. He couldn't be. He's related to you."

"I like that," he mused. He leaned back against the seat with a long sigh and held her close. "My God, what a day. When I came to find you, I had no idea in hell what I was going to walk into. Are you really all right?"

"Really. Had you been outside long?"

"Long enough to go crazy," he said. "I was afraid he'd killed you when I heard the shot. I don't know how I kept on breathing."

She smiled and snuggled closer to him, laying her weary head against his broad chest. "I thought that I might not see you again. It made me sad."

His arm contracted jerkily. He stared out the tinted window with eyes that barely registered the city traffic. "I've damned near made a tragic mistake, Amanda. I didn't realize until today that all my noble sacrifices might not have meant anything if you died. If I lost you."

Her heart leaped. "You yourself said it was only sex," she reminded him.

"You knew better," he said. "You knew I was lying through my teeth the whole time."

"Well, yes," she mused. "But it hurt, just the same."

He looked down at her. "There won't be any miracles, you know," he said. "No accidentally botched tests or switched test results. I've had six specialists on the case. They all agree that I'll never be able to give you a child." He hesitated. "Well, the natural way." He touched her cheek. "There's a small chance with in vitro fertilization—what they call test-tube babies. If you want to try it, later."

"All I ever wanted was you," she said simply. "You're very wrong if you think my interest in you is limited to your fertility."

He glanced away from her with faint embarrassment. "The thought occurred once or twice. Women want babies, don't they?"

She searched his averted face. "I wanted *you*. Just you, for so many reasons, Josh. I enjoy being with you, talking to you, sharing bad times and good ones. We think alike on all the important issues. The rest will give us a lot of arguments to make up after."

He chuckled. "You sound like a lady with commitment on her mind."

She lifted her face to his. "Oh, yes," she said softly. "Years and years of it. Any way you like. No strings—"

"No, you don't," he said, stopping her words with his mouth. He kissed her with lazy affection. "You're not getting away from me again. And I don't believe in long engagements. If we work fast, we can be married in three days."

"Married!"

"Don't look so shocked," he told her. "You might scare me off. You can have a small, intimate wedding."

Her head was spinning. Perhaps the ordeal had affected her. She said so.

"No, darling," he replied gently. "Not the ordeal. Me."

"And what about that busy love life you threatened to rekindle?" she asked, her eyes flashing.

He smiled ruefully. "That was a last ditch attempt to save you from me. I haven't slept since you left, or done much of anything except grieve for you," he said after a minute. His face sobered. "And I came very close to doing that for real today." He touched her hair tenderly, smoothing it away from her face. The look in his eyes was humbling. "Amanda, do you love me enough to take a chance on happiness?"

"You already knew the answer to that question before you ever asked it," she replied.

He searched her eyes slowly and nodded. "I've always known. That's why I had the tests in the first place. I wanted you more than anything on earth, except your own happiness. That came first."

"And then you tried to take away the one thing that *was* my happiness: you."

He drew her bruisingly close, careful of her arm, and rocked her against his strength. "I'll cherish you until they lower me down in the dark," he said roughly. "And the last thought I have...will be of you."

She felt the sting of tears in her eyes at the love and tenderness in that deep, quiet voice at her ear. She clung to him hungrily and gave him back the words. When his mouth searched for hers, it didn't have far to go. She met him halfway, as she always would now, for the rest of her life.

That night, lying close and contented in his arms in bed, Amanda drifted off to sleep. Their loving had been slow and tender and profound, a sharing of wonder and awed beauty and pleasure that transcended anything that had come before.

Afterward they'd talked a little about the newspaper and Ward Johnson's replacement. But they were hungry for each other, and in between whispers and endearments they'd sought fulfillment again and again.

While she slept Josh lay awake, watching her with unconcealed possession in his dark eyes. He hadn't felt so complete in all his life. His fondest, most secret dream lay beside him. Amanda had come full circle, from frightened child to responsible, competent woman. She could take anything life threw at her now, and he knew it. He felt a sense of accomplishment as he realized his part in her development. If there had been no obstacles, and he'd given in to his hunger for her earlier, he'd have stunted her growth. As it was, she had a life and a mind of her own, apart from him. If she ever had to rely on herself in the future, for any reason, he knew she could do it. He lay back and closed his eyes, smiling at his incredible good fortune. Sometimes, he thought, life was merciful.

Amanda's changes were implemented without further complications. Ward Johnson married Dora and eventually, when Scotty was released from jail, she became more of a mother to him than Gladys had ever been. Dora gained visitation rights with her own sons, frequently including them in outings.

A veteran reporter was hired to manage the newspaper while Amanda took over the job press, which grew into a major competitor for much larger enterprises in San Antonio. Years later her shop would absorb two others and become the biggest in the city.

Josh and Amanda were married the day the *Gazette* ran the exclusive story about the hostage situation that had resulted in Scotty Johnson's arrest. It was a kind story, as weekly newspaper stories often are. The tabloid stories that followed were not. But everyone weathered them, and eventually they became old news.

Having fulfilled the conditions of Harrison Todd's will by marrying Amanda, Josh signed over complete control of the *Todd Gazette* and job press to Amanda. He remarked dryly that he was afraid to ask which of the momentous events made her happiest. He didn't really have to. Amanda's answer was in her eyes.

★ ★ ★ ★ ★